I0584437

Ralph Waldo Emerson

Letters and Social Aims

Ralph Waldo Emerson

Letters and Social Aims

ISBN/EAN: 9783744765978

Printed in Europe, USA, Canada, Australia, Japan

Cover: Foto ©Andreas Hilbeck / pixelio.de

More available books at **www.hansebooks.com**

LETTERS AND SOCIAL AIMS

BY

RALPH WALDO EMERSON

BOSTON AND NEW YORK
HOUGHTON, MIFFLIN AND COMPANY
The Riverside Press, Cambridge

The Riverside Press, Cambridge, Mass., U. S. A.
Electrotyped and Printed by H. O. Houghton & Company.

CONTENTS.

NOTE.

—·—

It seems proper to mention here the circumstances under which this volume was put together, as they may have some bearing upon the estimate to be placed upon it. Some time perhaps in 1870, Mr. Emerson learned that a London publisher was intending, without consulting him, to make up a volume of his uncollected writings, from the "Dial" and elsewhere. He was much disturbed by this intelligence, and wrote to his friend, Mr. Moncure Conway, to stop the publication if possible. In this Mr. Conway succeeded, but only upon the agreement that Mr. Emerson would himself make such a collection, adding some new pieces, and would send advance-sheets to England, so that the book might appear simultaneously in both countries. This being settled, the American and the English publishers began to urge speed, and Mr. Emerson applied himself to the task, though with heavy heart, partly from a feeling of repugnance at being forced into an enterprise which he had not intended, but still more perhaps from a sense of inability, more real than he knew, which was beginning to make itself felt. He made, accordingly, but slow progress, so that in the summer of 1872 he had got ready little more than the first piece, Poetry and Imagination, the proof-sheets of which were in his hands, — indeed had been for some time in his hands, — when on the 24th of July his house was burned and all possibility of work put an end to for the time, not merely by the confusion of his papers and the destruction of his wonted surroundings, but yet more effectually by an illness resulting from the shock.

The proof-sheets showed that already before this accident his loss of memory and of mental grasp had gone so far as to make it unlikely that he would in any case have been able to accomplish what he had undertaken. Sentences, even whole pages, were repeated, and there was a confusion of order beyond what even he would have tolerated. Now, at any rate, nothing was to be thought of but rest and the attempt to restore the tone of his mind by some diversion. The Nile-tour was suggested and made feasible by kind friends, and he wrote to England explaining the necessity for some delay. Soon after his return home he heard of the death of the English publisher, and supposed himself free. But in 1875 he was informed that the claim had passed on to the successors of the London firm, and that they were asking what had become of their book. The old proof-sheets were again taken in hand, but again with a painful sense of incapacity to deal with them. By degrees and with much reluctance he admitted the necessity of some assistance. It was known to his family that he intended to make me his literary executor, and he now acceded to their asking me to help him with the book. Before long he had committed the business of selection and preparation for the press, almost entirely to me. Of course he was constantly consulted, and he would sometimes, upon urging, supply a needed word or sentence, but he was quite content to do as little as possible, and desired to leave everything in my hands.

This will appear to be of the more consequence in view of the fact that with the exception of four, viz., The Comic, Persian Poetry, Quotation and Originality, and Progress of Culture, the essays contained in this volume, though written in great part long before, had never been published: and, further, of the state of the manuscripts, which consisted of loose sheets, laid together in parcels, each marked on the cover with the title under which it was last read as a lecture, but often without any completely recoverable order or fixed limits. Mr. Emerson was in the habit of repeating, on different occasions, what was nominally the same lecture, in reality often varied by the introduction of part of some other, or of new matter. This, with his freedom of transition and breadth of scope, which were apt in any case to render the boundaries of the subject somewhat indistinct, made it often difficult or impossible for any one to determine with confidence to what particular lecture a given sheet or scrap originally belonged. Nor indeed did I attempt, in preparing the copy for the press, to adhere always to a single manuscript. To have attempted this would have been contrary to Mr. Emerson's wishes. What he desired was simply to bring together under the particular heading whatever could be found that seemed in place there, without regard to the connection in which it was found. This had been his own practice, and all his suggestions to me were to this effect. Most of the time that he spent (which was not very much) over the work, was spent in searching his note-books, new and old, for fresh matter that might be introduced with advantage. In this way it happened sometimes that writing of very different dates was brought together : *e. g.* the essay on Immortality, which has been cited as showing what were his latest opinions on that subject, contains passages written fifty years apart from each other. Then, as to the selection of the essays, there were, it is true, lists prepared by Mr. Emerson with a view to future volumes, but many of the papers had been lying by him for years unpublished, and it is open to any one to say that he never really decided upon publishing them, and, if he had been left to himself, never would have published them.

There is nothing here that he did not write, and he gave his full approval to whatever was done in the way of selection and arrangement; but I cannot say that he applied his mind very closely to the matter. He was pleased, in a general way, that the work should go on, but it may be a question exactly how far he sanctioned it.

J. E. CABOT.

August 27, 1883.

POETRY AND IMAGINATION.

POETRY AND IMAGINATION.

THE perception of matter is made the common sense, and for cause. This was the cradle, this the go-cart, of the human child. We must learn the homely laws of fire and water; we must feed, wash, plant, build. These are ends of necessity, and first in the order of nature. Poverty, frost, famine, disease, debt, are the beadles and guardsmen that hold us to common-sense. The intellect, yielded up to itself, cannot supersede this tyrannic necessity. The restraining grace of common-sense is the mark of all the valid minds, — of Æsop, Aristotle, Alfred, Luther, Shakspeare, Cervantes, Franklin, Napoleon. The common-sense which does not meddle with the absolute, but takes things at their word, — things as they appear, — believes in the existence of matter, not because we can touch it or conceive of it, but because it agrees with ourselves, and the universe does not jest with us, but is in earnest, is the house of health and life. In spite of all the joys of poets and the joys of saints, the most imaginative and abstracted person never

makes with impunity the least mistake in this particular, — never tries to kindle his oven with water,
nor carries a torch into a powder-mill, nor seizes
his wild charger by the tail. We should not pardon the blunder in another, nor endure it in ourselves.

But whilst we deal with this as finality, early
hints are given that we are not to stay here ; that
we must be making ready to go ; — a warning that
this magnificent hotel and conveniency we call Nature is not final. First innuendoes, then broad
hints, then smart taps are given, suggesting that
nothing stands still in nature but death ; that the
creation is on wheels, in transit, always passing into
something else, streaming into something higher ;
that matter is not what it appears ; — that chemistry can blow it all into gas. Faraday, the most
exact of natural philosophers, taught that when we
should arrive at the monads, or primordial elements
(the supposed little cubes or prisms of which all
matter was built up), we should not find cubes, or
prisms, or atoms, at all, but spherules of force. It
was whispered that the globes of the universe were
precipitates of something more subtle ; nay, somewhat was murmured in our ear that dwindled astronomy into a toy ; — that too was no finality ;
only provisional, a makeshift ; that under chemistry
was power and purpose : power and purpose ride

on matter to the last atom. It was steeped in thought, did everywhere express thought; that, as great conquerors have burned their ships when once they were landed on the wished-for shore, so the noble house of Nature we inhabit has temporary uses, and we can afford to leave it one day. The ends of all are moral, and therefore the beginnings are such. Thin or solid, everything is in flight. I believe this conviction makes the charm of chemistry, — that we have the same avoirdupois matter in an alembic, without a vestige of the old form; and in animal transformation not less, as in grub and fly, in egg and bird, in embryo and man; everything undressing and stealing away from its old into new form, and nothing fast but those invisible cords which we call laws, on which all is strung. Then we see that things wear different names and faces, but belong to one family; that the secret cords or laws show their well-known virtue through every variety, be it animal, or plant, or planet, and the interest is gradually transferred from the forms to the lurking method.

This hint, however conveyed, upsets our politics, trade, customs, marriages, nay, the common-sense side of religion and literature, which are all founded on low nature, — on the clearest and most economical mode of administering the material world, considered as final. The admission, never so covertly, that this is a makeshift, sets the dullest brain in ferment : our little sir, from his first tottering steps, as soon as he can crow, does not like to be practised upon, suspects that some one is " doing " him, and at this alarm everything is compromised ; gunpowder is laid under every man's breakfast-table.

But whilst the man is startled by this closer inspection of the laws of matter, his attention is called to the independent action of the mind; its strange suggestions and laws; a certain tyranny which springs up in his own thoughts, which have an order, method, and beliefs of their own, very different from the order which this common-sense uses.

Suppose there were in the ocean certain strong currents which drove a ship, caught in them, with a force that no skill of sailing with the best wind, and no strength of oars, or sails, or steam, could make any head against, any more than against the current of Niagara. Such currents, so tyrannical, exist in thoughts, those finest and subtilest of all waters, that as soon as once thought begins, it refuses to remember whose brain it belongs to ; what country, tradition, or religion; and goes whirling off — swim we merrily — in a direction self-chosen, by law of thought and not by law of kitchen clock or county committee. It has its own polarity. One of these vortices or self-directions of thought is the impulse to search resemblance, affinity, identity, in all its objects, and hence our science, from its rudest to its most refined theories.

The electric word pronounced by John Hunter a hundred years ago, *arrested and progressive development*, indicating the way upward from the invisible protoplasm to the highest organisms, gave the poetic key to Natural Science, of which the theories of Geoffroy St. Hilaire, of Oken, of Goethe, of Agassiz and Owen and Darwin in zoölogy and botany, are the fruits, — a hint whose power is not yet exhausted, showing unity and perfect order in physics.

The hardest chemist, the severest analyzer, scornful of all but dryest fact, is forced to keep the poetic curve of nature, and his result is like a myth of Theocritus. All multiplicity rushes to be resolved into unity. Anatomy, osteology, exhibit arrested or progressive ascent in each kind ; the lower pointing to the higher forms, the higher to the highest, from the fluid in an elastic sack, from radiate, mollusk, articulate, vertebrate, up to man ; as if the whole animal world were only a Hunterian museum to exhibit the genesis of mankind.

Identity of law, perfect order in physics, perfect parallelism between the laws of Nature and the laws of thought exist. In botany we have the like, the poetic perception of metamorphosis, — that the same vegetable point or eye which is the unit of the plant can be transformed at pleasure into every part, as bract, leaf, petal, stamen, pistil, or seed.

In geology, what a useful hint was given to the early inquirers on seeing in the possession of Professor Playfair a bough of a fossil tree which was perfect wood at one end and perfect mineral coal at the other. Natural objects, if individually described and out of connection, are not yet known, since they are really parts of a symmetrical universe, like words of a sentence; and if their true order is found, the poet can read their divine significance orderly as in a Bible. Each animal or vegetable form remembers the next inferior and predicts the next higher.

There is one animal, one plant, one matter, and one force. The laws of light and of heat translate each other; — so do the laws of sound and of color; and so galvanism, electricity, and magnetism are varied forms of the selfsame energy. While the student ponders this immense unity, he observes that all things in Nature, the animals, the mountain, the river, the seasons, wood, iron, stone, vapor, have a mysterious relation to his thoughts and his life; their growths, decays, quality and use so curiously resemble himself, in parts and in wholes,

that he is compelled to speak by means of them.
His words and his thoughts are framed by their
help. Every noun is an image. Nature gives him,
sometimes in a flattered likeness, sometimes in cari-
cature, a copy of every humor and shade in his
character and mind. The world is an immense
picture-book of every passage in human life. Every
object he beholds is the mask of a man.

> "The privates of man's heart
> They speken and sound in his ear
> As tho' they loud winds were;"

for the universe is full of their echoes.

Every correspondence we observe in mind and
matter suggests a substance older and deeper than
either of these old nobilities. We see the law
gleaming through, like the sense of a half-translated
ode of Hafiz. The poet who plays with it with
most boldness best justifies himself; is most profound and most devout. Passion adds eyes; is
a magnifying-glass. Sonnets of lovers are mad
enough, but are valuable to the philosopher, as are
prayers of saints, for their potent symbolism.

Science was false by being unpoetical. It assumed to explain a reptile or mollusk, and isolated
it, — which is hunting for life in graveyards. Reptile or mollusk or man or angel only exists in system, in relation. The metaphysician, the poet, only
sees each animal form as an inevitable step in the

path of the creating mind. The Indian, the hunter, the boy with his pets, have sweeter knowledge of these than the savant. We use semblances of logic until experience puts us in possession of real logic. The poet knows the missing link by the joy it gives. The poet gives us the eminent experiences only, — a god stepping from peak to peak, nor planting his foot but on a mountain.

Science does not know its debt to imagination. Goethe did not believe that a great naturalist could exist without this faculty. He was himself conscious of its help, which made him a prophet among the doctors. From this vision he gave brave hints to the zoölogist, the botanist, and the optician.

Poetry. — The primary use of a fact is low; the secondary use, as it is a figure or illustration of my thought, is the real worth. First the fact; second its impression, or what I think of it. Hence Nature was called "a kind of adulterated reason." Seas, forests, metals, diamonds and fossils interest the eye, but 't is only with some preparatory or predicting charm. Their value to the intellect appears only when I hear their meaning made plain in the spiritual truth they cover. The mind, penetrated with its sentiment or its thought, projects it outward on whatever it beholds. The lover sees re-

minders of his mistress in every beautiful object;
the saint, an argument for devotion in every natural process; and the facility with which Nature
lends itself to the thoughts of man, the aptness
with which a river, a flower, a bird, fire, day or
night, can express his fortunes, is as if the world
were only a disguised man, and, with a change
of form, rendered to him all his experience. We
cannot utter a sentence in sprightly conversation
without a similitude. Note our incessant use of
the word *like*, — like fire, like a rock, like thunder,
like a bee, " like a year without a spring." Conversation is not permitted without tropes ; nothing
but great weight in things can afford a quite literal
speech. It is ever enlivened by inversion and trope.
God himself does not speak prose, but communicates with us by hints, omens, inference, and dark
resemblances in objects lying all around us.

Nothing so marks a man as imaginative expressions. A figurative statement arrests attention, and
is remembered and repeated. How often has a
phrase of this kind made a reputation. Pythagoras's Golden Sayings were such, and Socrates's, and
Mirabeau's, and Burke's, and Bonaparte's. Genius
thus makes the transfer from one part of Nature
to a remote part, and betrays the rhymes and
echoes that pole makes with pole. Imaginative
minds cling to their images, and do not wish them

rashly rendered into prose reality, as children re-
sent your showing them that their doll Cinderella
is nothing but pine wood and rags ; and my young
scholar does not wish to know what the leopard,
the wolf, or Lucia, signify in Dante's Inferno, but
prefers to keep their veils on.   Mark the delight
of an audience in an image.   When some familiar
truth or fact appears in a new dress, mounted as
on a fine horse, equipped with a grand pair of
ballooning wings, we cannot enough testify our
surprise and pleasure.   It is like the new virtue
shown in some unprized old property, as when a
boy finds that his pocket-knife will attract steel
filings and take up a needle; or when the old horse-
block in the yard is found to be a Torso Hercules
of the Phidian age.   Vivacity of expression may
indicate this high gift, even when the thought is
of no great scope, as when Michel Angelo, praising
the *terra cottas*, said, " If this earth were to become
marble, woe to the antiques ! "   A happy symbol
is a sort of evidence that your thought is just.   I
had rather have a good symbol of my thought, or
a good analogy, than the suffrage of Kant or Plato.
If you agree with me, or if Locke or Montesquieu
agree, I may yet be wrong; but if the elm-tree
thinks the same thing, if running water, if burning
coal, if crystals, if alkalies, in their several fashions
say what I say, it must be true.   Thus a good sym-

bol is the best argument, and is a missionary to
persuade thousands. The Vedas, the Edda, the
Koran, are each remembered by their happiest figure. There is no more welcome gift to men than
a new symbol. That satiates, transports, converts
them. They assimilate themselves to it, deal with it
in all ways, and it will last a hundred years. Then
comes a new genius, and brings another. Thus the
Greek mythology called the sea " the tear of Sat-
urn." The return of the soul to God was described
as " a flask of water broken in the sea." Saint
John gave us the Christian figure of " souls washed
in the blood of Christ." The aged Michel Angelo
indicates his perpetual study as in boyhood, — " I
carry my satchel still." Machiavel described the
papacy as " a stone inserted in the body of Italy to
keep the wound open." To the Parliament debat-
ing how to tax America, Burke exclaimed, " Shear
the wolf." Our Kentuckian orator said of his dis-
sent from his companion, " I showed him the back
of my hand." And our proverb of the courteous
soldier reads : " An iron hand in a velvet glove."

This belief that the higher use of the material
world is to furnish us types or pictures to express
the thoughts of the mind, is carried to its logical
extreme by the Hindoos, who, following Buddha,
have made it the central doctrine of their religion
that what we call Nature, the external world, has

no real existence, — is only phenomenal. Youth, age, property, condition, events, persons, — self, even, — are successive *maias* (deceptions) through which Vishnu mocks and instructs the soul. I think Hindoo books the best gymnastics for the mind, as showing treatment. All European libraries might almost be read without the swing of this gigantic arm being suspected. But these Orientals deal with worlds and pebbles freely.

For the value of a trope is that the hearer is one : and indeed Nature itself is a vast trope, and all particular natures are tropes. As the bird alights on the bough, then plunges into the air again, so the thoughts of God pause but for a moment in any form. All thinking is analogizing, and it is the use of life to learn metonymy. The endless passing of one element into new forms, the incessant metamorphosis, explains the rank which the imagination holds in our catalogue of mental powers. The imagination is the reader of these forms. The poet accounts all productions and changes of Nature as the nouns of language, uses them representatively, too well pleased with their ulterior to value much their primary meaning. Every new object so seen gives a shock of agreeable surprise. The impressions on the imagination make the great days of life : the book, the landscape, or the personality which did not stay on the surface of the eye or ear but penetrated to the inward sense, agitates us, and is not forgotten. Walking, working, or talking, the sole question is how many strokes vibrate on this mystic string, — how many diameters are drawn quite through from matter to spirit; for whenever you enunciate a natural law you discover that you have enunciated a law of the mind. Chemistry, geology, hydraulics, are secondary science. The atomic theory is only an interior process *produced*, as geometers say, or the effect of a foregone metaphysical theory. Swedenborg saw gravity to be only an external of the irresistible attractions of affection and faith. Mountains and oceans we think we understand ; — yes, so long as they are contented to be such, and are safe with the geologist, — but when they are melted in Promethean alembics and come out men, and then, melted again, come out words, without any abatement, but with an exaltation of power !

In poetry we say we require the miracle. The bee flies among the flowers, and gets mint and marjoram, and generates a new product, which is not mint and marjoram, but honey ; the chemist mixes hydrogen and oxygen to yield a new product, which is not these, but water; and the poet listens to conversation and beholds all objects in nature, to give back, not them, but a new and transcendent whole.

Poetry is the perpetual endeavor to express the

spirit of the thing, to pass the brute body and search the life and reason which causes it to exist; — to see that the object is always flowing away, whilst the spirit or necessity which causes it subsists. Its essential mark is that it betrays in every word instant activity of mind, shown in new uses of every fact and image, in preternatural quickness or perception of relations. All its words are poems. It is a presence of mind that gives a miraculous command of all means of uttering the thought and feeling of the moment. The poet squanders on the hour an amount of life that would more than furnish the seventy years of the man that stands next him.

The term " genius," when used with emphasis, implies imagination; use of symbols, figurative speech. A deep insight will always, like Nature, ultimate its thought in a thing. As soon as a man masters a principle and sees his facts in relation to it, fields, waters, skies, offer to clothe his thoughts in images. Then all men understand him; Parthian, Mede, Chinese, Spaniard, and Indian hear their own tongue. For he can now find symbols of universal significance, which are readily rendered into any dialect; as a painter, a sculptor, a musician, can in their several ways express the same sentiment of anger, or love, or religion.

The thoughts are few, the forms many; the large

vocabulary or many-colored coat of the indigent unity. The *savans* are chatty and vain, but hold them hard to principle and definition, and they become mute and near-sighted. What is motion? what is beauty? what is matter? what is life? what is force? Push them hard and they will not be loquacious. They will come to Plato, Proclus, and Swedenborg. The invisible and imponderable is the sole fact. "Why changes not the violet earth into musk?" What is the term of the ever-flowing metamorphosis? I do not know what are the stoppages, but I see that a devouring unity changes all into that which changes not.

The act of imagination is ever attended by pure delight. It infuses a certain volatility and intoxication into all nature. It has a flute which sets the atoms of our frame in a dance. Our indeterminate size is a delicious secret which it reveals to us. The mountains begin to dislimn, and float in the air. In the presence and conversation of a true poet, teeming with images to express his enlarging thought, his person, his form, grows larger to our fascinated eyes. And thus begins that deification which all nations have made of their heroes in every kind, — saints, poets, lawgivers, and warriors.

Imagination. — Whilst common-sense looks at

things or visible nature as real and final facts, poetry, or the imagination which dictates it, is a second sight, looking through these, and using them
as types or words for thoughts which they signify.
Or is this belief a metaphysical whim of modern
times, and quite too refined? On the contrary, it
is as old as the human mind. Our best definition
of poetry is one of the oldest sentences, and claims
to come down to us from the Chaldæan Zoroaster,
who wrote it thus: " Poets are standing trans-
porters, whose employment consists in speaking to
the Father and to matter; in producing apparent
imitations of unapparent natures, and inscribing
things unapparent in the apparent fabrication of
the world ; " in other words, the world exists for
thought: it is to make appear things which hide :
mountains, crystals, plants, animals, are seen; that
which makes them is not seen: these, then, are
"apparent copies of unapparent natures." Bacon
expressed the same sense in his definition, " Poetry
accommodates the shows of things to the desires
of the mind ; " and Swedenborg, when he said,
" There is nothing existing in human thought, even
though relating to the most mysterious tenet of
faith, but has combined with it a natural and sen-
suous image." And again : "Names, countries, nations, and the like are not at all known to those
who are in heaven ; they have no idea of such

things, but of the realities signified thereby." A symbol always stimulates the intellect; therefore is poetry ever the best reading. The very design of imagination is to domesticate us in another, in a celestial nature.

This power is in the image because this power is in nature. It so affects, because it so is. All that is wondrous in Swedenborg is not his invention, but his extraordinary perception ; — that he was necessitated so to see. The world realizes the mind. Better than images is seen through them. The selection of the image is no more arbitrary than the power and significance of the image. The selection must follow fate. Poetry, if perfected, is the only verity; is the speech of man after the real, and not after the apparent.

Or shall we say that the imagination exists by sharing the ethereal currents ? The poet contemplates the central identity, sees it undulate and roll this way and that, with divine flowings, through remotest things; and, following it, can detect essential resemblances in natures never before compared. He can class them so audaciously because he is sensible of the sweep of the celestial stream, from which nothing is exempt. His own body is a fleeing apparition, — his personality as fugitive as the trope he employs. In certain hours we can almost pass our hand through our own body. I think the use or value of poetry to be the suggestion it affords of the flux or fugaciousness of the poet. The mind delights in measuring itself thus with matter, with history, and flouting both. A thought, any thought, pressed, followed, opened, dwarfs matter, custom, and all but itself. But this second sight does not necessarily impair the primary or common sense. Pindar, and Dante, yes, and the gray and timeworn sentences of Zoroaster, may all be parsed, though we do not parse them. The poet has a logic, though it be subtile. He observes higher laws than he transgresses. "Poetry must first be good sense, though it is something better."

This union of first and second sight reads nature to the end of delight and of moral use. Men are imaginative, but not overpowered by it to the extent of confounding its suggestions with external facts. We live in both spheres, and must not mix them. Genius certifies its entire possession of its thought, by translating it into a fact which perfectly represents it, and is hereby education. Charles James Fox thought " Poetry the great refreshment of the human mind, — the only thing, after all; that men first found out they had minds, by making and tasting poetry."

Man runs about restless and in pain when his condition or the objects about him do not fully match his thought. He wishes to be rich, to be old, to be young, that things may obey him. In the ocean, in fire, in the sky, in the forest, he finds facts adequate and as large as he. As his thoughts are deeper than he can fathom, so also are these. It is easier to read Sanscrit, to decipher the arrow-head character, than to interpret these familiar sights. It is even much to name them. Thus Thomson's " Seasons " and the best parts of many old and many new poets are simply enumerations by a person who felt the beauty of the common sights and sounds, without any attempt to draw a moral or affix a meaning.

The poet discovers that what men value as substances have a higher value as symbols; that Nature is the immense shadow of man. A man's action is only a picture-book of his creed. He does after what he believes. Your condition, your employment, is the fable of *you*. The world is thoroughly anthropomorphized, as if it had passed through the body and mind of man, and taken his mould and form. Indeed, good poetry is always personification, and heightens every species of force in nature by giving it a human volition. We are advertised that there is nothing to which man is not related; that everything is convertible into every other. The staff in his hand is the *radius vector* of the sun. The chemistry of this is the chemistry

of that. Whatever one act we do, whatever one
thing we learn, we are doing and learning all
things, — marching in the direction of universal
power. Every healthy mind is a true Alexander
or Sesostris, building a universal monarchy.

The senses imprison us, and we help them with
metres as limitary, — with a pair of scales and a
foot-rule and a clock. How long it took to find
out what a day was, or what this sun, that makes
days! It cost thousands of years only to make the
motion of the earth suspected. Slowly, by comparing thousands of observations, there dawned on
some mind a theory of the sun, — and we found
the astronomical fact. But the astronomy is in the
mind : the senses affirm that the earth stands still
and the sun moves. The senses collect the surface
facts of matter. The intellect acts on these brute
reports, and obtains from them results which are
the essence or intellectual form of the experiences.
It compares, distributes, generalizes and uplifts
them into its own sphere. It knows that these
transfigured results are not the brute experiences,
just as souls in heaven are not the red bodies they
once animated. Many transfigurations have befallen them. The atoms of the body were once
nebulæ, then rock, then loam, then corn, then
chyme, then chyle, then blood; and now the be-
holding and co-energizing mind sees the same refin-

ing and ascent to the third, the seventh, or the
tenth power of the daily accidents which the senses
report, and which make the raw material of knowledge. It was sensation; when memory came, it was
experience; when mind acted, it was knowledge;
when mind acted on it as knowledge, it was thought.

This metonymy, or seeing the same sense in
things so diverse, gives a pure pleasure. Every
one of a million times we find a charm in the metamorphosis. It makes us dance and sing. All men
are so far poets. When people tell me they do not
relish poetry, and bring me Shelley, or Aikin's
Poets, or I know not what volumes of rhymed
English, to show that it has no charm, I am quite
of their mind. But this dislike of the books only
proves their liking of poetry. For they relish
Æsop, — cannot forget him, or not use him; bring
them Homer's Iliad, and they like that; or the
Cid, and that rings well; read to them from Chaucer, and they reckon him an honest fellow. Lear
and Macbeth and Richard III. they know pretty
well without guide. Give them Robin Hood's ballads or Griselda, or Sir Andrew Barton, or Sir Patrick Spense, or Chevy Chase, or Tam O'Shanter,
and they like these well enough. They like to see
statues; they like to name the stars; they like to
talk and hear of Jove, Apollo, Minerva, Venus,
and the Nine. See how tenacious we are of the

old names. They like poetry without knowing it as such. They like to go to the theatre and be made to weep; to Faneuil Hall, and be taught by Otis, Webster, or Kossuth, or Phillips, what great hearts they have, what tears, what new possible enlargements to their narrow horizons. They like to see sunsets on the hills or on a lake shore. Now a cow does not gaze at the rainbow, or show or affect any interest in the landscape, or a peacock, or the song of thrushes.

Nature is the true idealist. When she serves us best, when, on rare days, she speaks to the imagination, we feel that the huge heaven and earth are but a web drawn around us, that the light, skies, and mountains are but the painted vicissitudes of the soul. Who has heard our hymn in the churches without accepting the truth, —

> " As o'er our heads the seasons roll,
>   And soothe with *change of bliss* the soul " ?

Of course, when we describe man as poet, and credit him with the triumphs of the art, we speak of the potential or ideal man, — not found now in any one person. You must go through a city or a nation, and find one faculty here, one there, to build the true poet withal. Yet all men know the portrait when it is drawn, and it is part of religion to believe its possible incarnation.

He is the healthy, the wise, the fundamental, the manly man, seer of the secret; against all the appearance he sees and reports the truth, namely that the soul generates matter. And poetry is the only verity, — the expression of a sound mind speaking after the ideal, and not after the apparent. As a power it is the perception of the symbolic character of things, and the treating them as representative: as a talent it is a magnetic tenaciousness of an image, and by the treatment demonstrating that this pigment of thought is as palpable and objective to the poet as is the ground on which he stands, or the walls of houses about him. And this power appears in Dante and Shakspeare. In some individuals this insight or second sight has an extraordinary reach which compels our wonder, as in Behmen, Swedenborg, and William Blake the painter.

William Blake, whose abnormal genius, Wordsworth said, interested him more than the conversation of Scott or of Byron, writes thus: "He who does not imagine in stronger and better lineaments and in stronger and better light than his perishing mortal eye can see, does not imagine at all. The painter of this work asserts that all his imaginations appear to him infinitely more perfect and more minutely organized than anything seen by his mortal eye. . . . I assert for myself that I do not behold the outward creation, and that to me it would be a hindrance, and not action. I question not my corporeal eye any more than I would question a window concerning a sight. I look through it, and not with it."

It is a problem of metaphysics to define the province of Fancy and Imagination. The words are often used, and the things confounded. Imagination respects the cause. It is the vision of an inspired soul reading arguments and affirmations in all nature of that which it is driven to say. But as soon as this soul is released a little from its passion, and at leisure plays with the resemblances and types, for amusement, and not for its moral end, we call its action Fancy. Lear, mad with his affliction, thinks every man who suffers must have the like cause with his own. "What, have his daughters brought him to this pass?" But when, his attention being diverted, his mind rests from this thought, he becomes fanciful with Tom, playing with the superficial resemblances of objects. Bunyan, in pain for his soul, wrote "Pilgrim's Progress;" Quarles, after he was quite cool, wrote "Emblems."

Imagination is central; fancy, superficial. Fancy relates to surface, in which a great part of life lies. The lover is rightly said to fancy the hair, eyes, complexion of the maid. Fancy is a wilful, imagination a spontaneous act; fancy, a play as with dolls and puppets which we choose to call men and women; imagination, a perception and affirming of a real relation between a thought and some material fact. Fancy amuses; imagination expands and exalts us. Imagination uses an organic classification. Fancy joins by accidental resemblance, surprises and amuses the idle, but is silent in the presence of great passion and action. Fancy aggregates; imagination animates. Fancy is related to color; imagination, to form. Fancy paints; imagination sculptures.

Veracity. — I do not wish, therefore, to find that my poet is not partaker of the feast he spreads, or that he would kindle or amuse me with that which does not kindle or amuse him. He must believe in his poetry. Homer, Milton, Hafiz, Herbert, Swedenborg, Wordsworth, are heartily enamored of their sweet thoughts. Moreover, they know that this correspondence of things to thoughts is far deeper than they can penetrate, — defying adequate expression; that it is elemental, or in the core of things. Veracity therefore is that which we require in poets, — that they shall say how it was with them, and not what might be said. And the fault of our popular poetry is that it is not sincere.

" What news? " asks man of man everywhere.

The only teller of news is the poet. When he sings, the world listens with the assurance that now a secret of God is to be spoken. The right poetic mood is or makes a more complete sensibility, piercing the outward fact to the meaning of the fact; shows a sharper insight: and the perception creates the strong expression of it, as the man who sees his way walks in it.

It is a rule in eloquence, that the moment the orator loses command of his audience, the audience commands him. So in poetry, the master rushes to deliver his thought, and the words and images fly to him to express it; whilst colder moods are forced to respect the ways of saying it, and insinuate, or, as it were, muffle the fact to suit the poverty or caprice of their expression, so that they only hint the matter, or allude to it, being unable to fuse and mould their words and images to fluid obedience. See how Shakspeare grapples at once with the main problem of the tragedy, as in Lear and Macbeth, and the opening of the Merchant of Venice.

All writings must be in a degree exoteric, written to a human *should* or *would*, instead of to the fatal *is :* this holds even of the bravest and sincerest writers. Every writer is a skater, and must go partly where he would, and partly where the skates carry him; or a sailor, who can only land where sails can be blown. And yet it is to be added that high poetry exceeds the fact, or nature itself, just as skates allow the good skater far more grace than his best walking would show, or sails more than riding. The poet writes from a real experience, the amateur feigns one. Of course one draws the bow with his fingers and the other with the strength of his body; one speaks with his lips and the other with a chest voice. Talent amuses, but if your verse has not a necessary and autobiographic basis, though under whatever gay poetic veils, it shall not waste my time.

For poetry is faith. To the poet the world is virgin soil; all is practicable; the men are ready for virtue; it is always time to do right. He is a true re-commencer, or Adam in the garden again. He affirms the applicability of the ideal law to this moment and the present knot of affairs. Parties, lawyers and men of the world will invariably dispute such an application, as romantic and dangerous: they admit the general truth, but they and their affair always constitute a case in bar of the statute. Free-trade, they concede, is very well as a principle, but it is never quite the time for its adoption without prejudicing actual interests. Chastity, they admit, is very well, — but then think of Mirabeau's passion and temperament! Eternal laws are very well, which admit no violation, — but so extreme were the times and manners of mankind, that you must admit miracles, for the times constituted a case. Of course, we know what you say, that legends are found in all tribes, — but this legend is different. And so throughout; the poet affirms the laws, prose busies itself with exceptions, — with the local and individual.

I require that the poem should impress me so that after I have shut the book it shall recall me to itself, or that passages should. And inestimable is the criticism of memory as a corrective to first impressions. We are dazzled at first by new words and brilliancy of color, which occupy the fancy and deceive the judgment. But all this is easily forgotten. Later, the thought, the happy image which expressed it and which was a true experience of the poet, recurs to mind, and sends me back in search of the book. And I wish that the poet should foresee this habit of readers, and omit all but the important passages. Shakspeare is made up of important passages, like Damascus steel made up of old nails. Homer has his own, —

"One omen is best, to fight for one's country ; "

and again, —

"They heal their griefs, for curable are the hearts of the noble."

Write, that I may know you. Style betrays you, as your eyes do. We detect at once by it whether the writer has a firm grasp on his fact or thought, — exists at the moment for that alone, or whether he has one eye apologizing, deprecatory, turned on his reader. In proportion always to his possession of his thought is his defiance of his readers. There is no choice of words for him who clearly sees the truth. That provides him with the best word.

Great design belongs to a poem, and is better than any skill of execution, — but how rare! I find it in the poems of Wordsworth, — Laodamia, and the Ode to Dion, and the plan of The Recluse. We want design, and do not forgive the bards if they have only the art of enamelling. We want an architect, and they bring us an upholsterer.

If your subject do not appear to you the flower of the world at this moment, you have not rightly chosen it. No matter what it is, grand or gay, national or private, if it has a natural prominence to you, work away until you come to the heart of it : then it will, though it were a sparrow or a spider-web, as fully represent the central law and draw all tragic or joyful illustration, as if it were the book of Genesis or the book of Doom. The subject — we must so often say it — is indifferent. Any word, every word in language, every circum- stance, becomes poetic in the hands of a higher thought.

The test or measure of poetic genius is the power
to read the poetry of affairs, — to fuse the circumstance of to-day; not to use Scott's antique superstitions, or Shakspeare's, but to convert those of
the nineteenth century and of the existing nations
into universal symbols. 'T is easy to repaint the
mythology of the Greeks, or of the Catholic Church,
the feudal castle, the crusade, the martyrdoms of
mediæval Europe; but to point out where the
same creative force is now working in our own
houses and public assemblies; to convert the vivid
energies acting at this hour in New York and Chi-
cago and San Francisco, into universal symbols,
requires a subtile and commanding thought. 'T is
boyish in Swedenborg to cumber himself with the
dead scurf of Hebrew antiquity, as if the Divine
creative energy had fainted in his own century.
American life storms about us daily, and is slow to
find a tongue. This contemporary insight is tran-
substantiation, the conversion of daily bread into
the holiest symbols; and every man would be a
poet if his intellectual digestion were perfect. The
test of the poet is the power to take the passing
day, with its news, its cares, its fears, as he shares
them, and hold it up to a divine reason, till he
sees it to have a purpose and beauty, and to be
related to astronomy and history and the eternal
order of the world. Then the dry twig blossoms
in his hand. He is calmed and elevated.

The use of "occasional poems" is to give leave to originality. Every one delights in the felicity frequently shown in our drawing - rooms. In a game-party or picnic poem each writer is released from the solemn rhythmic traditions which alarm and suffocate his fancy, and the result is that one of the partners offers a poem in a new style that hints at a new literature. Yet the writer holds it cheap, and could do the like all day. On the stage, the farce is commonly far better given than the tragedy, as the stock actors understand the farce, and do not understand the tragedy. The writer in the parlor has more presence of mind, more wit and fancy, more play of thought, on the incidents that occur at table or about the house, than in the politics of Germany or Rome. Many of the fine poems of Herrick, Jonson, and their contemporaries had this casual origin.

I know there is entertainment and room for talent in the artist's selection of ancient or remote subjects; as when the poet goes to India, or to Rome, or Persia, for his fable. But I believe nobody knows better than he that herein he consults his ease rather than his strength or his desire. He is very well convinced that the great moments of life are those in which his own house, his own body, the tritest and nearest ways and words and things have been illuminated into prophets and teachers.

What else is it to be a poet? What are his garland and singing-robes? What but a sensibility so keen that the scent of an elder-blow, or the timber-yard and corporation-works of a nest of pismires is event enough for him, — all emblems and personal appeals to him. His wreath and robe is to do what he enjoys; emancipation from other men's questions, and glad study of his own; escape from the gossip and routine of society, and the allowed right and practice of making better. He does not give his hand, but in sign of giving his heart; he is not affable with all, but silent, uncommitted, or in love, as his heart leads him. There is no subject that does not belong to him, — politics, economy, manufactures and stock-brokerage, as much as sunsets and souls; only, these things, placed in their true order, are poetry; displaced, or put in kitchen order, they are unpoetic. Malthus is the right organ of the English proprietors; but we shall never understand political economy until Burns or Béranger or some poet shall teach it in songs, and he will not teach Malthusianism.

Poetry is the *gai science.* The trait and test of the poet is that he builds, adds, and affirms. The critic destroys: the poet says nothing but what helps somebody; let others be distracted with cares, he is exempt. All their pleasures are tinged with pain. All his pains are edged with pleasure. The gladness he imparts he shares. As one of the old Minnesingers sung, —

> "Oft have I heard, and now believe it true,
> Whom man delights in, God delights in too."

Poetry is the consolation of mortal men. They live cabined, cribbed, confined in a narrow and trivial lot, — in wants, pains, anxieties and superstitions, in profligate politics, in personal animosities, in mean employments, — and victims of these; and the nobler powers untried, unknown. A poet comes who lifts the veil; gives them glimpses of the laws of the universe; shows them the circumstance as illusion; shows that nature is only a language to express the laws, which are grand and beautiful; — and lets them, by his songs, into some of the realities. Socrates, the Indian teachers of the Maia, the Bibles of the nations, Shakspeare, Milton, Hafiz, Ossian, the Welsh Bards; — these all deal with nature and history as means and symbols, and not as ends. With such guides they begin to see that what they had called pictures are realities, and the mean life is pictures. And this is achieved by words; for it is a few oracles spoken by perceiving men that are the texts on which religions and states are founded. And this perception has at once its moral sequence. Ben Jonson said, "The principal end of poetry is to inform men in the just reason of living."

Creation. — But there is a third step which poetry takes, and which seems higher than the others, namely, creation, or ideas taking forms of their own, — when the poet invents the fable, and invents the language which his heroes speak. He reads in the word or action of the man its yet untold results. His inspiration is power to carry out and complete the metamorphosis, which, in the imperfect kinds arrested for ages, in the perfecter proceeds rapidly in the same individual. For poetry is science, and the poet a truer logician. Men in the courts or in the street think themselves logical and the poet whimsical. Do they think there is chance or wilfulness in what he sees and tells? To be sure, we demand of him what he demands of himself, — veracity, first of all. But with that, he is the lawgiver, as being an exact reporter of the essential law. He knows that he did not make his thought, — no, his thought made him, and made the sun and the stars. Is the solar system good art and architecture? the same wise achievement is in the human brain also, can you only wile it from interference and marring. We cannot look at works of art but they teach us how near man is to creating. Michel Angelo is largely filled with the Creator that made and makes men. How much of the original craft remains in him, and he a mortal man! In him and the like perfecter brains the in·

stinct is resistless, knows the right way, is melodious, and at all points divine. The reason we set so high a value on any poetry, — as often on a line or a phrase as on a poem, — is that it is a new work of Nature, as a man is. It must be as new as foam and as old as the rock. But a new verse comes once in a hundred years; therefore Pindar, Hafiz, Dante, speak so proudly of what seems to the clown a jingle.

The writer, like the priest, must be exempted from secular labor. His work needs a frolic health; he must be at the top of his condition. In that prosperity he is sometimes caught up into a perception of means and materials, of feats and fine arts, of fairy machineries and funds of power hitherto utterly unknown to him, whereby he can transfer his visions to mortal canvas, or reduce them into iambic or trochaic, into lyric or heroic rhyme. These successes are not less admirable and astonishing to the poet than they are to his audience. He has seen something which all the mathematics and the best industry could never bring him unto. Now at this rare elevation above his usual sphere, he has come into new circulations, the marrow of the world is in his bones, the opulence of forms begins to pour into his intellect, and he is permitted to dip his brush into the old paint-pot with which birds, flowers, the human cheek, the living rock, the broad landscape, the ocean and the eternal sky were painted.

These fine fruits of judgment, poesy, and sentiment, when once their hour is struck, and the world is ripe for them, know as well as coarser how to feed and replenish themselves, and maintain their stock alive, and multiply; for roses and violets renew their race like oaks, and flights of painted moths are as old as the Alleghanies. The balance of the world is kept, and dewdrop and haze and the pencil of light are as long-lived as chaos and darkness.

Our science is always abreast of our self-knowledge. Poetry begins, or all becomes poetry, when we look from the centre outward, and are using all as if the mind made it. That only can we see which we are, and which we make. The weaver sees gingham; the broker sees the stock-list; the politician, the ward and county votes; the poet sees the horizon, and the shores of matter lying on the sky, the interaction of the elements, — the large effect of laws which correspond to the inward laws which he knows, and so are but a kind of extension of himself. " The attractions are proportional to the destinies." Events or things are only the fulfilment of the prediction of the faculties. Better men saw heavens and earths; saw noble instruments of noble souls. We see railroads, mills, and banks, and we pity the poverty of these dreaming Buddhists. There was as much creative force then as now, but it made globes and astronomic heavens, instead of broadcloth and wine-glasses.

The poet is enamored of thoughts and laws. These know their way, and, guided by them, he is ascending from an interest in visible things to an interest in that which they signify, and from the part of a spectator to the part of a maker. And as everything streams and advances, as every faculty and every desire is procreant, and every perception is a destiny, there is no limit to his hope. " Anything, child, that the mind covets, from the milk of a cocoa to the throne of the three worlds, thou mayest obtain, by keeping the law of thy members and the law of thy mind." It suggests that there is higher poetry than we write or read.

Rightly, poetry is organic. We cannot know things by words and writing, but only by taking a central position in the universe and living in its forms. We sink to rise : —

> " None any work can frame,
> Unless himself become the same. "

All the parts and forms of nature are the expression or production of divine faculties, and the same are in us. And the fascination of genius for us is this awful nearness to Nature's creations.

I have heard that the Germans think the creator of Trim and Uncle Toby, though he never wrote a verse, a greater poet than Cowper, and that Goldsmith's title to the name is not from his Deserted Village, but derived from the Vicar of Wakefield. Better examples are Shakspeare's Ariel, his Caliban, and his fairies in the Midsummer Night's Dream. Barthold Niebuhr said well, " There is little merit in inventing a happy idea or attractive situation, so long as it is only the author's voice which we hear. As a being whom we have called into life by magic arts, as soon as it has received existence acts independently of the master's impulse, so the poet creates his persons, and then watches and relates what they do and say. Such creation is poetry, in the literal sense of the term, and its possibility is an unfathomable enigma. The gushing fulness of speech belongs to the poet, and it flows from the lips of each of his magic beings in the thoughts and words peculiar to its nature." [1]

This force of representation so plants his figures before him that he treats them as real ; talks to them as if they were bodily there ; puts words in their mouth such as they should have spoken, and is affected by them as by persons. Vast is the difference between writing clean verses

[1] Niebuhr, *Letters*, etc., vol. iii. p. 196.

for magazines, and creating these new persons and situations, — new language with emphasis and reality. The humor of Falstaff, the terror of Macbeth, have each their swarm of fit thoughts and images, as if Shakspeare had known and reported the men, instead of inventing them at his desk. This power appears not only in the outline or portrait of his actors, but also in the bearing and behavior and style of each individual. Ben Jonson told Drummond that " Sidney did not keep a decorum in making every one speak as well as himself."

We all have one key to this miracle of the poet, and the dunce has experiences that may explain Shakspeare to him, — one key, namely, dreams. In dreams we are true poets; we create the persons of the drama; we give them appropriate figures, faces, costume; they are perfect in their organs, attitude, manners : moreover they speak after their own characters, not ours; — they speak to us, and we listen with surprise to what they say. Indeed, I doubt if the best poet has yet written any five-act play that can compare in thoroughness of invention with this unwritten play in fifty acts, composed by the dullest snorer on the floor of the watch-house.

Melody, Rhyme, Form. — Music and rhyme are

among the earliest pleasures of the child, and, in the history of literature, poetry precedes prose. Every one may see, as he rides on the highway through an uninteresting landscape, how a little water instantly relieves the monotony: no matter what objects are near it, — a gray rock, a grass-patch, an alder-bush, or a stake, — they become beautiful by being reflected. It is rhyme to the eye, and explains the charm of rhyme to the ear. Shadows please us as still finer rhymes. Architecture gives the like pleasure by the repetition of equal parts in a colonnade, in a row of windows, or in wings; gardens by the symmetric contrasts of the beds and walks. In society you have this figure in a bridal company, where a choir of white-robed maidens give the charm of living statues; in a funeral procession, where all wear black; in a regiment of soldiers in uniform.

The universality of this taste is proved by our habit of casting our facts into rhyme to remember them better, as so many proverbs may show. Who would hold the order of the almanac so fast but for the ding-dong,

"Thirty days hath September," etc.;

or of the Zodiac, but for

"The Ram, the Bull, the heavenly Twins," etc. ?

We are lovers of rhyme and return, period and

musical reflection. The babe is lulled to sleep by the nurse's song. Sailors can work better for their *yo-heave-o.* Soldiers can march better and fight better for the drum and trumpet. Metre begins with pulse-beat, and the length of lines in songs and poems is determined by the inhalation and exhalation of the lungs. If you hum or whistle the rhythm of the common English metres, — of the decasyllabic quatrain, or the octosyllabic with alternate sexisyllabic, or other rhythms, — you can easily believe these metres to be organic, derived from the human pulse, and to be therefore not proper to one nation, but to mankind. I think you will also find a charm heroic, plaintive, pathetic, in these cadences, and be at once set on searching for the words that can rightly fill these vacant beats. Young people like rhyme, drum-beat, tune, things in pairs and alternatives ; and, in higher degrees, we know the instant power of music upon our temperaments to change our mood, and give us its own ; and human passion, seizing these constitutional tunes, aims to fill them with appropriate words, or marry music to thought, believing, as we believe of all marriage, that matches are made in heaven, and that for every thought its proper melody or rhyme exists, though the odds are immense against our finding it, and only genius can rightly say the banns.

Another form of rhyme is iterations of phrase, as the record of the death of Sisera : —

" At her feet he bowed, he fell, he lay down : at her feet he bowed, he fell : where he bowed, there he fell down dead."

The fact is made conspicuous, nay, colossal, by this simple rhetoric : —

" They shall perish, but thou shalt endure : yea, all of them shall wax old like a garment ; as a vesture shalt thou change them, and they shall be changed : but thou art the same, and thy years shall have no end."

Milton delights in these iterations : —

> " Though fallen on evil days,
> On evil days though fallen, and evil tongues."

> " Was I deceived, or did a sable cloud
>   Turn forth its silver lining on the night ?
>   I did not err, there does a sable cloud
>   Turn forth its silver lining on the night."

Comus.

> " A little onward lend thy guiding hand,
>   To these dark steps a little farther on."

Samson.

So in our songs and ballads the refrain skilfully used, and deriving some novelty or better sense in each of many verses : —

> " Busk thee, busk thee, my bonny bonny bride,
>   Busk thee, busk thee, my winsome marrow."

HAMILTON.

Of course rhyme soars and refines with the growth of the mind. The boy liked the drum, the people liked an overpowering jewsharp tune. Later they like to transfer that rhyme to life, and to detect a melody as prompt and perfect in their daily affairs. Omen and coincidence show the rhythmical structure of man; hence the taste for signs, sortilege, prophecy and fulfilment, anniversaries, etc. By and by, when they apprehend real rhymes, namely, the correspondence of parts in nature, — acid and alkali, body and mind, man and maid, character and history, action and reaction, — they do not longer value rattles and ding-dongs, or barbaric word-jingle. Astronomy, Botany, Chemistry, Hydraulics and the elemental forces have their own periods and returns, their own grand strains of harmony not less exact, up to the primeval apothegm that " there is nothing on earth which is not in the heavens in a heavenly form, and nothing in the heavens which is not on the earth in an earthly form." They furnish the poet with grander pairs and alternations, and will require an equal expansion in his metres.

There is under the seeming poverty of metres an infinite variety, as every artist knows. A right ode (however nearly it may adopt conventional metre, as the Spenserian, or the heroic blank-verse, or one of the fixed lyric metres) will by any sprightliness be at once lifted out of conventionality, and will modify the metre. Every good poem that I know I recall by its rhythm also. Rhyme is a pretty good measure of the latitude and opulence of a writer. If unskilful, he is at once detected by the poverty of his chimes. A small, well-worn, sprucely brushed vocabulary serves him. Now try Spenser, Marlow, Chapman, and see how wide they fly for weapons, and how rich and lavish their profusion. In their rhythm is no manufacture, but a vortex, or musical tornado, which falling on words and the experience of a learned mind, whirls these materials into the same grand order as planets and moons obey, and seasons, and monsoons.

There are also prose poets. Thomas Taylor, the Platonist, for instance, is really a better man of imagination, a better poet, or perhaps I should say a better feeder to a poet, than any man between Milton and Wordsworth. Thomas Moore had the magnanimity to say, " If Burke and Bacon were not poets (measured lines not being necessary to constitute one), he did not know what poetry meant." And every good reader will easily recall expressions or passages in works of pure science which have given him the same pleasure which he seeks in professed poets. Richard Owen, the eminent paleontologist, said : —

" All hitherto observed causes of extirpation point

either to continuous slowly operating geologic changes, or to no greater sudden cause than the, so to speak, spectral appearance of mankind on a limited tract of land not before inhabited."

St. Augustine complains to God of his friends offering him the books of the philosophers : —

"And these were the dishes in which they brought to me, being hungry, the Sun and the Moon instead of Thee."

It would not be easy to refuse to Sir Thomas Browne's " Fragment on Mummies " the claim of poetry : —

" Of their living habitations they made little account, conceiving of them but as *hospitia,* or inns, while they adorned the sepulchres of the dead, and, planting thereon lasting bases, defied the crumbling touches of time, and the misty vaporousness of oblivion. Yet all were but Babel vanities. Time sadly overcometh all things, and is now dominant and sitteth upon a Sphinx, and looketh unto Memphis and old Thebes, while his sister Oblivion reclineth semi-somnous on a pyramid, gloriously triumphing, making puzzles of Titanian erections, and turning old glories into dreams. History sinketh beneath her cloud. The traveller as he paceth through those deserts asketh of her, Who builded them? and she mumbleth something, but what it is he heareth not."

Rhyme, being a kind of music, shares this advantage with music, that it has a privilege of speaking truth which all Philistia is unable to challenge. Music is the poor man's Parnassus. With the first note of the flute or horn, or the first strain of a song, we quit the world of common-sense and launch on the sea of ideas and emotions: we pour contempt on the prose you so magnify; yet the sturdiest Philistine is silent. The like allowance is the prescriptive right of poetry. You shall not speak ideal truth in prose uncontradicted: you may in verse. The best thoughts run into the best words; imaginative and affectionate thoughts into music and metre. We ask for food and fire, we talk of our work, our tools and material necessities, in prose; that is, without any elevation or aim at beauty; but when we rise into the world of thought, and think of these things only for what they signify, speech refines into order and harmony. I know what you say of mediæval barbarism and sleighbell-rhyme, but we have not done with music, no, nor with rhyme, nor must console ourselves with prose poets so long as boys whistle and girls sing.

Let Poetry then pass, if it will, into music and rhyme. That is the form which itself puts on. We do not enclose watches in wooden, but in crystal cases, and rhyme is the transparent frame that allows almost the pure architecture of thought to become visible to the mental eye. Substance is much, but so are mode and form much. The poet, like a delighted boy, brings you heaps of rainbow bubbles, opaline, air-borne, spherical as the world, instead of a few drops of soap and water. Victor Hugo says well, " An idea steeped in verse becomes suddenly more incisive and more brilliant : the iron becomes steel." Lord Bacon, we are told, " loved not to see poesy go on other feet than poetical dactyls and spondees ; " and Ben Jonson said that " Donne, for not keeping of accent, deserved hanging."

Poetry being an attempt to express, not the common-sense, — as the avoirdupois of the hero, or his structure in feet and inches, — but the beauty and soul in his aspect as it shines to fancy and feeling ; and so of all other objects in nature ; runs into fable, personifies every fact : — " the clouds clapped their hands," — " the hills skipped," — " the sky spoke." This is the substance, and this treatment always attempts a metrical grace. Outside of the nursery the beginning of literature is the prayers of a people, and they are always hymns, poetic, — the mind allowing itself range, and therewith is ever a corresponding freedom in the style, which becomes lyrical. The prayers of nations are rhythmic, have iterations and alliterations like the marriage-service and burial-service in our liturgies.

Poetry will never be a simple means, as when

history or philosophy is rhymed, or laureate odes on state occasions are written. Itself must be its own end, or it is nothing. The difference between poetry and stock poetry is this, that in the latter the rhythm is given and the sense adapted to it; while in the former the sense dictates the rhythm. I might even say that the rhyme is there in the theme, thought, and image themselves. Ask the fact for the form. For a verse is not a vehicle to carry a sentence as a jewel is carried in a case: the verse must be alive, and inseparable from its contents, as the soul of man inspires and directs the body, and we measure the inspiration by the music. In reading prose, I am sensitive as soon as a sentence drags; but in poetry, as soon as one word drags. Ever as the thought mounts, the expression mounts. 'T is cumulative also; the poem is made up of lines each of which fill the ear of the poet in its turn, so that mere synthesis produces a work quite superhuman.

Indeed, the masters sometimes rise above themselves to strains which charm their readers, and which neither any competitor could outdo, nor the bard himself again equal. Try this strain of Beaumont and Fletcher: —

> "Hence, all ye vain delights,
>   As short as are the nights
>   In which you spend your folly !

There's naught in this life sweet,
If men were wise to see 't,
But only melancholy.
Oh! sweetest melancholy!
Welcome, folded arms and fixed eyes,
A sigh that piercing mortifies,
A look that's fastened to the ground,
A tongue chained up without a sound;
Fountain-heads and pathless groves,
Places which pale Passion loves,
Midnight walks, when all the fowls
Are warmly housed, save bats and owls;
A midnight bell, a passing groan,
These are the sounds we feed upon,
Then stretch our bones in a still, gloomy valley.
Nothing's so dainty sweet as lovely melancholy."

Keats disclosed by certain lines in his "Hyperion" this inward skill; and Coleridge showed at least his love and appetency for it. It appears in Ben Jonson's songs, including certainly "The faery beam upon you," etc., Waller's "Go, lovely rose!" Herbert's "Virtue" and "Easter," and Lovelace's lines "To Althea" and "To Lucasta," and Collins's "Ode to Evening," all but the last verse, which is academical. Perhaps this dainty style of poetry is not producible to-day, any more than a right Gothic cathedral. It belonged to a time and taste which is not in the world.

As the imagination is not a talent of some men but is the health of every man, so also is this joy of musical expression. I know the pride of mathematicians and materialists, but they cannot conceal from me their capital want. The critic, the philosopher, is a failed poet. Gray avows that "he thinks even a bad verse as good a thing or better than the best observation that was ever made on it." I honor the naturalist; I honor the geometer, but he has before him higher power and happiness than he knows. Yet we will leave to the masters their own forms. Newton may be permitted to call Terence a play-book, and to wonder at the frivolous taste for rhymers; he only predicts, one would say, a grander poetry: he only shows that he is not yet reached; that the poetry which satisfies more youthful souls is not such to a mind like his, accustomed to grander harmonies; — this being a child's whistle to his ear; that the music must rise to a loftier strain, up to Handel, up to Beethoven, up to the thorough-base of the sea-shore, up to the largeness of astronomy: at last that great heart will hear in the music beats like its own; the waves of melody will wash and float him also, and set him into concert and harmony.

Bards and Trouveurs. — The metallic force of primitive words makes the superiority of the remains of the rude ages. It costs the early bard little talent to chant more impressively than the later, more cultivated poets. His advantage is that his words are things, each the lucky sound which described the fact, and we listen to him as we do to the Indian, or the hunter, or miner, each of whom represents his facts as accurately as the cry of the wolf or the eagle tells of the forest or the air they inhabit. The original force, the direct smell of the earth or the sea, is in these ancient poems, the Sagas of the North, the Nibelungen Lied, the songs and ballads of the English and Scotch.

I find or fancy more true poetry, the love of the vast and the ideal, in the Welsh and bardic fragments of Taliessin and his successors, than in many volumes of British Classics. An intrepid magniloquence appears in all the bards, as : —

"The whole ocean flamed as one wound."
King Regnar Lodbrok.

"God himself cannot procure good for the wicked."
Welsh Triad.

A favorable specimen is Taliessin's " Invocation of the Wind " at the door of Castle Teganwy : —

" Discover thou what it is, —
  The strong creature from before the flood,
  Without flesh, without bone, without head, without feet,
  It will neither be younger nor older than at the beginning ;
  It has no fear, nor the rude wants of created things.
  Great God ! how the sea whitens when it comes !
  It is in the field, it is in the wood,
  Without hand, without foot,
  Without age, without season,

It is always of the same age with the ages of ages,
And of equal breadth with the surface of the earth.
It was not born, it sees not,
And is not seen ; it does not come when desired ;
It has no form, it bears no burden,
For it is void of sin.
It makes no perturbation in the place where God wills it,
On the sea, on the land."

In one of his poems he asks : —
" Is there but one course to the wind ?
But one to the water of the sea ?
Is there but one spark in the fire of boundless energy ? "

He says of his hero, Cunedda, —
" He will assimilate, he will agree with the deep and the
     shallow."

To another, —

> " When I lapse to a sinful word,
>   May neither you, nor others hear."

Of an enemy, —

" The cauldron of the sea was bordered round by his
land, but it would not boil the food of a coward."

To an exile on an island he says, —

" The heavy blue chain of the sea didst thou, O just
man, endure."

Another bard in like tone says, —

" I am possessed of songs such as no son of man can
repeat ; one of them is called the ' Helper ; ' it will help
thee at thy need in sickness, grief, and all adversities.
I know a song which I need only to sing when men

have loaded me with bonds : when I sing it, my chains fall in pieces and I walk forth at liberty."

The Norsemen have no less faith in poetry and its power, when they describe it thus : —

" Odin spoke everything in rhyme. He and his temple-gods were called song-smiths. He could make his enemies in battle blind or deaf, and their weapons so blunt that they could no more cut than a willow-twig. Odin taught these arts in runes or songs, which are called incantations." [1]

The Crusades brought out the genius of France, in the twelfth century, when Pierre d'Auvergne said, —

" I will sing a new song which resounds in my breast : never was a song good or beautiful which resembled any other."

And Pons de Capdeuil declares, —

" Since the air renews itself and softens, so must my heart renew itself, and what buds in it buds and grows outside of it."

There is in every poem a height which attracts more than other parts, and is best remembered. Thus, in " Morte d'Arthur," I remember nothing so well as Sir Gawain's parley with Merlin in his wonderful prison : —

"After the disappearance of Merlin from King Ar-

[1] Heimskringla, Vol. I. p. 221.

thur's court he was seriously missed, and many knights set out in search of him. Among others was Sir Gawain, who pursued his search till it was time to return to the court. He came into the forest of Broceliande, lamenting as he went along. Presently he heard the voice of one groaning on his right hand ; looking that way, he could see nothing save a kind of smoke which seemed like air, and through which he could not pass ; and this impediment made him so wrathful that it deprived him of speech. Presently he heard a voice which said, 'Gawain, Gawain, be not out of heart, for everything which must happen will come to pass.' And when he heard the voice which thus called him by his right name, he replied, 'Who can this be who hath spoken to me?' 'How,' said the voice, 'Sir Gawain, know you me not ? You were wont to know me well, but thus things are interwoven and thus the proverb says true, "Leave the court and the court will leave you." So is it with me. Whilst I served King Arthur, I was well known by you and by other barons, but because I have left the court, I am known no longer, and put in forgetfulness, which I ought not to be if faith reigned in the world.' When Sir Gawain heard the voice which spoke to him thus, he thought it was Merlin, and he answered, 'Sir, certes I ought to know you well, for many times I have heard your words. I pray you appear before me so that I may be able to recognize you.' 'Ah, sir,' said Merlin, 'you will never see me more, and that grieves me, but I cannot remedy it, and when you shall have departed from this place, I shall nevermore speak to you nor to

any other person, save only my mistress; for never other
person will be able to discover this place for anything
which may befall; neither shall I ever go out from
hence, for in the world there is no such strong tower as
this wherein I am confined; and it is neither of wood,
nor of iron, nor of stone, but of air, without anything
else; and made by enchantment so strong that it can
never be demolished while the world lasts; neither can
I go out, nor can any one come in, save she who hath
enclosed me here and who keeps me company when it
pleaseth her: she cometh when she listeth, for her will
is here.' 'How, Merlin, my good friend,' said Sir Gawain, 'are you restrained so strongly that you cannot
deliver yourself nor make yourself visible unto me; how
can this happen, seeing that you are the wisest man in
the world?' 'Rather,' said Merlin, 'the greatest fool;
for I well knew that all this would befall me, and I have
been fool enough to love another more than myself, for
I taught my mistress that whereby she hath imprisoned
me in such a manner that none can set me free.' 'Certes,
Merlin,' replied Sir Gawain, 'of that I am right sorrowful, and so will King Arthur, my uncle, be, when he
shall know it, as one who is making search after you
throughout all countries.' 'Well,' said Merlin, 'it must
be borne, for never will he see me, nor I him; neither
will any one speak with me again after you, it would be
vain to attempt it; for you yourself, when you have
turned away, will never be able to find the place: but
salute for me the king and the queen and all the barons,
and tell them of my condition. You will find the king

at Carduel in Wales; and when you arrive there you will find there all the companions who departed with you, and who at this day will return. Now then go in the name of God, who will protect and save the King Arthur, and the realm of Logres, and you also, as the best knights who are in the world.' With that Sir Gawain departed joyful and sorrowful; joyful because of what Merlin had assured him should happen to him, and sorrowful that Merlin had thus been lost."

Morals.—We are sometimes apprised that there is a mental power and creation more excellent than anything which is commonly called philosophy and literature; that the high poets, that Homer, Milton, Shakspeare, do not fully content us. How rarely they offer us the heavenly bread! The most they have done is to intoxicate us once and again with its taste. They have touched this heaven and retain afterwards some sparkle of it: they betray their belief that such discourse is possible. There is something — our brothers on this or that side of the sea do not know it or own it; the eminent scholars of England, historians and reviewers, romancers and poets included, might deny and blaspheme it, — which is setting us and them aside and the whole world also, and planting itself. To true poetry we shall sit down as the result and justification of the age in which it appears, and think lightly of histories and statutes. None of your parlor or piano verse, none of your carpet poets, who are content to amuse, will satisfy us. Power, new power, is the good which the soul seeks. The poetic gift we want, as the health and supremacy of man, — not rhymes and sonneteering, not bookmaking and bookselling; surely not cold spying and authorship.

Is not poetry the little chamber in the brain where is generated the explosive force which, by gentle shocks, sets in action the intellectual world? Bring us the bards who shall sing all our old ideas out of our heads, and new ones in; men-making poets; poetry which, like the verses inscribed on Balder's columns in Breidablik, is capable of restoring the dead to life; — poetry like that verse of Saadi, which the angels testified "met the approbation of Allah in Heaven;"— poetry which finds its rhymes and cadences in the rhymes and iterations of nature, and is the gift to men of new images and symbols, each the ensign and oracle of an age; that shall assimilate men to it, mould itself into religions and mythologies, and impart its quality to centuries; — poetry which tastes the world and reports of it, upbuilding the world again in the thought; —

> "Not with tickling rhymes,
>   But high and noble matter, such as flies
>   From brains entranced, and filled with ecstasies."

Poetry must be affirmative. It is the piety of

the intellect. "Thus saith the Lord," should begin
the song.   The poet who shall use nature as his
hieroglyphic must have an adequate message to
convey thereby.   Therefore when we speak of the
Poet in any high sense, we are driven to such exam
ples as Zoroaster and Plato, St. John and Menu,
with their moral burdens.   The Muse shall be the
counterpart of Nature, and equally rich.   I find her
not often in books.   We know Nature and figure
her exuberant, tranquil, magnificent in her fertility,
coherent; so that every creation is omen of every
other.   She is not proud of the sea, of the stars,
of space or time, or man or woman.   All her kinds
share the attributes of the selectest extremes.   But
in current literature I do not find her.   Literature
warps away from life, though at first it seems to
bind it.   In the world of letters how few commanding oracles!   Homer did what he could ; Pindar,
Æschylus, and the Greek Gnomic poets and the
tragedians.   Dante was faithful when not carried
away by his fierce hatreds.   But in so many al-
coves of English poetry I can count only nine or
ten authors who are still inspirers and lawgivers
to their race.

The supreme value of poetry is to educate us to a
height beyond itself, or which it rarely reaches ; —
the subduing mankind to order and virtue.   He is
the true Orpheus who writes his ode, not with syl-

lables, but men. "In poetry," said Goethe, "only
the really great and pure advances us, and this exists as a second nature, either elevating us to itself,
or rejecting us." The poet must let Humanity sit
with the Muse in his head, as the charioteer sits
with the hero in the Iliad. "Show me," said Sa-
rona in the novel, "one wicked man who has written poetry, and I will show you where his poetry is
not poetry ; or rather, I will show you in his poetry no poetry at all." [1]

I have heard that there is a hope which precedes
and must precede all science of the visible or the
invisible world ; and that science is the realization
of that hope in either region. I count the genius
of Swedenborg and Wordsworth as the agents of a
reform in philosophy, the bringing poetry back to
nature, — to the marrying of nature and mind, un-
doing the old divorce in which poetry had been
famished and false, and nature had been suspected
and pagan. The philosophy which a nation receives, rules its religion, poetry, politics, arts,
trades, and whole history. A good poem — say
Shakspeare's Macbeth, or Hamlet, or the Tempest
— goes about the world offering itself to reasonable
men, who read it with joy and carry it to their
reasonable neighbors. Thus it draws to it the wise
and generous souls, confirming their secret thoughts,

---

[1] "Counterparts." Vol. I. p. 67.

and, through their sympathy, really publishing itself.   It affects the characters of its readers by for-
mulating their opinions and feelings, and inevitably
prompting their daily action.   If they build ships,
they write " Ariel " or " Prospero " or " Ophelia "
on the ship's stern, and impart a tenderness and
mystery to matters of fact.   The ballad and romance work on the hearts of boys, who recite the
rhymes to their hoops or their skates if alone, and
these heroic songs or lines are remembered and determine many practical choices which they make
later.   Do you think Burns has had no influence
on the life of men and women in Scotland, — has
opened no eyes and ears to the face of nature and
the dignity of man and the charm and excellence
of woman ?

We are a little civil, it must be owned, to Homer
and Æschylus, to Dante and Shakspeare, and give
them the benefit of the largest interpretation.   We
must be a little strict also, and ask whether, if we
sit down at home, and do not go to Hamlet, Hamlet will come to us ? whether we shall find our
tragedy written in his, — our hopes, wants, pains,
disgraces, described to the life, — and the way
opened to the paradise which ever in the best hour
beckons us ?   But our overpraise and idealization
of famous masters is not in its origin a poor Bos-
wellism, but an impatience of mediocrity.   The

praise we now give to our heroes we shall unsay when we make larger demands. How fast we outgrow the books of the nursery, — then those that satisfied our youth. What we once admired as poetry has long since come to be a sound of tin pans; and many of our later books we have outgrown. Perhaps Homer and Milton will be tin pans yet. Better not to be easily pleased. The poet should rejoice if he has taught us to despise his song; if he has so moved us as to lift us, — to open the eye of the intellect to see farther and better.

In proportion as a man's life comes into union with truth, his thoughts approach to a parallelism with the currents of natural laws, so that he easily expresses his meaning by natural symbols, or uses the ecstatic or poetic speech. By successive states of mind all the facts of nature are for the first time interpreted. In proportion as his life departs from this simplicity, he uses circumlocution, — by many words hoping to suggest what he cannot say. Vexatious to find poets, who are by excellence the thinking and feeling of the world, deficient in truth of intellect and of affection. Then is conscience unfaithful, and thought unwise. To know the merit of Shakspeare, read Faust. I find Faust a little too modern and intelligible. We can find such a fabric at several mills, though a little inferior. Faust abounds in the disagreeable. The vice is

prurient, learned, Parisian. In the presence of
Jove, Priapus may be allowed as an offset, but here
he is an equal hero. The egotism, the wit, is cal-
culated. The book is undeniably written by a
master, and stands unhappily related to the whole
modern world; but it is a very disagreeable chapter of literature, and accuses the author as well as
the times. Shakspeare could no doubt have been
disagreeable, had he less genius, and if ugliness had
attracted him. In short, our English nature and
genius has made us the worst critics of Goethe, —

> " We, who speak the tongue
> That Shakspeare spake, the faith and manners hold
> Which Milton held."

It is not style or rhymes, or a new image more
or less that imports, but sanity; that life should
not be mean; that life should be an image in every
part beautiful; that the old forgotten splendors of
the universe should glow again for us; — that we
should lose our wit, but gain our reason. And
when life is true to the poles of nature, the streams
of truth will roll through us in song.

Transcendency. — In a cotillon some persons
dance and others await their turn when the music
and the figure come to them. In the dance of God
there is not one of the chorus but can and will
begin to spin, monumental as he now looks, when·

ever the music and figure reach his place and duty. O celestial Bacchus! drive them mad, — this multitude of vagabonds, hungry for eloquence, hungry for poetry, starving for symbols, perishing for want of electricity to vitalize this too much pasture, and in the long delay indemnifying themselves with the false wine of alcohol, of politics, or of money.

Every man may be, and at some time a man is, lifted to a platform whence he looks beyond sense to moral and spiritual truth, and in that mood deals sovereignly with matter, and strings worlds like beads upon his thought. The success with which this is done can alone determine how genuine is the inspiration. The poet is rare because he must be exquisitely vital and sympathetic, and, at the same time, immovably centred. In good society, nay, among the angels in heaven, is not everything spoken in fine parable, and not so servilely as it befell to the sense? All is symbolized. Facts are not foreign, as they seem, but related. Wait a little and we see the return of the remote hyperbolic curve. The solid men complain that the idealist leaves out the fundamental facts; the poet complains that the solid men leave out the sky. To every plant there are two powers; one shoots down as rootlet, and one upward as tree. You must have eyes of science to see in the seed ·its nodes; you must have the vivacity of the poet to perceive

in the thought its futurities. The poet is representative, — whole man, diamond-merchant, sym-
bolizer, emancipator; in him the world projects a
scribe's hand and writes the adequate genesis. The
nature of things is flowing, a metamorphosis. The
free spirit sympathizes not only with the actual
form, but with the power or possible forms ; but for
obvious municipal or parietal uses God has given
us a bias or a rest on to-day's forms. Hence the
shudder of joy with which in each clear moment we
recognize the metamorphosis, because it is always
a conquest, a surprise from the heart of things.
One would say of the force in the works of nature,
all depends on the battery. If it give one shock,
we shall get to the fish form, and stop; if two
shocks, to the bird ; if three, to the quadruped ; if
four, to the man. Power of generalizing differences
men. The number of successive saltations the nimble thought can make, measures the difference between the highest and lowest of mankind. The
habit of saliency, of not pausing but going on, is a
sort of importation or domestication of the Divine
effort in a man. After the largest circle has been
drawn, a larger can be drawn around it. The
problem of the poet is to unite freedom with pre-
cision; to give the pleasure of color, and be not
less the most powerful of sculptors. Music seems
to you sufficient, or the subtle and delicate scent of

lavender; but Dante was free imagination, — all wings, — yet he wrote like Euclid. And mark the equality of Shakspeare to the comic, the tender and sweet, and to the grand and terrible. A little more or less skill in whistling is of no account. See those weary pentameter tales of Dryden and others. Turnpike is one thing and blue sky another. Let the poet, of all men, stop with his inspiration. The inexorable rule in the muses' court, *either inspiration or silence*, compels the bard to report only his supreme moments. It teaches the enormous force of a few words, and in proportion to the inspiration checks loquacity. Much that we call poetry is but polite verse. The high poetry which shall thrill and agitate mankind, restore youth and health, dissipate the dreams under which men reel and stagger, and bring in the new thoughts, the sanity and heroic aims of nations, is deeper hid and longer postponed than was America or Australia, or the finding of steam or of the galvanic battery. We must not conclude against poetry from the defects of poets. They are, in our experience, men of every degree of skill, — some of them only once or twice receivers of an inspiration, and presently falling back on a low life. The drop of *ichor* that tingles in their veins has not yet refined their blood and cannot lift the whole man to the digestion and function of ichor, — that is, to godlike nature.

Time will be when ichor shall be their blood, when what are now glimpses and aspirations shall be the routine of the day. Yet even partial ascents to poetry and ideas are forerunners, and announce the dawn. In the mire of the sensual life, their religion, their poets, their admiration of heroes and benefactors, even their novel and newspaper, nay, their superstitions also, are hosts of ideals, — a cordage of ropes that hold them up out of the slough. Poetry is inestimable as a lonely faith, a lonely protest in the uproar of atheism.

But so many men are ill-born or ill-bred, — the brains are so marred, so imperfectly formed, unheroically, brains of the sons of fallen men, that the doctrine is imperfectly received. One man sees a spark or shimmer of the truth and reports it, and his saying becomes a legend or golden proverb for ages, and other men report as much, but none wholly and well. Poems! — we have no poem. Whenever that angel shall be organized and appear on earth, the Iliad will be reckoned a poor ballad-grinding. I doubt never the riches of nature, the gifts of the future, the immense wealth of the mind. O yes, poets we shall have, mythology, symbols, religion, of our own. We too shall know how to take up all this industry and empire, this Western civilization, into thought, as easily as men did when arts were few; but not by holding it high, but by holding it low. The intellect uses and is not used, — uses London and Paris and Berlin, East and West, to its end. The only heart that can help us is one that draws, not from our society, but from itself, a counterpoise to society. What if we find partiality and meanness in us? The grandeur of our life exists in spite of us, — all over and under and within us, in what of us is inevitable and above our control. Men are facts as well as persons, and the involuntary part of their life is so much as to fill the mind and leave them no countenance to say aught of what is so trivial as their selfish thinking and doing. Sooner or later that which is now life shall be poetry, and every fair and manly trait shall add a richer strain to the song.

SOCIAL AIMS.

MUCH ill-natured criticism has been directed on American manners. I do not think it is to be resented. Rather, if we are wise, we shall listen and mend. Our critics will then be our best friends, though they did not mean it. But in every sense the subject of manners has a constant interest to thoughtful persons. Who does not delight in fine manners? Their charm cannot be predicted or overstated. 'T is perpetual promise of more than can be fulfilled. It is music and sculpture and picture to many who do not pretend to appreciation of those arts. It is even true that grace is more beautiful than beauty. Yet how impossible to overcome the obstacle of an unlucky temperament and acquire good manners, unless by living with the well-bred from the start; and this makes the value of wise forethought to give ourselves and our children as much as possible the habit of cultivated society.

'T is an inestimable hint that I owe to a few persons of fine manners, that they make behavior the very first sign of force, — behavior, and not performance, or talent, or, much less, wealth. Whilst almost everybody has a supplicating eye turned on events and things and other persons, a few natures are central and forever unfold, and these alone charm us. He whose word or deed you cannot predict, who answers you without any supplication in his eye, who draws his determination from within, and draws it instantly, — that man rules.

The staple figure in novels is the man of *aplomb*, who sits, among the young aspirants and desperates, quite sure and compact, and, never sharing their affections or debilities, hurls his word like a bullet when occasion requires, knows his way, and carries his points. They may scream or applaud, he is never engaged or heated. Napoleon is the type of this class in modern history; Byron's heroes in poetry. But we for the most part are all drawn into the *charivari;* we chide, lament, cavil, and recriminate.

I think Hans Andersen's story of the cobweb cloth woven so fine that it was invisible, — woven for the king's garment, — must mean manners, which do really clothe a princely nature. Such a one can well go in a blanket, if he would. In the gymnasium or on the sea-beach his superiority does not leave him. But he who has not this fine garment of behavior is studious of dress, and then not less of house and furniture and pictures and gar dens, in all which he hopes to lie *perdu*, and not be exposed.

" Manners are stronger than laws." Their vast convenience I must always admire. The perfect defence and isolation which they effect makes an insuperable protection. Though the person so clothed wrestle with you, or swim with you, lodge in the same chamber, eat at the same table, he is yet a thousand miles off, and can at any moment finish with you. Manners seem to say, *You are you, and I am I.* In the most delicate natures, fine temperament and culture build this impassable wall. Balzac finely said : " Kings themselves cannot force the exquisite politeness of distance to capitulate, hid behind its shield of bronze."

Nature values manners. See how she has prepared for them. Who teaches manners of majesty, of frankness, of grace, of humility, — who but the adoring aunts and cousins that surround a young child ? The babe meets such courting and flattery as only kings receive when adult; and, trying experiments, and at perfect leisure with these posture-masters and flatterers all day, he throws himself into all the attitudes that correspond to theirs. Are they humble? he is composed. Are they eager? he is nonchalant. Are they encroaching? he is dignified and inexorable. And this scene is daily repeated in hovels as well as in high houses.

Nature is the best posture-master. An awkward man is graceful when asleep, or when hard at work, or agreeably amused. The attitudes of children are gentle, persuasive, royal, in their games and in their house-talk and in the street, before they have learned to cringe. 'T is impossible but thought disposes the limbs and the walk, and is masterly or secondary. No art can contravene it or conceal it. Give me a thought, and my hands and legs and voice and face will all go right. And we are awkward for want of thought. The inspiration is scanty, and does not arrive at the extremities.

It is a commonplace of romances to show the ungainly manners of the pedant who has lived too long in college. Intellectual men pass for vulgar, and are timid and heavy with the elegant. But if the elegant are also intellectual, instantly the hesitating scholar is inspired, transformed, and exhibits the best style of manners. An intellectual man, though of feeble spirit, is instantly reinforced by being put into the company of scholars, and, to the surprise of everybody, becomes a lawgiver. We think a man unable and desponding. It is only that he is misplaced. Put him with new companions, and they will find in him excellent qualities, unsuspected accomplishments, and the joy of life. 'T is a great point in a gallery, how you hang pictures; and not less in society, how you seat your party. The circumstance of circumstance is timing and placing. When a man meets his accurate mate, society begins, and life is delicious.

What happiness they give, — what ties they form! Whilst one man by his manners pins me to the wall, with another I walk among the stars. One man can, by his voice, lead the cheer of a regiment; another will have no following. Nature made us all intelligent of these signs, for our safety and our happiness. Whilst certain faces are illumined with intelligence, decorated with invitation, others are marked with warnings: certain voices are hoarse and truculent; sometimes they even bark. There is the same difference between heavy and genial manners as between the perceptions of octogenarians and those of young girls who see everything in the twinkling of an eye.

Manners are the revealers of secrets, the betrayers of any disproportion or want of symmetry in mind and character. It is the law of our constitution that every change in our experience instantly indicates itself on our countenance and carriage, as the lapse of time tells itself on the face of a clock. We may be too obtuse to read it, but the record is there. Some men may be obtuse to read it, but some men are not obtuse and do read it. In Borrow's "Lavengro," the gypsy instantly detects, by his companion's face and behavior, that some good fortune has befallen him, and that he has money. We say, in these days, that credit is to be abolished in trade: is it? When a stranger comes to buy goods of you, do you not look in his face and answer according to what you read there? Credit is to be abolished? Can't you abolish faces and character, of which credit is the reflection? As long as men are born babes they will live on credit for the first fourteen or eighteen years of their life. Every innocent man has in his countenance a promise to pay, and hence credit. Less credit will there be? You are mistaken. There will always be more and more. Character *must* be trusted; and just in proportion to the morality of a people will be the expansion of the credit system.

There is even a little rule of prudence for the young experimenter which Dr. Franklin omitted to set down, yet which the youth may find useful, — Do not go to ask your debtor the payment of a debt on the day when you have no other resource. He will learn by your air and tone how it is with you, and will treat you as a beggar. But work and starve a little longer. Wait till your affairs go better and you have other means at hand; you will then ask in a different tone, and he will treat your claim with entire respect.

Now we all wish to be graceful, and do justice to ourselves by our manners; but youth in America is wont to be poor and hurried, not at ease, or not in society where high behavior could be taught. But the sentiment of honor and the wish to serve make all our pains superfluous. Life is not so short but that there is always time enough for courtesy. Self-command is the main elegance. "Keep cool, and you command everybody," said St. Just; and the wily old Talleyrand would still say, *Surtout, messieurs, pas de zèle,* — "Above all, gentlemen, no heat."

Why have you statues in your hall, but to teach you that, when the door-bell rings, you shall sit like them. "Eat at your table as you would eat at the table of the king," said Confucius. It is an excellent custom of the Quakers, if only for a school of manners, — the silent prayer before meals. It has the effect to stop mirth, and introduce a moment of reflection. After the pause, all resume their usual intercourse from a vantage-ground. What a check to the violent manners which sometimes come to the table, — of wrath, and whining, and heat in trifles!

'T is a rule of manners to avoid exaggeration. A lady loses as soon as she admires too easily and too much. In man or woman, the face and the person lose power when they are on the strain to express admiration. A man makes his inferiors his superiors by heat. Why need you, who are not a gossip, talk as a gossip, and tell eagerly what the neighbors or the journals say? State your opinion without apology. The attitude is the main point, assuring your companion that, come good news or come bad, you remain in good heart and good mind, which is the best news you can possibly communicate. Self-control is the rule. You have in you there a noisy, sensual savage, which you are to keep down, and turn all his strength to beauty. For example, what a seneschal and detective is laughter! It seems to require several generations of education to train a squeaking or a shouting habit out of a man. Sometimes, when in almost all expressions the Choctaw and the slave have been worked out of him, a coarse nature still betrays itself in his contemptible squeals of joy. It is necessary for the purification of drawing-rooms that these entertaining explosions should be under strict control. Lord Chesterfield had early made this discovery, for he says, "I am sure that since I had the use of my reason, no human being has ever heard me laugh." I know that there go two to this game, and, in the presence of certain formidable wits, savage nature must sometimes rush out in some disorder.

To pass to an allied topic, one word or two in regard to dress, in which our civilization instantly shows itself. No nation is dressed with more good sense than ours. And everybody sees certain moral benefit in it. When the young European emigrant, after a summer's labor, puts on for the first time a new coat, he puts on much more. His good and becoming clothes put him on thinking that he must behave like people who are so dressed; and silently and steadily his behavior mends. But quite another class of our own youth I should remind, of dress in general, that some people need it and others need it not. Thus a king or a general does not need a fine coat, and a commanding person may save himself all solicitude on that point. There are always slovens in State Street or Wall Street, who are not less considered. If a man have manners and talent he may dress roughly and carelessly. It is only when mind and character slumber that the dress can be seen. If the intellect were always awake, and every noble sentiment, the man might go in huckaback or mats, and his dress would be admired and imitated. Remember George Herbert's maxim, "This coat with my discretion will be brave." If, however, a man has not firm nerves and has keen sensibility, it is perhaps a wise economy to go to a good shop and dress himself irreproachably. He can then dismiss all care from his mind, and may easily find that performance an addition of confidence, a fortification that turns the scale in social encounters, and allows him to go gayly into conversations where else he had been dry and embarrassed. I am not ignorant, — I have heard with admiring submission the experience of the lady who declared that "the sense of being perfectly well - dressed gives a feeling of inward tranquillity which religion is powerless to bestow."

Thus much for manners : but we are not content with pantomime ; we say, This is only for the eyes. We want real relations of the mind and the heart; we want friendship; we want knowledge; we want virtue; a more inward existence to read the history of each other. Welfare requires one or two companions of intelligence, probity, and grace, to wear out life with, — persons with whom we can speak a few reasonable words every day, by whom we can measure ourselves, and who shall hold us fast to good sense and virtue ; and these we are always in search of. He must be inestimable to us to whom we can say what we cannot say to ourselves. Yet now and then we say things to our mates, or hear things from them, which seem to put it out of the power of the parties to be strangers again. "Either death or a friend," is a Persian proverb. I suppose I give the experience of many when I give my own. A few times in my life it has happened to me to meet persons of so good a nature and so good breeding that every topic was open and discussed without possibility of offence, — persons who could not be shocked. One of my friends said in speaking of certain associates, "There is not one of them but I can offend at any moment." But to the company I am now considering, were no terrors, no vulgarity. All topics were broached, — life, love, marriage, sex, hatred, suicide, magic, theism, art, poetry, religion, myself, thyself, all selves, and whatever else, with a security and vivacity which belonged to the nobility of the parties and to their brave truth. The life of these persons was conducted in the same calm and affirmative manner as their discourse. Life with them was an experiment continually varied, full of results, full of grandeur, and by no means the hot and hurried business which passes in the world. The delight in good company, in pure, brilliant, social atmosphere; the incomparable satisfaction of a society in which everything can be safely said, in which every member returns a true echo, in which a wise freedom, an ideal republic of sense, simplicity, knowledge, and thorough good-meaning abide, — doubles the value of life. It is this that justifies to each the jealousy with which the doors are kept. Do not look sourly at the set or the club which does not choose you. Every highly-organized person knows the value of the social barriers, since the best society has often been spoiled to him by the intrusion of bad companions. He of all men would keep the right of choice sacred, and feel that the exclusions are in the interest of the admissions, though they happen at this moment to thwart his wishes.

The hunger for company is keen, but it must be discriminating, and must be economized. 'T is a defect in our manners that they have not yet reached the prescribing a limit to visits. That every well-dressed lady or gentleman should be at liberty to exceed ten minutes in his or her call on serious people, shows a civilization still rude. A universal etiquette should fix an iron limit after which a moment should not be allowed without explicit leave granted on request of either the giver or receiver of the visit. There is inconvenience in such strictness, but vast inconvenience in the want of it. To trespass on a public servant is to trespass on a nation's time. Yet presidents of the United States are afflicted by rude Western and Southern gossips (I hope it is only by them) until the gossip's immeasurable legs are tired of sitting ; then he strides out and the nation is relieved.

It is very certain that sincere and happy conversation doubles our powers ; that in the effort to unfold our thought to a friend we make it clearer to ourselves, and surround it with illustrations that help and delight us. It may happen that each hears from the other a better wisdom than any one else will ever hear from either. But these ties are taken care of by Providence to each of us. A wise man once said to me that "all whom he knew, met:"—meaning that he need not take pains to introduce the persons whom he valued to each other: they were sure to be drawn together as by gravitation. The soul of a man must be the servant of another. The true friend must have an attraction to whatever virtue is in us. Our chief want in life,—is it not somebody who can make us do what we can? And we are easily great with the loved and honored associate. We come out of our eggshell existence and see the great dome arching over us; see the zenith above and the nadir under us.

Speech is power: speech is to persuade, to convert, to compel. It is to bring another out of his bad sense into your good sense. You are to be missionary and carrier of all that is good and noble. Virtues speak to virtues, vices to vices,— each to their own kind in the people with whom we deal. If you are suspiciously and dryly on your guard, so is he or she. If you rise to frankness and generosity, they will respect it now or later.

In this art of conversation, Woman, if not the queen and victor, is the lawgiver. If every one recalled his experiences, he might find the best in the speech of superior women;—which was better than song, and carried ingenuity, character, wise counsel and affection, as easily as the wit with which it was adorned. They are not only wise themselves, they make us wise. No one can be a master in conversation who has not learned much from women; their presence and inspiration are essential to its success. Steele said of his mistress, that " to have loved her was a liberal education." Shenstone gave no bad account of this influence in his description of the French woman : " There is a quality in which no woman in the world can compete with her, — it is the power of intellectual irritation. She will draw wit out of a fool. She strikes with such address the chords of self-love, that she gives unexpected vigor and agility to fancy, and electrifies a body that appeared non-electric." Coleridge esteems cultivated women as the depositaries and guardians of " English undefiled ; " and Luther commends that accomplishment of "pure German speech " of his wife.

Madame de Staël, by the unanimous consent of all who knew her, was the most extraordinary converser that was known in her time, and it was a time full of eminent men and women; she knew all distinguished persons in letters or society in England, Germany, and Italy, as well as in France ; though she said, with characteristic nationality, " Conversation, like talent, exists only in France." Madame de Staël valued nothing but conversation. When they showed her the beautiful Lake Leman, she exclaimed, " O for the gutter of the Rue de Bac ! " the street in Paris in which her house stood. And she said one day, seriously, to M. Molé, "If it were not for respect to human opinions, I would not open my window to see the Bay of Naples for the first time, whilst I would go five hundred leagues to talk with a man of genius whom I had not seen." Sainte-Beuve tells us of the privileged circle at Coppet, that after making an excursion one day, the party returned in two coaches from Chambéry to Aix, on the way to Coppet. The first coach had many rueful accidents to relate, — a terrific thunder-storm, shocking roads, and danger and gloom to the whole company. The party in the second coach, on arriving, heard this story with surprise ; — of thunder-storm, of steeps, of mud, of danger, they knew nothing ; no, they had forgotten earth, and breathed a purer air : such a conversation between Madame de Staël and Madame Récamier and Benjamin Constant and Schlegel ! they were all in a state of delight. The intoxication of the conversation had made them insensible to all notice of weather or rough roads. Madame de Tessé said, "If I were Queen, I should command Madame de Staël to talk to me every day." Conversation fills all gaps, supplies all deficiencies. What a good trait is that recorded of Madame de Maintenon, that, during dinner, the servant slipped to her side, "Please, madame, one anecdote more, for there is no roast to-day."

Politics, war, party, luxury, avarice, fashion, are all asses with loaded panniers to serve the kitchen of Intellect, the king. There is nothing that does not pass into lever or weapon.

And yet there are trials enough of nerve and character, brave choices enough of taking the part of truth and of the oppressed against the oppressor, in privatest circles. A right speech is not well to be distinguished from action. Courage to ask questions; courage to expose our ignorance. The great gain is, not to shine, not to conquer your companion, — then you learn nothing but conceit, — but to find a companion who knows what you do not; to tilt with him and be overthrown, horse and foot, with utter destruction of all your logic and learning. There is a defeat that is useful. Then you can see the real and the counterfeit, and will never accept the counterfeit again. You will adopt the art of war that has defeated you. You will ride to battle horsed on the very logic which you found irresistible. You will accept the fertile truth, instead of the solemn customary lie.

Let nature bear the expense. The attitude, the tone, is all. Let our eyes not look away, but meet. Let us not look east and west for materials of conversation, but rest in presence and unity. A just feeling will fast enough supply fuel for discourse, if speaking be more grateful than silence. When people come to see us, we foolishly prattle, lest we be inhospitable. But things said for conversation are chalk eggs. Don't *say* things. What you *are* stands over you the while, and thunders so that I cannot hear what you say to the contrary. A lady of my acquaintance said, "I don't care so much for what they say as I do for what makes them say it."

The main point is to throw yourself on the truth, and say, with Newton, "There's no contending against facts." When Molyneux fancied that the observations of the nutation of the earth's axis destroyed Newton's theory of gravitation, he tried to break it softly to Sir Isaac, who only answered, "It may be so, there's no arguing against facts and experiments."

But there are people who cannot be cultivated, — people on whom speech makes no impression; swainish, morose people, who must be kept down and quieted as you would those who are a little tipsy; others, who are not only swainish, but are prompt to take oath that swainishness is the only culture; and though their odd wit may have some salt for you, your friends would not relish it. Bolt these out. And I have seen a man of genius who made me think that if other men were like him co-operation were impossible. Must we always talk for victory, and never once for truth, for comfort, and joy? Here is centrality and penetration, strong understanding, and the higher gifts, the insight of the real, or from the real, and the moral rectitude which belongs to it: but all this and all his resources of wit and invention are lost to me in every experiment that I make to hold intercourse with his mind; always some weary, captious paradox to fight you with, and the time and temper wasted. And beware of jokes; too much temperance cannot be used: inestimable for sauce, but corrupting for food, we go away hollow and ashamed. As soon as the company give in to this enjoyment, we shall have no Olympus. True wit never made us laugh. Mahomet seems to have borrowed by anticipation of several centuries a leaf from the mind of Swedenborg, when he wrote in the Koran: —

" On the day of resurrection, those who have indulged in ridicule will be called to the door of Paradise, and have it shut in their faces when they reach it. Again, on their turning back, they will be called to another door, and again, on reaching it, will see it closed against them; and so on, *ad infinitum*, without end."

Shun the negative side. Never worry people with your contritions, nor with dismal views of politics or society. Never name sickness: even if you could trust yourself on that perilous topic, beware of unmuzzling a valetudinarian, who will soon give you your fill of it.

The law of the table is Beauty, — a respect to the common soul of all the guests. Everything is unseasonable which is private to two or three or any portion of the company. Tact never violates for a moment this law; never intrudes the orders of the house, the vices of the absent, or a tariff of expenses, or professional privacies; as we say, we never "talk shop" before company. Lovers abstain from caresses and haters from insults whilst they sit in one parlor with common friends.

Stay at home in your mind. Don't recite other people's opinions. See how it lies there in you; and if there is no counsel, offer none. What we want is not your activity or interference with your mind, but your content to be a vehicle of the simple truth. The way to have large occasional views, as in a political or social crisis, is to have large habitual views. When men consult you, it is not that they wish you to stand tip toe and pump your brains, but to apply your habitual view, your wisdom, to the present question, forbearing all pedantries and the very name of argument; for in good conversation parties don't speak to the words, but to the meanings of each other.

Manners first, then conversation. Later, we see that as life was not in manners, so it is not in

talk. Manners are external; talk is occasional;
these require certain material conditions, human
labor for food, clothes, house, tools, and, in short,
plenty and ease, — since only so can certain finer
and finest powers appear and expand. In a whole
nation of Hottentots there shall not be one valuable
man, — valuable out of his tribe. In every million
of Europeans or of Americans there shall be thousands who would be valuable on any spot on the
globe.

The consideration the rich possess in all societies
is not without meaning or right. It is the approval
given by the human understanding to the act of
creating value by knowledge and labor. It is the
sense of every human being that man should have
this dominion of nature, should arm himself with
tools and force the elements to drudge for him and
give him power. Every one must seek to secure
his independence; but he need not be rich. The
old Confucius in China admitted the benefit, but
stated the limitation : " If the search for riches were
sure to be successful, though I should become a
groom with whip in hand to get them, I will do so.
As the search may not be successful, I will follow
after that which I love." There is in America a
general conviction in the minds of all mature men,
that every young man of good faculty and good
habits can by perseverance attain to an adequate

estate; if he have a turn for business, and a quick eye for the opportunities which are always offering for investment, he can come to wealth, and in such good season as to enjoy as well as transmit it.

Every human society wants to be officered by a best class, who shall be masters instructed in all the great arts of life; shall be wise, temperate, brave, public men, adorned with dignity and accomplishments. Every country wishes this, and each has taken its own method to secure such service to the state. In Europe, ancient and modern, it has been attempted to secure the existence of a superior class by hereditary nobility, with estates transmitted by primogeniture and entail. But in the last age, this system has been on its trial, and the verdict of mankind is pretty nearly pronounced. That method secured permanence of families, firmness of customs, a certain external culture and good taste; gratified the ear with preserving historic names: but the heroic father did not surely have heroic sons, and still less surely heroic grandsons; wealth and ease corrupted the race.

In America, the necessity of clearing the forest, laying out town and street, and building every house and barn and fence, then church and town-house, exhausted such means as the Pilgrims brought, and made the whole population poor; and the like necessity is still found in each new

settlement in the Territories. These needs gave
their character to the public debates in every village and State. I have been often impressed at
our country town-meetings with the accumulated
virility, in each village, of five or six or eight or ten
men, who speak so well, and so easily handle the
affairs of the town. I often hear the business of a
little town (with which I am most familiar) discussed with a clearness and thoroughness, and with
a generosity too, that would have satisfied me had
it been in one of the larger capitals. I am sure each
one of my readers has a parallel experience. And
every one knows that in every town or city is
always to be found a certain number of public-
spirited men who perform, unpaid, a great amount
of hard work in the interest of the churches, of
schools, of public grounds, works of taste and refinement. And as in civil duties, so in social power
and duties. Our gentlemen of the old school, that
is, of the school of Washington, Adams, and Hamilton, were bred after English types, and that style
of breeding furnished fine examples in the last generation; but, though some of us have seen such, I
doubt they are all gone. But nature is not poorer
to-day. With all our haste, and slipshod ways, and
flippant self-assertion, I have seen examples of new
grace and power in address that honor the country.
It was my fortune not long ago, with my eyes di-

rected on this subject, to fall in with an American to be proud of. I said never was such force, good meaning, good sense, good action, combined with such domestic lovely behavior, such modesty and persistent preference for others. Wherever he moved he was the benefactor. It is of course that he should ride well, shoot well, sail well, keep house well, administer affairs well; but he was the best talker, also, in the company: what with a per- petual practical wisdom, with an eye always to the working of the thing, what with the multitude and distinction of his facts (and one detected continu- ally that he had a hand in everything that has been done), and in the temperance with which he parried all offence and opened the eyes of the per- son he talked with without contradicting him. Yet I said to myself, How little this man suspects, with his sympathy for men and his respect for lettered and scientific people, that he is not likely, in any company, to meet a man superior to himself. And I think this is a good country that can bear such a creature as he is.

The young men in America at this moment take little thought of what men in England are thinking or doing. That is the point which decides the wel- fare of a people; *which way does it look?* If to any other people, it is not well with them. If occu- pied in its own affairs and thoughts and men, with

a heat which excludes almost the notice of any
other people, — as the Jews, the Greeks, the Persians, the Romans, the Arabians, the French, the
English, at their best times have been, — they are
sublime ; and we know that in this abstraction they
are executing excellent work.   Amidst the calami-
ties which war has brought on our country this one
benefit has accrued, — that our eyes are withdrawn
from England, withdrawn from France, and look
homeward.   We have come to feel that " by ourselves our safety must be bought; " to know the
vast resources of the continent, the good-will that
is in the people, their conviction of the great moral
advantages of freedom, social equality, education
and religious culture, and their determination to
hold these fast, and, by them, to hold fast the country and penetrate every square mile of it with this
American civilization.

The consolation and happy moment of life, aton-
ing for all short-comings, is sentiment; a flame of
affection or delight in the heart, burning up suddenly for its object ; — as the love of the mother
for her child ; of the child for its mate ; of the youth
for his friend ; of the scholar for his pursuit; of the
boy for sea-life, or for painting, or in the passion
for his country; or in the tender-hearted philan-
thropist to spend and be spent for some romantic
charity, as Howard for the prisoner, or John Brown

for the slave. No matter what the object is, so it be good, this flame of desire makes life sweet and tolerable. It reinforces the heart that feels it, makes all its acts and words gracious and interesting. Now society in towns is infested by persons who, seeing that the sentiments please, counterfeit the expression of them. These we call sentimentalists, — talkers who mistake the description for the thing, saying for having. They have, they tell you, an intense love of nature; poetry, — O, they adore poetry, — and roses, and the moon, and the cavalry regiment, and the governor; they love liberty, " dear liberty ! " they worship virtue, " dear virtue ! " Yes, they adopt whatever merit is in good repute, and almost make it hateful ' with their praise. The warmer their expressions, the colder we feel; we shiver with cold. A little experience acquaints us with the unconvertibility of the sentimentalist, the soul that is lost by mimicking soul. Cure the drunkard, heal the insane, mollify the homicide, civilize the Pawnee, but what lessons can be devised for the debauchee of sentiment? Was ever one converted? The innocence and ignorance of the patient is the first difficulty; he believes his disease is blooming health. A rough realist or a phalanx of realists would be prescribed; but that is like proposing to mend your bad road with diamonds. Then poverty, famine, war, imprisonment, might be tried. Another cure would be to fight fire with fire, to match a sentimentalist with a sentimentalist. I think each might begin to suspect that something was wrong.

Would we codify the laws that should reign in households, and whose daily transgression annoys and mortifies us and degrades our household life, we must learn to adorn every day with sacrifices. Good manners are made up of petty sacrifices. Temperance, courage, love, are made up of the same jewels. Listen to every prompting of honor. "As soon as sacrifice becomes a duty and necessity to the man, I see no limit to the horizon which opens before me. " [1]

Of course those people, and no others, interest us, who believe in their thought, who are absorbed, if you please to say so, in their own dream. They only can give the key and leading to better society : those who delight in each other only because both delight in the eternal laws ; who forgive nothing to each other ; who, by their joy and homage to these, are made incapable of conceit, which destroys almost all the fine wits. Any other affection between men than this geometric one of relation to the same thing, is a mere mush of materialism.

These are the bases of civil and polite society ; namely, manners, conversation, lucrative labor, and

[1] Ernest Renan.

public action ; whether political, or in the leading of social institutions. We have much to regret, much to mend, in our society ; but I believe that with all liberal and hopeful men there is a firm faith in the beneficent results which we really enjoy ; that intelligence, manly enterprise, good education, virtuous life and elegant manners have been and are found here, and, we hope, in the next generation will still more abound.

ELOQUENCE.

ELOQUENCE.

I DO not know any kind of history, except the event of a battle, to which people listen with more interest than to any anecdote of eloquence ; and the wise think it better than a battle. It is a triumph of pure power, and it has a beautiful and prodigious surprise in it. For all can see and understand the means by which a battle is gained : they count the armies, they see the cannon, the musketry, the cavalry, and the character and advantages of the ground, so that the result is often predicted by the observer with great certainty before the charge is sounded. Not so in a court of law, or in a legislature. Who knows before the debate begins what the preparation, or what the means are of the combatants? The facts, the reasons, the logic, — above all, the flame of passion and the continuous energy of will which is presently to be let loose on this ·bench of judges, or on this miscellaneous assembly gathered from the streets, — are all invisible and unknown. Indeed, much power is to be exhibited which is not yet called into existence, but is to be suggested on the spot by the unexpected turn things may take, — at the appearance of new evidence, or by the exhibition of an unlooked-for bias in the judges or in the audience. It is eminently the art which only flourishes in free countries. It is an old proverb that "Every people has its prophet;" and every class of the people has. Our community runs through a long scale of mental power, from the highest refinement to the borders of savage ignorance and rudeness. There are not only the wants of the intellectual and learned and poetic men and women to be met, but also the vast interests of property, public and private, of mining, of manufactures, of trade, of railroads, etc. These must have their advocates of each improvement and each interest. Then the political questions, which agitate millions, find or form a class of men by nature and habit fit to discuss and deal with these measures, and make them intelligible and acceptable to the electors. So of education, of art, of philanthropy.

Eloquence shows the power and possibility of man. There is one of whom we took no note, but on a certain occasion it appears that he has a secret virtue never suspected, — that he can paint what has occurred and what must occur, with such clearness to a company, as if they saw it done before their eyes. By leading their thought he leads their will, and can make them do gladly what an hour ago they would not believe that they could be led to do at all: he makes them glad or angry or penitent at his pleasure; of enemies makes friends, and fills desponding men with hope and joy. After Sheridan's speech in the trial of Warren Hastings, Mr. Pitt moved an adjournment, that the House might recover from the overpowering effect of Sheridan's oratory. Then recall the delight that sudden eloquence gives, — the surprise that the moment is so rich. The orator is the physician. Whether he speaks in the Capitol or on a cart, he is the benefactor that lifts men above themselves, and creates a higher appetite than he satisfies. The orator is he whom every man is seeking when he goes into the courts, into the conventions, into any popular assembly, — though often disappointed, yet never giving over the hope. He finds himself perhaps in the Senate, when the forest has cast out some wild, black-browed bantling to show the same energy in the crowd of officials which he had learned in driving cattle to the hills, or in scrambling through thickets in a winter forest, or through the swamp and river for his game. In the folds of his brow, in the majesty of his mien, Nature has marked her son; and in that artificial and perhaps unworthy place and company shall remind you of the lessons taught him in earlier days by the torrent in the gloom of the pine-woods, when he was the companion of the mountain cattle, of jays and foxes, and a hunter of the bear. Or you may find him in some lowly Bethel, by the seaside, where a hard-featured, scarred, and wrinkled Methodist becomes the poet of the sailor and the fisherman, whilst he pours out the abundant streams of his thought through a language all glittering and fiery with imagination ; a man who never knew the looking-glass or the critic; a man whom college drill or patronage never made, and whom praise cannot spoil, — a man who conquers his audience by infusing his soul into them, and speaks by the right of being the person in the assembly who has the most to say, and so makes all other speakers appear little and cowardly before his face. For the time, his exceeding life throws all other gifts into shade, — philosophy speculating on its own breath, taste, learning, and all, — and yet how every listener gladly consents to be nothing in his presence, and to share this surprising emanation, and be steeped and ennobled in the new wine of this eloquence! It instructs in the power of man over men ; that a man is a mover ; to the extent of his being, a power; and, in contrast with the efficiency he suggests, our actual life and society appears a dormitory. Who can wonder at its influence on young and ardent minds ? Uncommon boys follow uncommon men , and I think every one of us can remember when our first experiences made us for a time the victim and worshipper of the first master of this art whom we happened to hear in the court-house or in the caucus.

We reckon the bar, the senate, journalism, and the pulpit, peaceful professions; but you cannot escape the demand for courage in these, and certainly there is no true orator who is not á hero. His attitude in the rostrum, on the platform, requires that he counterbalance his auditory. He is challenger, and must answer all comers. The orator must ever stand with forward foot, in the attitude of advancing. His speech must be just ahead of the assembly, ahead of the whole human race, or it is superfluous. His speech is not to be distinguished from action. It is the electricity of action. It is action, as the general's word of command or chart of battle is action. I must feel that the speaker compromises himself to his auditory, comes for something, — it is a cry on the perilous edge of the fight, — or let him be silent. You go to a town-meeting where the people are called to some disagreeable duty, such as, for example, often occurred during the war, at the occasion of a new draft. They come unwillingly; they have spent their money once or twice very freely. They have sent their best men; the young and ardent, those of a martial temper, went at the first draft, or the second, and it is not easy to see who else can be spared or can be induced to go. The silence and coldness after the meeting is opened and the purpose of it stated, are not encouraging. When a good man rises in the cold and malicious assembly, you think, Well, sir, it would be more prudent to be silent; why not rest, sir, on your good record? Nobody doubts your talent and power, but for the present business, we know all about it, and are tired of being pushed into patriotism by people who stay at home. But he, taking no counsel of past things but only of the inspiration of his to-day's feeling, surprises them with his tidings, with his better knowledge, his larger view, his steady gaze at the new and future event whereof they had not thought, and they are interested like so many children, and carried off out of all recollection of their malignant considerations, and he gains his victory by prophecy, where they expected repetition. He knew very well beforehand that they were looking behind and that he was looking ahead, and therefore it was wise to speak. Then the observer says, What a godsend is this manner of man to a town! and he, what a faculty! He is put together like a Waltham watch, or like a locomotive just finished at the Tredegar works.

No act indicates more universal health than eloquence. The special ingredients of this force are clear perceptions; memory; power of statement; logic; imagination, or the skill to clothe your thought in natural images; passion, which is the *heat;* and then a grand will, which, when legitimate and abiding, we call *character*, the height of manhood. As soon as a man shows rare power of expression, like Chatham, Erskine, Patrick Henry, Webster, or Phillips, all the great interests, whether of state or of property, crowd to him to be their spokesman, so that he is at once a potentate, a ruler of men. A worthy gentleman, Mr. Alexander, listening to the debates of the General Assembly of the Scottish Kirk in Edinburgh, and eager to speak to the questions but utterly failing in his endeavors, —delighted with the talent shown by Dr. Hugh Blair, went to him and offered him one thousand pounds sterling if he would teach him to speak with propriety in public. If the performance of the advocate reaches any high success it is paid in England with dignities in the professions, and in the State with seats in the cabinet, earldoms, and woolsacks. And it is easy to see that the great and daily growing interests at stake in this country must pay proportional prices to their spokesmen and defenders. It does not surprise us then to learn from Plutarch what great sums were paid at Athens to the teachers of rhetoric; and if the pupils got what they paid for, the lessons were cheap.

But this power which so fascinates and astonishes and commands is only the exaggeration of a talent which is universal. All men are competitors in this art. We have all attended meetings called for some object in which no one had beforehand any warm interest. Every speaker rose unwillingly, and even his speech was a bad excuse; but it is only the first plunge which is formidable; and deep interest or sympathy thaws the ice, loosens the tongue, and will carry the cold and fearful presently into self-possession and possession of the audience. Go into an assembly well excited, some angry political meeting on the eve of a crisis. Then it appears that eloquence is as natural as swimming, — an art which all men might learn, though so few do. It only needs that they should be once well pushed off into the water, overhead, without corks, and, after a mad struggle or two they find their poise and the use of their arms, and henceforward they possess this new and wonderful element.

The most hard - fisted, disagreeably restless, thought-paralyzing companion sometimes turns out in a public assembly to be a fluent, various, and effective orator. Now you find what all that excess of power which so chafed and fretted you in a *tête-à-tête* with him was for. What is peculiar in it is a certain creative heat, which a man attains to

perhaps only once in his life. Those whom we admire — the great orators — have some *habit* of heat,
and moreover a certain control of it, an art of hus-
banding it, — as if their hand was on the organ-
stop, and could now use it temperately, and now
let out all the length and breadth of the power. I
remember that Jenny Lind, when in this country,
complained of concert-rooms and town-halls, that
they did not give her room enough to unroll her
voice, and exulted in the opportunity given her in
the great halls she found sometimes built over a
railroad depot. And this is quite as true of the
action of the mind itself, that a man of this talent
sometimes finds himself cold and slow in private
company, and perhaps a heavy companion; but
give him a commanding occasion and the inspiration of a great multitude, and he surprises by new
and unlooked-for powers. Before, he was out of
place, and unfitted as a cannon in a parlor. To be
sure there are physical advantages, — some eminently leading to this art. I mentioned Jenny
Lind's voice. A good voice has a charm in speech
as in song; sometimes of itself enchains attention,
and indicates a rare sensibility, especially when
trained to wield all its powers. The voice, like the
face, betrays the nature and disposition, and soon
indicates what is the range of the speaker's mind.
Many people have no ear for music, but every one

has an ear for skilful reading. Every one of us has at some time been the victim of a well-toned and cunning voice, and perhaps been repelled once for all by a harsh, mechanical speaker. The voice, indeed, is a delicate index of the state of mind. I have heard an eminent preacher say that he learns from the first tones of his voice on a Sunday morning whether he is to have a successful day. A singer cares little for the words of the song; he will make any words glorious. I think the like rule holds of the good reader. In the church I call him only a good reader who can read sense and poetry into any hymn in the hymn-book. Plutarch, in his enumeration of the ten Greek orators, is careful to mention their excellent voices, and the pains bestowed by some of them in training these. What character, what infinite variety belong to the voice! sometimes it is a flute, sometimes a trip-hammer; what range of force! In moments of clearer thought or deeper sympathy, the voice will attain a music and penetration which surprises the speaker as much as the auditor; he also is a sharer of the higher wind that blows over his strings. I believe that some orators go to the assembly as to a closet where to find their best thoughts. The Persian poet Saadi tells us that a person with a disagreeable voice was reading the Koran aloud, when a holy man, passing by, asked what was his monthly stipend. He answered, " Nothing at all." " But why then do you take so much trouble?" He replied, " I read for the sake of God." The other rejoined, " For God's sake, do not read; for if you read the Koran in this manner you will destroy the splendor of Islamism." Then there are persons of natural fascination, with certain frankness, winning manners, almost endearments in their style; like Bouillon, who could almost persuade you that a quartan ague was wholesome; like Louis XI. of France, whom Commines praises for "the gift of managing all minds by his accent and the caresses of his speech;" like Galiani, Voltaire, Robert Burns, Barclay, Fox, and Henry Clay. What must have been the discourse of St. Bernard, when mothers hid their sons, wives their husbands, companions their friends, lest they should be led by his eloquence to join the monastery.

It is said that one of the best readers in his time was the late President John Quincy Adams. I have heard that no man could read the Bible with such powerful effect. I can easily believe it, though I never heard him speak in public until his fine voice was much broken by age. But the wonders he could achieve with that cracked and disobedient organ showed what power might have belonged to it in early manhood. If " indignation makes verses," as Horace says, it is not less true that a good indignation makes an excellent speech. In the early years of this century, Mr. Adams, at that time a member of the United States Senate at Washington, was elected Professor of Rhetoric and Oratory in Harvard College. When he read his first lectures in 1806, not only the students heard him with delight, but the hall was crowded by the Professors and by unusual visitors. I remember, when, long after, I entered college, hearing the story of the numbers of coaches in which his friends came from Boston to hear him. On his return in the winter to the Senate at Washington, he took such ground in the debates of the following session as to lose the sympathy of many of his constituents in Boston. When, on his return from Washington, he resumed his lectures in Cambridge, his class attended, but the coaches from Boston did not come, and indeed many of his political friends deserted him. In 1809 he was appointed Minister to Russia, and resigned his chair in the University. His last lecture, in taking leave of his class, contained some nervous allusions to the treatment he had received from his old friends, which showed how much it had stung him, and which made a profound impression on the class. Here is the concluding paragraph, which long resounded in Cambridge : —

"At no hour of your life will the love of letters ever oppress you as a burden, or fail you as a resource. In the vain and foolish exultation of the heart, which the brighter prospects of life will sometimes excite, the pensive portress of Science shall call you to the sober pleasures of her holy cell. In the mortifications of disappointment, her soothing voice shall whisper serenity and peace. In social converse with the mighty dead of ancient days, you will never smart under the galling sense of dependence upon the mighty living of the present age. And in your struggles with the world, should a crisis ever occur when even friendship may deem it prudent to desert you, when even your country may seem ready to abandon herself and you, when priest and Levite shall come and look on you and pass by on the other side, seek refuge, my *un*failing friends, and be assured you shall find it, in the friendship of Lælius and Scipio, in the patriotism of Cicero, Demosthenes, and Burke, as well as in the precepts and example of Him whose law is love, and who taught us to remember injuries only to forgive them."

The orator must command the whole scale of the language, from the most elegant to the most low and vile. Every one has felt how superior in force is the language of the street to that of the academy. The street must be one of his schools. Ought not the scholar to be able to convey his meaning in terms as short and strong as the porter or truckman uses to convey his? And Lord Chesterfield thought that "without being instructed in the dialect of the *Halles* no man could be a complete master of French." The speech of the man in the street is invariably strong, nor can you mend it by making it what you call parliamentary. You say, " If he could only express himself ; " but he does already, better than any one can for him, — can always get the ear of an audience to the exclusion of everybody else. Well, this is an example in point. That something which each man was created to say and do, he only or he best can tell you, and has a right to supreme attention so far. The power of their speech is, that it is perfectly understood by all ; and I believe it to be true that when any orator at the bar or in the Senate rises in his thought, he descends in his language, — that is, when he rises to any height of thought or of passion he comes down to a language level with the ear of all his audience. It is the merit of John Brown and of Abraham Lincoln — one at Charlestown, one at Gettysburg — in the two best specimens of eloquence we have had in this country. And observe that all poetry is written in the oldest and simplest English words. Dr. Johnson said, " There is in every nation a style which never becomes obsolete, a certain mode of phraseology so consonant to the analogy and principles of its respective language as to remain settled and unaltered. This style is to be sought in the common intercourse of life among those who speak only to be understood, without ambition of elegance. The polite are always catching modish innovations, and the learned forsake the vulgar, when the vulgar is right; but there is a conversation above grossness and below refinement, where propriety resides."

But all these are the gymnastics, the education of eloquence, and not itself. They cannot be too much considered and practised as preparation, but the powers are those I first named. If I should make the shortest list of the qualifications of the orator, I should begin with *manliness ;* and perhaps it means here presence of mind. Men differ so much in control of their faculties! You can find in many, and indeed in all, a certain fundamental equality. Fundamentally all feel alike and think alike, and at a great heat they can all express themselves with an almost equal force. But it costs a great heat to enable a heavy man to come up with those who have a quick sensibility. Thus we have all of us known men who lose their talents, their wit, their fancy, at any sudden call. Some men, on such pressure, collapse, and cannot rally. If they are to put a thing in proper shape, fit for the occasion and the audience, their mind is a blank. Something which any boy would tell with color and vivacity they can only stammer out with hard literalness, — say it in the very words they heard, and no other. This fault is very incident to men of study, — as if the more

they had read the less they knew. Dr. Charles
Chauncy was, a hundred years ago, a man of
marked ability among the clergy of New England.
But when once going to preach the Thursday lecture in Boston (which in those days people walked
from Salem to hear), on going up the pulpit-
stairs he was informed that a little boy had fallen
into Frog Pond on the Common and was drowned,
and the doctor was requested to improve the sad
occasion. The doctor was much distressed, and in
his prayer he hesitated, he tried to make soft approaches, he prayed for Harvard College, he prayed
for the schools, he implored the Divine Being "to—
to—to bless to them all the boy that was this morning drowned in Frog Pond." Now this is not want
of talent or learning, but of manliness. The doctor,
no doubt, shut up in his closet and his theology, had
lost some natural relation to men, and quick application of his thought to the course of events. I should
add what is told of him, — that he so disliked the
" sensation " preaching of his time, that he had
once prayed that " he might never be eloquent ; "
and, it appears, his prayer was granted. On the
other hand, it would be easy to point to many masters whose readiness is sure ; as the French say of
Guizot, that " what Guizot learned this morning he
has the air of having known from all eternity."
This unmanliness is so common a result of our half-

education, — teaching a youth Latin and metaphysics and history, and neglecting to give him the
rough training of a boy, — allowing him to skulk
from the games of ball and skates and coasting
down the hills on his sled, and whatever else would
lead him and keep him on even terms with boys, so
that he can meet them as an equal, and lead in his
turn, — that I wish his guardians to consider that
they are thus preparing him to play a contemptible
part when he is full-grown. In England they send
the most delicate and protected child from his lux-
urious home to learn to rough it with boys in the
public schools. A few bruises and scratches will do
him no harm if he has thereby learned not to be
afraid. It is this wise mixture of good drill in
Latin grammar with good drill in cricket, boating,
and wrestling, that is the boast of English education, and of high importance to the matter in hand.

Lord Ashley, in 1666, while the bill for regulat-
ing trials in cases of high treason was pending,
attempting to utter a premeditated speech in Parliament in favor of that clause of the bill which
allowed the prisoner the benefit of counsel, fell into
such a disorder that he was not able to proceed;
but, having recovered his spirits and the command
of his faculties, he drew such an argument from
his own confusion as more advantaged his cause
than all the powers of eloquence could have done.

" For," said he, " if I, who had no personal concern in the question, was so overpowered with my own apprehensions that I could not find words to express myself, what must be the case of one whose life depended on his own abilities to defend it ? " This happy turn did great service in promoting that excellent bill.

These are ascending stairs, — a good voice, winning manners, plain speech, chastened, however, by the schools into correctness ; but we must come to the main matter, of power of statement, — know your fact ; hug your fact. For the essential thing is heat, and heat comes of sincerity. Speak what you do know and believe ; and are personally in it ; and are answerable for every word. Eloquence is *the power to translate a truth into language perfectly intelligible to the person to whom you speak.* He who would convince the worthy Mr. Dunderhead of any truth which Dunderhead does not see, must be a master of his art. Declamation is common ; but such possession of thought as is here required, such practical chemistry as the conversion of a truth written in God's language into a truth in Dunderhead's language, is one of the most beautiful and cogent weapons that are forged in the shop of the Divine Artificer.

It was said of Robespierre's audience, that though they understood not the words, they understood a fury in the words, and caught the contagion. This leads us to the high class, the men of character, who bring an overpowering personality into court, and the cause they maintain borrows importance from an illustrious advocate. Absoluteness is' required, and he must have it or simulate it. If the cause be unfashionable, he will make it fashiona-able. 'T is the best man in the best training. If he does not know your fact, he will show that it is not worth the knowing. Indeed, as great generals do not fight many battles, but conquer by tactics, so all eloquence is a war of posts. What is said is the least part of the oration. It is the attitude taken, the unmistakable sign, never so casually given, in tone of voice, or manner, or word, that a greater spirit speaks from you than is spoken to in him.

But I say, *provided your cause is really honest.* There is always the previous question: How came you on that side? Your argument is ingenious, your language copious, your illustrations brilliant, but your major proposition palpably absurd. Will you establish a lie? You are a very elegant writer, but you can't write up what gravitates down.

An ingenious metaphysical writer, Dr. Stirling, of Edinburgh, has noted that intellectual works in any department breed each other, by what he calls *zymosis,* i. e. fermentation; thus in the Elizabethan

Age there was a dramatic *zymosis*, when all the genius ran in that direction, until it culminated in Shakspeare ; so in Germany we have seen a metaphysical *zymosis* culminating in Kant, Schelling, Schleiermacher, Schopenhauer, Hegel, and so ending.   To this we might add the great eras not only of painters but of orators.   The historian Paterculus says of Cicero, that only in Cicero's lifetime was any great eloquence in Rome ; so it was said that no member of either house of the British Parliament will be ranked among the orators, whom Lord North did not see, or who did not see Lord North.   But I should rather say that when a great sentiment, as religion or liberty, makes itself deeply felt in any age or country, then great orators appear.   As the Andes and Alleghanies indicate the line of the fissure in the crust of the earth along which they were lifted, so the great ideas that suddenly expand at some moment the mind of mankind, indicate themselves by orators.

If there ever was a country where eloquence was a power, it is the United States.   Here is room for every degree of it, on every one of its ascending stages, — that of useful speech, in our commercial, manufacturing, railroad, and educational conventions ; that of political advice and persuasion on the grandest theatre, reaching, as all good men trust, into a vast future, and so compelling the best thought and noblest administrative ability that the citizen can offer. And here are the service of science, the demands of art, and the lessons of religion to be brought home to the instant practice of thirty millions of people. Is it not worth the ambition of every generous youth to train and arm his mind with all the resources of knowledge, of method, of grace, and of character, to serve such a constituency ?

RESOURCES.

RESOURCES.

MEN are made up of potencies. We are magnets in an iron globe. We have keys to all doors. We are all inventors, each sailing out on a voyage of discovery, guided each by a private chart, of which there is no duplicate. The world is all gates, all opportunities, strings of tension waiting to be struck; the earth sensitive as iodine to light; the most plastic and impressionable medium, alive to every touch, and, whether searched by the plough of Adam, the sword of Cæsar, the boat of Columbus, the telescope of Galileo, or the surveyor's chain of Picard, or the submarine telegraph, — to every one of these experiments it makes a gracious response. I am benefited by every observation of a victory of man over nature; by seeing that wisdom is better than strength; by seeing that every healthy and resolute man is an organizer, a method coming into a confusion and drawing order out of it. We are touched and cheered by every such example. We like to see the inexhaustible riches of Nature, and the access of every soul to her magazines.

These examples wake an infinite hope, and call every man to emulation. A low, hopeless spirit puts out the eyes; skepticism is slow suicide. A philosophy which sees only the worst; believes neither in virtue nor in genius; which says 't is all of no use, life is eating us up, 't is only question who shall be last devoured, — dispirits us; the sky shuts down before us. A Schopenhauer, with logic and learning and wit, teaching pessimism, — teaching that this is the worst of all possible worlds, and inferring that sleep is better than waking, and death than sleep, — all the talent in the world cannot save him from being odious. But if instead of these negatives you give me affirmatives; if you tell me that there is always life for the living; that what man has done man can do; that this world belongs to the energetic; that there is always a way to everything desirable; that every man is provided, in the new bias of his faculty, with a key to nature, and that man only rightly knows himself as far as he has experimented on things, — I am invigorated, put into genial and working temper; the horizon opens, and we are full of good-will and gratitude to the Cause of Causes. I like the sentiment of the poor woman who, coming from a wretched garret in an inland manufacturing town for the first time to the sea-shore, gazing at the ocean, said she was " glad for once in her life to see something which there was enough of. "

Our Copernican globe is a great factory or shop of power, with its rotating constellations, times, and tides. The machine is of colossal size; the diameter of the water-wheel, the arms of the levers and the volley of the battery out of all mechanic measure; and it takes long to understand its parts and its workings. This pump never sucks; these screws are never loose; this machine is never out of gear. The vat, the piston, the wheels and tires, never wear out, but are self-repairing. Is there any load which water cannot lift? If there be, try steam; or if not that, try electricity. Is there any exhausting of these means? Measure by barrels the spending of the brook that runs through your field. Nothing is great but the inexhaustible wealth of Nature. She shows us only surfaces, but she is million fathoms deep. What spaces! what durations! dealing with races as merely preparations of somewhat to follow; or, in humanity, millions of lives of men to collect the first observations on which our astronomy is built; millions of lives to add only sentiments and guesses, which at last, gathered in by an ear of sensibility, make the furniture of the poet. See how children build up a language; how every traveller, every laborer, every impatient boss who sharply shortens the phrase or the word to give his order quicker, reducing it to the lowest possible terms, and there it must stay, — improves the national tongue. What power does Nature not owe to her duration, of amassing infinitesimals into cosmical forces!

The marked events in history, as the emigration of a colony to a new and more delightful coast; the building of a large ship; the discovery of the mariner's compass, which perhaps the Phœnicians made; the arrival among an old stationary nation of a more instructed race, with new arts: — each of these events electrifies the tribe to which it befalls; supples the tough barbarous sinew, and brings it into that state of sensibility which makes the transition to civilization possible and sure. By his machines man can dive and remain under water like a shark; can fly like a hawk in the air; can see atoms like a gnat; can see the system of the universe like Uriel, the angel of the sun; can carry whatever loads a ton of coal can lift; can knock down cities with his fist of gunpowder; can recover the history of his race by the medals which the deluge, and every creature, civil or savage or brute, has involuntarily dropped of its existence; and divine the future possibility of the planet and its inhabitants by his perception of laws of nature. Ah! what a plastic little creature he is! so shifty, so adaptive! his body a chest of tools, and he making himself comfortable in every climate, in every condition.

Here in America are all the wealth of soil, of timber, of mines, and of the sea, put into the possession of a people who wield all these wonderful machines, have the secret of steam, of electricity; and have the power and habit of invention in their brain. We Americans have got suppled into the state of melioration. Life is always rapid here, but what acceleration to its pulse in ten years, — what in the four years of the war! We have seen the railroad and telegraph subdue our enormous geography; we have seen the snowy deserts on the northwest, seats of Esquimaux, become lands of promise. When our population, swarming west, had reached the boundary of arable land, — as if to stimulate our energy, on the face of the sterile waste beyond, the land was suddenly in parts found covered with gold and silver, floored with coal. It was thought a fable, what Guthrie, a traveller in Persia, told us, that "in Taurida, in any piece of ground where springs of naphtha (or petroleum) obtain, by merely sticking an iron tube in the earth and applying a light to the upper end, the mineral oil will burn till the tube is decomposed, or for a vast number of years." But we have found the Taurida in Pennsylvania and Ohio. If they have not the lamp of Aladdin, they have the Aladdin oil. Resources of America! why, one thinks of St. Simon's saying, "The Golden Age is not behind,

but before you." Here is man in the Garden of
Eden; here the Genesis and the Exodus. We
have seen slavery disappear like a painted scene in
a theatre; we have seen the most healthful revolution in the politics of the nation, — the Constitution
not only amended, but construed in a new spirit.
We have seen China opened to European and
American ambassadors and commerce; the like in
Japan : our arts and productions begin to penetrate
both. As the walls of a modern house are perfo-
rated with water-pipes, sound-pipes, gas-pipes, heat-
pipes, — so geography and geology are yielding to
man's convenience, and we begin to perforate and
mould the old ball, as a carpenter does with wood.
All is ductile and plastic. We are working the
new Atlantic telegraph. American energy is over-
riding every venerable maxim of political science.
America is such a garden of plenty, such a mag-
azine of power, that at her shores all the common
rules of political economy utterly fail. Here is
bread, and wealth, and power, and education for
every man who has the heart to use his opportunity.
The creation of power had never any parallel. It
was thought that the immense production of gold
would make gold cheap as pewter. But the immense expansion of trade has wanted every ounce
of gold, and it has not lost its value.

See how nations of customers are formed. The

disgust of California has not been able to drive nor kick the Chinaman back to his home ; and now it turns out that he has sent home to China American food and tools and luxuries, until he has taught his people to use them, and a new market has grown up for our commerce. The emancipation has brought a whole nation of negroes as customers to buy all the articles which once their few masters bought, and every manufacturer and producer in the North has an interest in protecting the negro as the consumer of his wares.

The whole history of our civil war is rich in a thousand anecdotes attesting the fertility of resource, the presence of mind, the skilled labor of our people. At Annapolis a regiment, hastening to join the army, found the locomotives broken, the railroad destroyed, and no rails. The commander called for men in the ranks who could rebuild the road. Many men stepped forward, searched in the water, found the hidden rails, laid the track, put the disabled engine together and continued their journey. The world belongs to the energetic man. His will gives him new eyes. He sees expedients and means where we saw none. The invalid sits shivering in lamb's-wool and furs ; the woodsman knows how to make warm garments out of cold and wet themselves. The Indian, the sailor, the hunter, only these know the power of the hands, feet, teeth, eyes and ears.

It is out of the obstacles to be encountered that they make the means of destroying them. The sailor by his boat and sail makes a ford out of deepest waters. The hunter, the soldier, rolls himself in his blanket, and the falling snow, which he did not have to bring in his knapsack, is his eider-down, in which he sleeps warm till the morning. Nature herself gives the hint and the example, if we have wit to take it. See how Nature keeps the lakes warm by tucking them up under a blanket of ice, and the ground under a cloak of snow. The old forester is never far from shelter; no matter how remote from camp or city, he carries Bangor with him. A sudden shower cannot wet him, if he cares to be dry; he draws his boat ashore, turns it over in a twinkling against a clump of alders, with cat-briers which keep up the lee-side, crawls under it with his comrade, and lies there till the shower is over, happy in his stout roof. The boat is full of water, and resists all your strength to drag it ashore and empty it. The fisherman looks about him, puts a round stick of wood underneath, and it rolls as on wheels at once. Napoleon says, the Corsicans at the battle of Golo, not having had time to cut down the bridge, which was of stone, made use of the bodies of their dead to form an intrenchment. Malus, known for his discoveries in the polarization of light, was captain of a corps of engineers in Bonaparte's

Egyptian campaign, which was heinously unprovided and exposed. " Wanting a picket to which to
attach my horse," he says, " I tied him to my leg.
I slept, and dreamed peaceably of the pleasures of
Europe." M. Tissenet had learned among the Indians to understand their language, and, coming
among a wild party of Illinois, he overheard them
say that they would scalp him. He said to them,
" Will you scalp me ? Here is my scalp," and confounded them by lifting a little periwig he wore.
He then explained to them that he was a great med-
icine-man, and that they did great wrong in wishing
to harm him, who carried them all in his heart.
So he opened his shirt a little and showed to each
of the savages in turn the reflection of his own eye-
ball in a small pocket-mirror which he had hung
next to his skin. He assured them that if they
should provoke him he would burn up their rivers
and their forests ; and taking from his portmanteau
a small phial of white brandy, he poured it into a
cup, and lighting a straw at the fire in the wigwam,
he kindled the brandy (which they believed to be
water), and burned it up before their eyes. Then
taking up a chip of dry pine, he drew a burning-
glass from his pocket and set the chip on fire.

What a new face courage puts on everything!
A determined man, by his very attitude and the
tone of his voice, puts a stop to defeat, and begins

to conquer. " For they can conquer who believe they can." Every one hears gladly that cheerful voice. He reveals to us the enormous power of one man over masses of men; that one man whose eye commands the end in view and the means by which it can be attained, is not only better than ten men or a hundred men, but victor over all mankind who do not see the issue and the means. " When a man is once possessed with fear," said the old French Marshal Montluc, "and loses his judgment, as all men in a fright do, he knows not what he does. And it is the principal thing you are to beg at the hands of Almighty God, to preserve your understanding entire; for what danger soever there may be, there is still one way or other to get off, and perhaps to your honor. But when fear has once possessed you, God ye good even! You think you are flying towards the poop when you are running towards the prow, and for one enemy think you have ten before your eyes, as drunkards who see a thousand candles at once."

Against the terrors of the mob, which, intoxicated with passion, and once suffered to gain the ascendant, is diabolic and chaos come again, good sense has many arts of prevention and of relief. Disorganization it confronts with organization, with police, with military force. But in earlier stages of the disorder it applies milder and nobler remedies. The natural offset of terror is ridicule. And we have noted examples among our orators, who have on conspicuous occasions handled and controlled, and, best of all, converted a malignant mob, by superior manhood, and by a wit which disconcerted and at last delighted the ringleaders. What can a poor truckman, who is hired to groan and to hiss, do, when the orator shakes him into convulsions of laughter so that he cannot throw his egg? If a good story will not answer, still milder remedies sometimes serve to disperse a mob. Try sending round the contribution-box. Mr. Marshall, the eminent manufacturer at Leeds, was to preside at a Free-Trade festival in that city; it was threatened that the operatives, who were in bad humor, would break up the meeting by a mob. Mr. Marshall was a man of peace; he had the pipes laid from the waterworks of his mill, with a stop-cock by his chair from which he could discharge a stream that would knock down an ox, and sat down very peacefully to his dinner, which was not disturbed.

See the dexterity of the good aunt in keeping the young people all the weary holiday busy and diverted without knowing it: the story, the pictures, the ballad, the game, the cuckoo-clock, the stereoscope, the rabbits, the mino bird, the popcorn, and Christmas hemlock spurting in the fire. The children never suspect how much design goes

to it, and that this unfailing fertility has been re-
hearsed a hundred times, when the necessity came
of finding for the little Asmodeus a rope of sand to
twist. She relies on the same principle that makes
the strength of Newton, — alternation of employment. See how he refreshed himself, resting from
the profound researches of the calculus by astronomy; from astronomy by optics; from optics by
chronology. It is a law of chemistry that every
gas is a vacuum to every other gas; and when the
mind has exhausted its energies for one employment, it is still fresh and capable of a different
task. We have not a toy or trinket for idle amusement but somewhere it is the one thing needful,
for solid instruction or to save the ship or army.
In the Mammoth Cave in Kentucky, the torches
which each traveller carries make a dismal funeral
procession, and serve no purpose but to see the
ground. When now and then the vaulted roof
rises high overhead and hides all its possibilities in
lofty depths, 't is but gloom on gloom. But the
guide kindled a Roman candle, and held it here
and there shooting its fireballs successively into
each crypt of the groined roof, disclosing its starry
splendor, and showing for the first time what that
plaything was good for.

Whether larger or less, these strokes and all ex-
ploits rest at last on the wonderful structure of the

mind. And we learn that our doctrine of resources must be carried into higher application, namely, to the intellectual sphere. But every power in energy speedily arrives at its limits, and requires to be husbanded: the law of light, which Newton said proceeded by "fits of easy reflection and transmission;" the come-and-go of the pendulum, is the law of mind; alternation of labors is its rest.

I should like to have the statistics of bold experimenting on the husbandry of mental power. In England men of letters drink wine; in Scotland, whiskey; in France, light wines; in Germany, beer. In England everybody rides in the saddle; in France the theatre and the ball occupy the night. In this country we have not learned how to repair the exhaustions of our climate. Is not the seaside necessary in summer? Games, fishing, bowling, hunting, gymnastics, dancing, — are not these needful to you? The chapter of pastimes is very long. There are better games than billiards and whist. It was a pleasing trait in Goethe's romance, that Makaria retires from society "to astronomy and her correspondence."

I do not know that the treatise of Brillat Savarin on the Physiology of Taste deserves its fame. I know its repute, and I have heard it called the France of France. But the subject is so large and exigent, that a few particulars, and those the pleas-

ures of the epicure, cannot satisfy. I know many
men of taste whose single opinions and practice
would interest much more. It should be extended
to gardens and grounds, and mainly one thing
should be illustrated : that life in the country
wants all things on a low tone, — wants coarse
clothes, old shoes, no fleet horse that a man cannot
hold, but an old horse that will stand tied in a pasture half a day without risk, so allowing the picnic-
party the full freedom of the woods. Natural history is, in the country, most attractive ; at once elegant, immortal, always opening new resorts. The
first care of a man settling in the country should
be to open the face of the earth to himself by a
little knowledge of nature, or a great deal, if he
can ; of birds, plants, rocks, astronomy ; in short,
the art of taking a walk. This will draw the sting
out of frost, dreariness out of November and March,
and the drowsiness out of August. To know the
trees is, as Spenser says of the ash, "for nothing
ill." Shells, too ; how hungry I found myself, the
other day, at Agassiz's Museum, for their names!
But the uses of the woods are many, and some of
them for the scholar high and peremptory. When
his task requires the wiping out from memory

> "all trivial fond records
> That youth and observation copied there,"

he must leave the house, the streets, and the club,

and go to wooded uplands, to the clearing and the brook. Well for him if he can say with the old minstrel, " I know where to find a new song."

If I go into the woods in winter, and am shown the thirteen or fourteen species of willow that grow in Massachusetts, I learn that they quietly expand in the warmer days, or when nobody is looking at them, and, though insignificant enough in the general bareness of the forest, yet a great change takes place in them between fall and spring; in the first relentings of March they hasten, and long before anything else is ready, these osiers hang out their joyful flowers in contrast to all the woods. You cannot tell when they do bud and blossom, these vivacious trees, so ancient, for they are almost the oldest of all. Among fossil remains, the willow and the pine appear with the ferns. They bend all day to every wind; the cart-wheel in the road may crush them; every passenger may strike off a twig with his cane; every boy cuts them for a whistle; the cow, the rabbit, the insect, bite the sweet and tender bark; yet, in spite of accident and enemy, their gentle persistency lives when the oak is shattered by storm, and grows in the night and snow and cold. When I see in these brave plants this vigor and immortality in weakness, I find a sudden relief and pleasure in observing the mighty law of vegetation, and I think it more grateful and health-giving than any news I am likely to find of man in the journals, and better than Washington politics.

It is easy to see that there is no limit to the chapter of Resources. I have not, in all these rambling sketches, gone beyond the beginning of my list. Resources of Man, — it is the inventory of the world, the roll of arts and sciences; it is the whole of memory, the whole of invention; it is all the power of passion, the majesty of virtue, and the omnipotence of will.

But the one fact that shines through all this plenitude of powers is, that as is the receiver, so is the gift; that all these acquisitions are victories of the good brain and brave heart; that the world belongs to the energetic, belongs to the wise. It is in vain to make a paradise but for good men. The tropics are one vast garden; yet man is more miserably fed and conditioned there than in the cold and stingy zones. The healthy, the civil, the industrious, the learned, the moral race, — Nature herself only yields her secret to these. And the resources of America and its future will be immense only to wise and virtuous men.

THE COMIC.

THE COMIC.

A TASTE for fun is all but universal in our species, which is the only joker in nature. The rocks, the plants, the beasts, the birds, neither do anything ridiculous, nor betray a perception of anything absurd done in their presence. And as the lower nature does not jest, neither does the highest. The Reason pronounces its omniscient yea and nay, but meddles never with degrees or fractions; and it is in comparing fractions with essential integers or wholes that laughter begins.

Aristotle's definition of the ridiculous is, "what is out of time and place, without danger." If there be pain and danger, it becomes tragic; if not, comic. I confess, this definition, though by an admirable definer, does not satisfy me, does not say all we know.

The essence of all jokes, of all comedy, seems to be an honest or well-intended halfness; a non-performance of what is pretended to be performed, at the same time that one is giving loud pledges of performance. The balking of the intellect, the frustrated expectation, the break of continuity in the intellect, is comedy ; and it announces itself physically in the pleasant spasms we call laughter.

With the trifling exception of the stratagems of a few beasts and birds, there is no seeming, no half-ness in nature, until the appearance of man. Un-conscious creatures do the whole will of wisdom. An oak or a chestnut undertakes no function it can-not execute ; or if there be phenomena in botany which we call abortions, the abortion is also a function of nature, and assumes to the intellect the like completeness with the further function to which in different circumstances it had attained. The same rule holds true of the animals. Their ac-tivity is marked by unerring good-sense. But man, through his access to Reason, is capable of the per-ception of a whole and a part. Reason is the whole, and whatsoever is not that is a part. The whole of nature is agreeable to the whole of thought, or to the Reason ; but separate any part of nature and attempt to look at it as a whole by itself, and the feeling of the ridiculous begins. The perpetual game of humor is to look with considerate good-nature at every object in existence, *aloof*, as a man might look at a mouse, comparing it with the eter-nal Whole ; enjoying the figure which each self-satisfied particular creature cuts in the unrespecting All, and dismissing it with a benison. Separate any object, as a particular bodily man, a horse, a turnip, a flour-barrel, an umbrella, from the connection of things, and contemplate it alone, standing there in absolute nature, it becomes at once comic ; no useful, no respectable qualities can rescue it from the ludicrous.

In virtue of man's access to Reason, or the Whole, the human form is a pledge of wholeness, suggests to our imagination the perfection of truth or goodness, and exposes by contrast any halfness or imperfection. We have a primary association between perfectness and this form. But the facts that occur when actual men enter do not make good this anticipation ; a discrepancy which is at once detected by the intellect, and the outward sign is the muscular irritation of laughter.

Reason does not joke, and men of reason do not ; a prophet, in whom the moral sentiment predominates, or a philosopher, in whom the love of truth predominates, these do not joke, but they bring the standard, the ideal whole, exposing all actual defect ; and hence the best of all jokes is the sympathetic contemplation of things by the understanding from the philosopher's point of view. There is no joke so true and deep in actual life as when some pure idealist goes up and down among the institutions of society, attended by a man who knows the world, and who, sympathizing with the philoso-

pher's scrutiny, sympathizes also with the confusion
and indignation of the detected, skulking institutions.   His perception of disparity, his eye wandering perpetually from the rule to the crooked, lying,
thieving fact, makes the eyes run over with laughter.

This is the radical joke of life and then of literature.   The presence of the ideal of right and of
truth in all action makes the yawning delinquen-
cies of practice remorseful to the conscience, tragic
to the interest, but droll to the intellect.   The activity of our sympathies may for a time hinder our
perceiving the fact intellectually, and so deriving
mirth from it ; but all falsehoods, all vices seen at
sufficient distance, seen from the point where our
moral sympathies do not interfere, become ludicrous.   The comedy is in the intellect's perception
of discrepancy.   And whilst the presence of the
ideal discovers the difference, the comedy is enhanced whenever that ideal is embodied visibly in
a man.   Thus Falstaff, in Shakspeare, is a character of the broadest comedy, giving himself unre-
servedly to his senses, coolly ignoring the Reason,
whilst he invokes its name, pretending to patriotism and to parental virtues, not with any intent to
deceive, but only to make the fun perfect by enjoying the confusion betwixt reason and the negation
of reason, — in other words, the rank rascaldom he

is calling by its name. Prince Hal stands by, as the acute understanding, who sees the Right, and sympathizes with it, and in the heyday of youth feels also the full attractions of pleasure, and is thus eminently qualified to enjoy the joke. At the same time he is to that degree under the Reason that it does not amuse him as much as it amuses another spectator.

If the essence of the Comic be the contrast in the intellect between the idea and the false performance, there is good reason why we should be affected by the exposure. We have no deeper interest than our integrity, and that we should be made aware by joke and by stroke of any lie we entertain. Besides, a perception of the Comic seems to be a balance-wheel in our metaphysical structure. It appears to be an essential element in a fine character. Wherever the intellect is constructive, it will be found. We feel the absence of it as a defect in the noblest and most oracular soul. The perception of the Comic is a tie of sympathy with other men, a pledge of sanity, and a protection from those perverse tendencies and gloomy insanities in which fine intellects sometimes lose themselves. A rogue alive to the ludicrous is still convertible. If that sense is lost, his fellow-men can do little for him.

It is true the sensibility to the ludicrous may run

into excess. Men celebrate their perception of halfness and a latent lie by the peculiar explosions of
laughter. So painfully susceptible are some men
to these impressions, that if a man of wit come into
the room where they are, it seems to take them out
of themselves with violent convulsions of the face
and sides, and obstreperous roarings of the throat.
How often and with what unfeigned compassion we
have seen such a person receiving like a willing
martyr the whispers into his ear of a man of wit.
The victim who has just received the discharge, if
in a solemn company, has the air very much of a
stout vessel which has just shipped a heavy sea;
and though it does not split it, the poor bark is for
the moment critically staggered. The peace of society and the decorum of tables seem to require
that next to a notable wit should always be posted
a phlegmatic bolt-upright man, able to stand without movement of muscle whole broadsides of this
Greek fire. It is a true shaft of Apollo, and traverses the universe, and unless it encounter a mystic
or a dumpish soul, goes everywhere heralded and
harbingered by smiles and greetings. Wit makes
its own welcome, and levels all distinctions. No
dignity, no learning, no force of character, can
make any stand against good wit. It is like ice,
on which no beauty of form, no majesty of carriage
can plead any immunity, — they must walk gin-

gerly, according to the laws of ice, or down they must go, dignity and all. "Dost thou think, because thou art virtuous, there shall be no more cakes and ale?" Plutarch happily expresses the value of the jest as a legitimate weapon of the philosopher. "Men cannot exercise their rhetoric unless they speak, but their philosophy even whilst they are silent or jest merrily ; for as it is the highest degree of injustice not to be just and yet seem so, so it is the top of wisdom to philosophize yet not appear to do it, and in mirth to do the same with those that are serious and seem in earnest ; for as in Euripides, the Bacchæ, though unprovided of iron weapons, and unarmed, wounded their invaders with the boughs of trees which they carried, thus the very jests and merry talk of true philosophers move those that are not altogether insensible, and unusually reform."

In all the parts of life, the occasion of laughter is some seeming, some keeping of the word to the ear and eye, whilst it is broken to the soul. Thus, as the religious sentiment is the most vital and sublime of all our sentiments, and capable of the most prodigious effects, so is it abhorrent to our whole nature, when, in the absence of the sentiment, the act or word or officer volunteers to stand in its stead. To the sympathies this is shocking, and occasions grief. But to the intellect the lack of the

sentiment gives no pain; it compares incessantly
the sublime idea with the bloated nothing which
pretends to be it, and the sense of the disproportion
is comedy.   And as the religious sentiment is the
most real and earnest thing in nature, being a mere
rapture, and excluding, when it appears, all other
considerations, the vitiating this is the greatest lie.
Therefore, the oldest gibe of literature is the ridicule of false religion.   This is the joke of jokes.
In religion, the sentiment is all; the ritual or ceremony indifferent.   But the inertia of men inclines
them, when the sentiment sleeps, to imitate that
thing it did; it goes through the ceremony omitting
only the will, makes the mistake of the wig for the
head, the clothes for the man.   The older the mistake and the more overgrown the particular form is,
the more ridiculous to the intellect.   Captain John
Smith, the discoverer of New England, was not
wanting in humor.   The Society in London which
had contributed their means to convert the savages,
hoping doubtless to see the Keokuks, Black Hawks,
Roaring Thunders, and Tustanuggees of that day
converted into church - wardens and deacons at
least, pestered the gallant rover with frequent so-
licitations out of England touching the conversion
of the Indians, and the enlargement of the Church.
Smith, in his perplexity how to satisfy the Society,
sent out a party into the swamp, caught an Indian,

and sent him home in the first ship to London, telling the Society they might convert one themselves.

The satire reaches its climax when the actual Church is set in direct contradiction to the dictates of the religious sentiment, as in the sketch of our Puritan politics in Hudibras : —

> "Our brethren of New England use
> Choice malefactors to excuse,
> And hang the guiltless in their stead,
> Of whom the churches have less need ;
> As lately happened, in a town
> Where lived a cobbler, and but one,
> That out of doctrine could cut use,
> And mend men's lives as well as shoes.
> This precious brother having slain,
> In times of peace, an Indian,
> Not out of malice, but mere zeal
> (Because he was an infidel),
> The mighty Tottipottymoy
> Sent to our elders an envoy,
> Complaining loudly of the breach
> Of league held forth by Brother Patch,
> Against the articles in force
> Between both churches, his and ours,
> For which he craved the saints to render
> Into his hands, or hang the offender ;
> But they, maturely having weighed
> They had no more but him o' th' trade
> (A man that served them in the double
> Capacity to teach and cobble),

Resolved to spare him ; yet to do
The Indian Hoghan Moghan too
Impartial justice, in his stead did
Hang an old weaver that was bedrid."

In science the jest at pedantry is analogous to that in religion which lies against superstition. A classification or nomenclature used by the scholar only as a memorandum of his last lesson in the laws of nature, and confessedly a makeshift, a bivouac for a night, and implying a march and a conquest to-morrow, — becomes through indolence a barrack and a prison, in which the man sits down immovably, and wishes to detain others. The physiologist Camper humorously confesses the effect of his studies in dislocating his ordinary associations. " I have been employed," he says, " six months on the *Cetacea ;* I understand the osteology of the head of all these monsters, and have made the combination with the human head so well that everybody now appears to me narwhale, porpoise, or marsouins. Women, the prettiest in society, and those whom I find less comely, they are all either narwhales or porpoises to my eyes." I chanced the other day to fall in with an odd illustration of the remark I had heard, that the laws of disease are as beautiful as the laws of health ; I was hastening to visit an old and honored friend, who, I was informed, was in a dying condition, when I met his physician, who accosted me in great spirits, with joy sparkling in his eyes. " And how is my friend, the reverend Doctor ? " I inquired. " O, I saw him this morning; it is the most correct apoplexy I have ever seen : face and hands livid, breathing stertorous, all the symptoms perfect." And he rubbed his hands with delight, for in the country we cannot find every day a case that agrees with the diagnosis of the books. I think there is malice in a very trifling story which goes about, and which I should not take any notice of, did I not suspect it to contain some satire upon my brothers of the Natural History Society. It is of a boy who was learning his alphabet. " That letter is A," said the teacher; " A," drawled the boy. " That is B," said the teacher ; " B," drawled the boy, and so on. " That is W, " said the teacher. " The devil ! " exclaimed the boy, " is that W ? "

The pedantry of literature belongs to the same category. In both cases there is a lie, when the mind, seizing a classification to help it to a sincerer knowledge of the fact, stops in the classification ; or learning languages and reading books to the end of a better acquaintance with man, stops in the languages and books : in both the learner seems to be wise, and is not.

The same falsehood, the same confusion of the sympathies because a pretension is not made good, points the perpetual satire against poverty, since, according to Latin poetry and English doggerel,

> " Poverty does nothing worse
> Than to make man ridiculous."

In this instance the halfness lies in the pretension of the parties to some consideration on account of their condition. If the man is not ashamed of his poverty, there is no joke. The poorest man who stands on his manhood destroys the jest. The poverty of the saint, of the rapt philosopher, of the naked Indian, is not comic. The lie is in the surrender of the man to his appearance; as if a man should neglect himself and treat his shadow on the wall with marks of infinite respect. It affects us oddly, as to see things turned upside down, or to see a man in a high wind run after his hat, which is always droll. The relation of the parties is inverted, — hat being for the moment master, the by-standers cheering the hat. The multiplication of artificial wants and expenses in civilized life, and the exaggeration of all trifling forms, present innumerable occasions for this discrepancy to expose itself. Such is the story told of the painter Astley, who, going out of Rome one day with a party for a ramble in the Campagna and the weather proving hot, refused to take off his coat when his companions threw off theirs, but sweltered on; which, exciting remark, his comrades playfully forced off his coat, and behold on the back of his waistcoat a gay cascade was thundering down the rocks with foam and rainbow, very refreshing in so sultry a day ; — a picture of his own, with which the poor painter had been fain to repair the shortcomings of his wardrobe. The same astonishment of the intellect at the disappearance of the man out of nature, through some superstition of his house or equipage, as if truth and virtue should be bowed out of creation by the clothes they wore, is the secret of all the fun that circulates concerning eminent fops and fashionists, and, in like manner, of the gay Rameau of Diderot, who believes in nothing but hunger, and that the sole end of art, virtue, and poetry is to put something for mastication between the upper and lower mandibles.

Alike in all these cases and in the instance of cowardice or fear of any sort, from the loss of life to the loss of spoons, the majesty of man is violated. He whom all things should serve, serves some one of his own tools. In fine pictures the head sheds on the limbs the expression of the face. In Raphael's Angel driving Heliodorus from the Temple, the crest of the helmet is so remarkable, that but for the extraordinary energy of the face, it would draw the eye too much ; but the countenance of the celestial messenger subordinates it, and we see it not. In poor pictures the limbs and trunk degrade the face. So among the women in the street, you shall see one whose bonnet and dress are one thing, and the lady herself quite another, wearing withal an expression of meek submission to her bonnet and dress; and another whose dress obeys and heightens the expression of her form.

More food for the Comic is afforded whenever the personal appearance, the face, form, and manners, are subjects of thought with the man himself. No fashion is the best fashion for those matters which will take care of themselves. This is the butt of those jokes of the Paris drawing-rooms, which Napoleon reckoned so formidable, and which are copiously recounted in the French Mémoires. A lady of high rank, but of lean figure, had given the Countess Dulauloy the nickname of " Le Grenadier tricolore," in allusion to her tall figure, as well as to her republican opinions ; the Countess retaliated by calling Madame "the Venus of the Père-Lachaise," a compliment to her skeleton which did not fail to circulate. " Lord C.," said the Countess of Gordon, " O, he is a perfect comb, all teeth and back." The Persians have a pleasant story of Tamerlane which relates to the same particulars : "Timur was an ugly man; he had a blind eye and a lame foot. One day when Chodscha was with him, Timur scratched his head, since the hour of the barber was come, and commanded that the barber should be called. Whilst he was shaven, the barber gave him a looking-glass in his hand. Timur saw himself in the mirror and found his face quite too ugly. Therefore he began to weep; Chodscha also set himself to weep, and so they wept for two hours. On this, some courtiers began to comfort Timur, and entertained him with strange stories in order to make him forget all about it. Timur ceased weeping, but Chodscha ceased not, but began now first to weep amain, and in good earnest. At last said Timur to Chodscha, 'Hearken! I have looked in the mirror, and seen myself ugly. Thereat I grieved, because, although I am Caliph, and have also much wealth, and many wives, yet still I am so ugly; therefore have I wept. But thou, why weepest thou without ceasing?' Chodscha answered, 'If thou hast only seen thy face once, and at once seeing hast not been able to contain thyself, but hast wept, what should we do, — we who see thy face every day and night? If we weep not, who should weep? Therefore have I wept.' Timur almost split his sides with laughing."

Politics also furnish the same mark for satire. What is nobler than the expansive sentiment of patriotism, which would find brothers in a whole nation? But when this enthusiasm is perceived to end in the very intelligible maxims of trade, so much for so much, the intellect feels again the half·

man. Or what is fitter than that we should espouse and carry a principle against all opposition? But when the men appear who ask our votes as representatives of this ideal, we are sadly out of countenance.

But there is no end to this analysis. We do nothing that is not laughable whenever we quit our spontaneous sentiment. All our plans, managements, houses, poems, if compared with the wisdom and love which man represents, are equally imperfect and ridiculous. But we cannot afford to part with any advantages. We must learn by laughter, as well as by tears and terrors; explore the whole of nature, the farce and buffoonery in the yard below, as well as the lessons of poets and philosophers upstairs in the hall, and get the rest and refreshment of the shaking of the sides. But the Comic also has its own speedy limits. Mirth quickly becomes intemperate, and the man would soon die of inanition, as some persons have been tickled to death. The same scourge whips the joker and the enjoyer of the joke. When Carlini was convulsing Naples with laughter, a patient waited on a physician in that city, to obtain some remedy for excessive melancholy, which was rapidly consuming his life. The physician endeavored to cheer his spirits, and advised him to go to the theatre and see Carlini. He replied, " I am Carlini. "

QUOTATION AND ORIGINALITY.

QUOTATION AND ORIGINALITY.

WHOEVER looks at the insect world, at flies, aphides, gnats, and innumerable parasites, and even at the infant mammals, must have remarked the extreme content they take in suction, which constitutes the main business of their life. If we go into a library or news-room, we see the same function on a higher plane, performed with like ardor, with equal impatience of interruption, indicating the sweetness of the act. In the highest civilization the book is still the highest delight. He who has once known its satisfactions is provided with a resource against calamity. Like Plato's disciple who has perceived a truth, " he is preserved from harm until another period. " In every man's memory, with the hours when life culminated are usually associated certain books which met his views. Of a large and powerful class we might ask with confidence, What is the event they most desire ? what gift? What but the book that shall come, which they have sought through all libraries, through all languages, that shall be to their mature eyes what many a tinsel-covered toy pamphlet was to their childhood, and shall speak to the imagination? Our high respect for a well-read man is praise enough of literature. If we encountered a man of rare intellect, we should ask him what books he read. We expect a great man to be a good reader; or in proportion to the spontaneous power should be the assimilating power. And though such are a more difficult and exacting class, they are not less eager. "He that borrows the aid of an equal understanding," said Burke, "doubles his own; he that uses that of a superior elevates his own to the stature of that he contemplates."

We prize books, and they prize them most who are themselves wise. Our debt to tradition through reading and conversation is so massive, our protest or private addition so rare and insignificant, — and this commonly on the ground of other reading or hearing, — that, in a large sense, one would say there is no pure originality. All minds quote. Old and new make the warp and woof of every moment. There is no thread that is not a twist of these two strands. By necessity, by proclivity, and by delight, we all quote. We quote not only books and proverbs, but arts, sciences, religion, customs, and laws; nay, we quote temples and houses, tables and chairs by imitation. The Patent-Office Commissioner knows that all machines in use have been invented and re-invented over and over ; that the mariner's compass, the boat, the pendulum, glass, movable types, the kaleidoscope, the railway, the power-loom, etc., have been many times found and lost, from Egypt, China, and Pompeii down ; and if we have arts which Rome wanted, so also Rome had arts which we have lost ; that the invention of yesterday of making wood indestructible by means of vapor of coal-oil or paraffine was suggested by the Egyptian method which has preserved its mummy-cases four thousand years.

The highest statement of new philosophy complacently caps itself with some prophetic maxim from the oldest learning. There is something mortifying in this perpetual circle. This extreme economy argues a very small capital of invention. The stream of affection flows broad and strong ; the practical activity is a river of supply ; but the dearth of design accuses the penury of intellect. How few thoughts ! In a hundred years, millions of men and not a hundred lines of poetry, not a theory of philosophy that offers a solution of the great problems, not an art of education that fulfils the conditions. In this delay and vacancy of thought we must make the best amends we can by seeking the wisdom of others to fill the time.

If we confine ourselves to literature, 't is easy to see that the debt is immense to past thought.

None escapes it. The originals are not original. There is imitation, model, and suggestion, to the very archangels, if we knew their history. The first book tyrannizes over the second. Read Tasso, and you think of Virgil; read Virgil, and you think of Homer; and Milton forces you to reflect how narrow are the limits of human invention. The " Paradise Lost " had never existed but for these precursors ; and if we find in India or Arabia a book out of our horizon of thought and tradition, we are soon taught by new researches in its native country to discover its foregoers, and its latent, but real connection with our own Bibles.

Read in Plato and you shall find Christian dogmas, and not only so, but stumble on our evangelical phrases. Hegel pre-exists in Proclus, and, long before, in Heraclitus and Parmenides. Whoso knows Plutarch, Lucian, Rabelais, Montaigne and Bayle will have a key to many supposed originalities. Rabelais is the source of many a proverb, story, and jest, derived from him into all modern languages ; and if we knew Rabelais's reading we should see the rill of the Rabelais river. Swedenborg, Behmen, Spinoza, will appear original to uninstructed and to thoughtless persons : their originality will disappear to such as are either well-read or thoughtful ; for scholars will recognize their dogmas as reappearing in men of a similar intel-

lectual elevation throughout history. Albert, the
" wonderful doctor," St. Buonaventura, the " se-
raphic doctor," Thomas Aquinas, the " angelic doctor " of the thirteenth century, whose books made
the sufficient culture of these ages, Dante absorbed,
and he survives for us. " Renard the Fox, " a
German poem of the thirteenth century, was long
supposed to be the original work, until Grimm
found fragments of another original a century older.
M. Le Grand showed that in the old Fabliaux were
the originals of the tales of Molière, La Fontaine,
Boccaccio, and of Voltaire.

Mythology is no man's work ; but, what we daily
observe in regard to the *bon-mots* that circulate in
society, — that every talker helps a story in repeating it, until, at last, from the slenderest fila-
ment of fact a good fable is constructed, — the
same growth befalls mythology : the legend is
tossed from believer to poet, from poet to believer,
everybody adding a grace or dropping a fault or
rounding the form, until it gets an ideal truth.

Religious literature, the psalms and liturgies of
churches, are of course of this slow growth, — a
fagot of selections gathered through ages, leaving
the worse and saving the better, until it is at last
the work of the whole communion of worshippers.
The Bible itself is like an old Cremona ; it has been
played upon by the devotion of thousands of years

until every word and particle is public and tun-
able.   And whatever undue reverence may have
been claimed for it by the prestige of philonic inspiration, the stronger tendency we are describing
is likely to undo.   What divines had assumed as
the distinctive revelations of Christianity, theologic
criticism has matched by exact parallelisms from
the Stoics and poets of Greece and Rome.   Later,
when Confucius and the Indian scriptures were
made known, no claim to monopoly of ethical wisdom could be thought of; and the surprising results of the new researches into the history of
Egypt have opened to us the deep debt of the
churches of Rome and England to the Egyptian
hierology.

The borrowing is often honest enough, and comes
of magnanimity and stoutness.   A great man quotes
bravely, and will not draw on his invention when
his memory serves him with a word as good.   What
he quotes, he fills with his own voice and humor,
and the whole cyclopædia of his table-talk is presently believed to be his own.   Thirty years ago,
when Mr. Webster at the bar or in the Senate
filled the eyes and minds of young men, you might
often hear cited as Mr. Webster's three rules : first,
never to do to-day what he could defer till to-morrow ; secondly, never to do himself what he could
make another do for him ; and, thirdly, never to

pay any debt to-day. Well, they are none the worse for being already told, in the last generation, of Sheridan; and we find in Grimm's *Mémoires* that Sheridan got them from the witty D'Argenson; who, no doubt, if we could consult him, could tell of whom he first heard them told. In our own college days we remember hearing other pieces of Mr. Webster's advice to students, — among others, this : that, when he opened a new book, he turned to the table of contents, took a pen, and sketched a sheet of matters and topics, what he knew and what he thought, before he read the book. But we find in Southey's " Commonplace Book " this said of the Earl of Strafford : " I learned one rule of him," says Sir G. Radcliffe, " which I think worthy to be remembered. When he met with a well-penned oration or tract upon any subject, he framed a speech upon the same argument, inventing and disposing what seemed fit to be said upon that subject, before he read the book; then, reading, compared his own with the author's, and noted his own defects and the author's art and fulness ; whereby he drew all that ran in the author more strictly, and might better judge of his own wants to supply them." I remember to have heard Mr. Samuel Rogers, in London, relate, among other anecdotes of the Duke of Wellington, that a lady having expressed in his presence a passionate wish to witness a great victory, he replied: "Madam, there is nothing so dreadful as a great victory, —excepting a great defeat." But this speech is also D'Argenson's, and is reported by Grimm. So the sarcasm attributed to Baron Alderson upon Brougham, "What a wonderful versatile mind has Brougham! he knows politics, Greek, history, science; if he only knew a little of law, he would know a little of everything." You may find the original of this gibe in Grimm, who says that Louis XVI., going out of chapel after hearing a sermon from the Abbé Maury, said, " *Si l'Abbé nous avait parlé un peu de religion, il nous aurait parlé de tout.*" A pleasantry which ran through all the newspapers a few years since, taxing the eccentricities of a gifted family connection in New England, was only a theft of Lady Mary Wortley Montagu's *mot* of a hundred years ago, that "the world was made up of men and women and Herveys."

Many of the historical proverbs have a doubtful paternity. Columbus's egg is claimed for Brunelleschi. Rabelais's dying words, "I am going to see the great Perhaps" (*le grand Peut-être*), only repeats the "IF" inscribed on the portal of the temple at Delphi. Goethe's favorite phrase, "the open secret," translates Aristotle's answer to Alexander, "These books are published and not published." Madame de Staël's "Architecture is frozen music" is borrowed from Goethe's "dumb music," which is Vitruvius's rule, that "the architect must not only understand drawing, but music." Wordsworth's hero acting "on the plan which pleased his childish thought," is Schiller's "Tell him to reverence the dreams of his youth," and earlier, Bacon's "*Consilia juventutis plus divinitatis habent.*"

In romantic literature examples of this vamping abound. The fine verse in the old Scotch ballad of "The Drowned Lovers,"

> "Thou art roaring ower loud, Clyde water,
>   Thy streams are ower strang ;
> Make me thy wrack when I come back,
>   But spare me when I gang,"

is a translation of Martial's epigram on Hero and Leander, where the prayer of Leander is the same : —

> "Parcite dum propero, mergite dum redeo."

Hafiz furnished Burns with the song of "John Barleycorn," and furnished Moore with the original of the piece,

> "When in death I shall calm recline
> Oh, bear my heart to my mistress dear," etc.

There are many fables which, as they are found in every language, and betray no sign of being borrowed, are said to be agreeable to the human mind. Such are " The Seven Sleepers," " Gyges's Ring," " The Travelling Cloak," " The Wandering Jew," "The Pied Piper," "Jack and his Beanstalk," the "Lady Diving in the Lake and Rising in the Cave," — whose omnipresence only indicates how easily a good story crosses all frontiers. The popular incident of Baron Munchausen, who hung his bugle up by the kitchen fire and the frozen tune thawed out, is found in Greece in Plato's time. Antiphanes, one of Plato's friends, laughingly compared his writings to a city where the words froze in the air as soon as they were pronounced, and the next summer, when they were warmed and melted by the sun, the people heard what had been spoken in the winter. It is only within this century that England and America discovered that their nursery-tales were old German and Scandinavian stories; and now it appears that they came from India, and are the property of all the nations descended from the Aryan race, and have been warbled and babbled between nurses and children for unknown thousands of years.

If we observe the tenacity with which nations cling to their first types of costume, of architecture, of tools and methods in tillage, and of decoration, — if we learn how old are the patterns of our shawls, the capitals of our columns, the fret, the beads, and other ornaments on our walls, the alter-

nate lotus-bud and leaf-stem of our iron fences, —
we shall think very well of the first men, or ill of
the latest.

Now shall we say that only the first men were
well alive, and the existing generation is invalided
and degenerate? Is all literature eavesdropping,
and all art Chinese imitation? our life a custom,
and our body borrowed, like a beggar's dinner, from
a hundred charities? A more subtle and severe
criticism might suggest that some dislocation has
befallen the race ; that men are off their centre ;
that multitudes of men do not live with Nature,
but behold it as exiles. People go out to look at
sunrises and sunsets who do not recognize their
own, quietly and happily, but know that it is foreign to them. As they do by books, so they *quote*
the sunset and the star, and do not make them
theirs. Worse yet, they live as foreigners in the
world of truth, and quote thoughts, and thus disown them. Quotation confesses inferiority. In
opening a new book we often discover, from the un-
guarded devotion with which the writer gives his
motto or text, all we have to expect from him. If
Lord Bacon appears already in the preface, I go
and read the " Instauration " instead of the new
book.

The mischief is quickly punished in general and
in particular. Admirable mimics have nothing of

their own. In every kind of parasite, when Nature has finished an aphis, a teredo, or a vampire bat, — an excellent sucking-pipe to tap another animal, or a mistletoe or dodder among plants, — the self-supplying organs wither and dwindle, as being superfluous. In common prudence there is an early limit to this leaning on an original. In literature, quotation is good only when the writer whom I follow goes my way, and, being better mounted than I, gives me a cast, as we say; but if I like the gay equipage so well as to go out of my road, I had better have gone afoot.

But it is necessary to remember there are certain considerations which go far to qualify a reproach too grave. This vast mental indebtedness has every variety that pecuniary debt has, — every variety of merit. The capitalist of either kind is as hungry to lend as the consumer to borrow; and the transaction no more indicates intellectual turpitude in the borrower than the simple fact of debt involves bankruptcy. On the contrary, in far the greater number of cases the transaction is honorable to both. Can we not help ourselves as discreetly by the force of two in literature? Certainly it only needs two well placed and well tempered for co-operation, to get somewhat far transcending any private enterprise! Shall we converse as spies? Our very abstaining to repeat and credit the fine remark of our friend is thievish. Each man of thought is surrounded by wiser men than he, if they cannot write as well. Cannot he and they combine? Cannot they sink their jealousies in God's love, and call their poem Beaumont and Fletcher, or the Theban Phalanx's? The city will for nine days or nine years make differences and sinister comparisons: there is a new and more excellent public that will bless the friends. Nay, it is an inevitable fruit of our social nature. The child quotes his father, and the man quotes his friend. Each man is a hero and an oracle to somebody, and to that person whatever he says has an enhanced value. Whatever we think and say is wonderfully better for our spirits and trust, in another mouth. There is none so eminent and wise but he knows minds whose opinion confirms or qualifies his own, and men of extraordinary genius acquire an almost absolute ascendant over their nearest companions. The Comte de Crillon said one day to M. d'Allonville, with French vivacity, "If the universe and I professed one opinion and M. Necker expressed a contrary one, I should be at once convinced that the universe and I were mistaken."

Original power is usually accompanied with assimilating power, and we value in Coleridge his excellent knowledge and quotations perhaps as much, possibly more, than his original suggestions. If an author give us just distinctions, inspiring lessons, or imaginative poetry, it is not so important to us whose they are. If we are fired and guided by these, we know him as a benefactor, and shall return to him as long as he serves us so well. We may like well to know what is Plato's and what is Montesquieu's or Goethe's part, and what thought was always dear to the writer himself ; but the worth of the sentences consists in their radiancy and equal aptitude to all intelligence. They fit all our facts like a charm. We respect ourselves the more that we know them.

Next to the originator of a good sentence is the first quoter of it. Many will read the book before one thinks of quoting a passage. As soon as he has done this, that line will be quoted east and west. Then there are great ways of borrowing. Genius borrows nobly. When Shakspeare is charged with debts to his authors, Landor replies: " Yet he was more original than his originals. He breathed upon dead bodies and brought them into life." And we must thank Karl Ottfried Müller for the just remark, " Poesy, drawing within its circle all that is glorious and inspiring, gave itself but little concern as to where its flowers originally grew." So Voltaire usually imitated, but with such superiority that Dubuc said : " He is like the false Amphitryon; although the stranger, it is always he who has the air of being master of the house." Wordsworth, as soon as he heard a good thing, caught it up, meditated upon it, and very soon reproduced it in his conversation and writing. If De Quincey said, "That is what I told you," he replied, "No: that is mine, — mine, and not yours." On the whole, we like the valor of it. 'T is on Marmontel's principle, "I pounce on what is mine, wherever I find it;" and on Bacon's broader rule, "I take all knowledge to be my province." It betrays the consciousness that truth is the property of no individual, but is the treasure of all men. And inasmuch as any writer has ascended to a just view of man's condition, he has adopted this tone. In so far as the receiver's aim is on life, and not on literature, will be his indifference to the source. The nobler the truth or sentiment, the less imports the question of authorship. It never troubles the simple seeker from whom he derived such or such a sentiment. Whoever expresses to us a just thought makes ridiculous the pains of the critic who should tell him where such a word had been said before. "It is no more according to Plato than according to me." Truth is always present: it only needs to lift the iron lids of the mind's eye to read its oracles. But the moment there is the purpose of display, the fraud is exposed.

In fact, it is as difficult to appropriate the thoughts of others, as it is to invent. Always some steep transition, some sudden alteration of temperature, or of point of view, betrays the foreign interpolation.

There is, besides, a new charm in such intellectual works as, passing through long time, have had a multitude of authors and improvers. We admire that poetry which no man wrote, — no poet less than the genius of humanity itself, — which is to be read in a mythology, in the effect of a fixed or national style of pictures, of sculptures, or drama, or cities, or sciences, on us. Such a poem also is language. Every word in the language has once been used happily. The ear, caught by that felicity, retains it, and it is used again and again, as if the charm belonged to the word and not to the life of thought which so enforced it. These profane uses, of course, kill it, and it is avoided. But a quick wit can at any time reinforce it, and it comes into vogue again. Then people quote so differently : one finding only what is gaudy and popular ; another, the heart of the author, the report of his select and happiest hour ; and the reader sometimes giving more to the citation than he owes to it. Most of the classical citations you shall hear or read in the current journals or speeches were not drawn from the originals, but from previous quotations in English books ; and you can easily pronounce, from the use and relevancy of the sentence, whether it had not done duty many times before, — whether your jewel was got from the mine or from an auctioneer. We are as much informed of a writer's genius by what he selects as by what he originates. We read the quotation with his eyes, and find a new and fervent sense; as a passage from one of the poets, well recited, borrows new interest from the rendering. As the journals say, " the italics are ours." The profit of books is according to the sensibility of the reader. The profoundest thought or passion sleeps as in a mine until an equal mind and heart finds and publishes it. The passages of Shakspeare that we most prize were never quoted until within this century; and Milton's prose, and Burke, even, have their best fame within it. Every one, too, remembers his friends by their favorite poetry or other reading.

Observe also that a writer appears to more advantage in the pages of another book than in his own. In his own he waits as a candidate for your approbation; in another's he is a lawgiver.

Then another's thoughts have a certain advantage with us simply because they are another's. There is an illusion in a new phrase. A man hears a fine sentence out of Swedenborg, and wonders at the wisdom, and is very merry at heart that he has now got so fine a thing. Translate it out of the new words into his own usual phrase, and he will wonder again at his own simplicity, such tricks do fine words play with us.

It is curious what new interest an old author acquires by official canonization in Tiraboschi, or Dr. Johnson, or Von Hammer-Purgstall, or Hallam, or other historian of literature. Their registration of his book, or citation of a passage, carries the sentimental value of a college diploma. Hallam, though never profound, is a fair mind, able to appreciate poetry unless it becomes deep, being always blind and deaf to imaginative and analogy-loving souls, like the Platonists, like Giordano Bruno, like Donne, Herbert, Crashaw, and Vaughan; and Hallam cites a sentence from Bacon or Sidney, and distinguishes a lyric of Edwards or Vaux, and straightway it commends itself to us as if it had received the Isthmian crown.

It is a familiar expedient of brilliant writers, and not less of witty talkers, the device of ascribing their own sentence to an imaginary person, in order to give it weight, — as Cicero, Cowley, Swift, Landor, and Carlyle have done. And Cardinal de Retz, at a critical moment in the Parliament of Paris, described himself in an extemporary Latin sentence, which he pretended to quote from a classic author, and which told admirably well. It is a curious reflex effect of this enhancement of our thought by citing it from another, that many men can write better under a mask than for themselves; as Chatterton in archaic ballad, Le Sage in Spanish costume, Macpherson as " Ossian ; " and, I doubt not, many a young barrister in chambers in London, who forges good thunder for the "Times," but never works as well under his own name. This is a sort of dramatizing talent ; as it is not rare to find great powers of recitation, without the least original eloquence, — or people who copy drawings with admirable skill, but are incapable of any design.

In hours of high mental activity we sometimes do the book too much honor, reading out of it better things than the author wrote, — reading, as we say, between the lines. You have had the like experience in conversation : the wit was in what you heard, not in what the speakers said. Our best thought came from others. We heard in their words a deeper sense than the speakers put into them, and could express ourselves in other people's phrases to finer purpose than they knew. In Moore's Diary, Mr. Hallam is reported as mentioning at dinner one of his friends who had said, " I don't know how it is, a thing that falls flat from me seems quite an excellent joke when given at second-hand by Sheridan. I never like my own *bon-mots* until he adopts them." Dumont was exalted by being used by Mirabeau, by Bentham, and by Sir Philip Francis, who, again, was less than his own "Junius;" and James Hogg (except in his poems "Kilmeny" and "The Witch of Fife") is but a third-rate author, owing his fame to his effigy colossalized through the lens of John Wilson, — who, again, writes better under the domino of "Christopher North" than in his proper clothes. The bold theory of Delia Bacon, that Shakspeare's plays were written by a society of wits, — by Sir Walter Raleigh, Lord Bacon, and others around the Earl of Southampton, — had plainly for her the charm of the superior meaning they would acquire when read under this light; this idea of the authorship controlling our appreciation of the works themselves. We once knew a man overjoyed at the notice of his pamphlet in a leading newspaper. What range he gave his imagination! Who could have written it? Was it not Colonel Carbine, or Senator Tonitrus, or, at the least, Professor Maximilian? Yes, he could detect in the style that fine Roman hand. How it seemed the very voice of the refined and discerning public, inviting merit at last to consent to fame, and come up and take place in the reserved and authentic chairs! He carried the journal with haste to the sympathizing Cousin Matilda, who is so proud of all we do. But what dismay when the good Matilda, pleased with his pleasure, confessed she had written the criticism, and carried it with her own hands to the post-office! "Mr. Wordsworth," said Charles Lamb, "allow me to introduce to you my only admirer."

Swedenborg threw a formidable theory into the world, that every soul existed in a society of souls, from which all its thoughts passed into it, as the blood of the mother circulates in her unborn child; and he noticed that, when in his bed, alternately sleeping and waking, — sleeping, he was surrounded by persons disputing and offering opinions on the one side and on the other side of a proposition; waking, the like suggestions occurred for and against the proposition as his own thoughts; sleeping again, he saw and heard the speakers as before: and this as often as he slept or waked. And if we expand the image, does it not look as if we men were thinking and talking out of an enormous antiquity, as if we stood, not in a coterie of prompters that filled a sitting-room, but in a circle of intelligences that reached through all thinkers, poets, inventors, and wits, men and women, English, German, Celt, Aryan, Ninevite, Copt, — back to the first geometer, bard, mason, carpenter, planter, shepherd, — back to the first negro, who, with more health or better perception, gave a shriller sound or name for the thing he saw and dealt with? Our benefactors are as many as the children who invented speech, word by word. Language is a city

to the building of which every human being brought
a stone; yet he is no more to be credited with the
grand result than the acaleph which adds a cell to
the coral reef which is the basis of the continent.

Πάντα ῥεῖ: all things are in flux. It is inevitable
that you are indebted to the past. You are fed and
formed by it. The old forest is decomposed for
the composition of the new forest. The old animals have given their bodies to the earth to furnish
through chemistry the forming race, and every individual is only a momentary fixation of what was
yesterday another's, is to-day his, and will belong
to a third to-morrow. So it is in thought. Our
knowledge is the amassed thought and experience
of innumerable minds : our language, our science,
our religion, our opinions, our fancies we inherited.
Our country, customs, laws, our ambitions, and our
notions of fit and fair, — all these we never made,
we found them ready-made ; we but quote them.
Goethe frankly said, " What would remain to me
if this art of appropriation were derogatory to genius ? Every one of my writings has been furnished
to me by a thousand different persons, a thousand
things : wise and foolish have brought me, without
suspecting it, the offering of their thoughts, faculties, and experience. My work is an aggregation
of beings taken from the whole of nature ; it bears
the name of Goethe."

But there remains the indefeasible persistency of the individual to be himself. One leaf, one blade of grass, one meridian, does not resemble another. Every mind is different; and the more it is unfolded, the more pronounced is that difference. He must draw the elements into him for food, and, if they be granite and silex, will prefer them cooked by sun and rain, by time and art, to his hand. But, however received, these elements pass into the substance of his constitution, will be assimilated, and tend always to form, not a partisan, but a possessor of truth. To all that can be said of the preponderance of the Past, the single word Genius is a sufficient reply. The divine resides in the new. The divine never quotes, but is, and creates. The profound apprehension of the Present is Genius, which makes the Past forgotten. Genius believes its faintest presentiment against the testimony of all history; for it knows that facts are not ultimates, but that a state of mind is the ancestor of everything. And what is Originality? It is being, being one's self, and reporting accurately what we see and are. Genius is in the first instance, sensibility, the capacity of receiving just impressions from the external world, and the power of co-ordinating these after the laws of thought. It implies Will, or original force, for their right distribution and expression. If to this the sentiment of piety be added, if the thinker feels that the thought most strictly his own is not his own, and recognizes the perpetual suggestion of the Supreme Intellect, the oldest thoughts become new and fertile whilst he speaks them.

Originals never lose their value. There is always in them a style and weight of speech, which the immanence of the oracle bestowed, and which cannot be counterfeited. Hence the permanence of the high poets. Plato, Cicero, and Plutarch cite the poets in the manner in which Scripture is quoted in our churches. A phrase or a single word is adduced, with honoring emphasis, from Pindar, Hesiod, or Euripides, as precluding all argument, because thus had they said : importing that the bard spoke not his own, but the words of some god. True poets have always ascended to this lofty platform, and met this expectation. Shakspeare, Milton, Wordsworth, were very conscious of their responsibilities. When a man thinks happily, he finds no foot-track in the field he traverses. All spontaneous thought is irrespective of all else. Pindar uses this haughty defiance, as if it were impossible to find his sources: " There are many swift darts within my quiver, which have a voice for those with understanding ; but to the crowd they need interpreters. He is gifted with genius who knoweth much by natural talent."

Our pleasure in seeing each mind take the subject to which it has a proper right is seen in mere fitness in time. He that comes second must needs quote him that comes first. The earliest describers of savage life, as Captain Cook's account of the Society Islands, or Alexander Henry's travels among our Indian tribes, have a charm of truth and just point of view. Landsmen and sailors freshly come from the most civilized countries, and with no false expectation, no sentimentality yet about wild life, healthily receive and report what they saw, — seeing what they must, and using no choice; and no man suspects the superior merit of the description, until Chateaubriand, or Moore, or Campbell, or Byron, or the artists, arrive, and mix so much art with their picture that the incomparable advantage of the first narrative appears. For the same reason we dislike that the poet should choose an antique or far-fetched subject for his muse, as if he avowed want of insight. The great deal always with the nearest. Only as braveries of too prodigal power can we pardon it, when the life of genius is so redundant that out of petulance it flings its fire into some old mummy, and, lo! it walks and blushes again here in the street.

We cannot overstate our debt to the Past, but the moment has the supreme claim. The Past is for us; but the sole terms on which it can become ours are its subordination to the Present. Only an inventor knows how to borrow, and every man is or should be an inventor. We must not tamper with the organic motion of the soul. 'T is certain that thought has its own proper motion, and the hints which flash from it, the words overheard at unawares by the free mind, are trustworthy and fertile when obeyed and not perverted to low and selfish account. This vast memory is only raw material. The divine gift is ever the instant life, which receives and uses and creates, and can well bury the old in the omnipotency with which Nature decomposes all her harvest for recomposition.

PROGRESS OF CULTURE.

PROGRESS OF CULTURE.

ADDRESS READ BEFORE THE Φ B K SOCIETY AT CAM-
BRIDGE, JULY 18, 1867.

WE meet to-day under happy omens to our ancient society, to the commonwealth of letters, to
the country, and to mankind. No good citizen but
shares the wonderful prosperity of the Federal
Union. The heart still beats with the public pulse
of joy that the country has withstood the rude
trial which threatened its existence, and thrills with
the vast augmentation of strength which it draws
from this proof. The storm which has been re-
sisted is a crown of honor and a pledge of strength
to the ship. We may be well contented with our
fair inheritance. Was ever such coincidence of advantages in time and place as in America to-day?
— the fusion of races and religions; the hungry
cry for men which goes up from the wide continent; the answering facility of immigration, per-
mitting every wanderer to choose his climate and
government. Men come hither by nations. Science surpasses the old miracles of mythology, to

fly with them over the sea, and to send their mes-
sages under it.   They come from crowded, anti-
quated kingdoms to the easy sharing of our simple
forms.   Land without price is offered to the settler,
cheap education to his children.   The temper of
our people delights in this whirl of life.   Who
would live in the stone age, or the bronze, or the
iron, or the lacustrine ?   Who does not prefer the
age of steel, of gold, of coal, petroleum, cotton,
steam, electricity, and the spectroscope ?

> " Prisca juvent alios, ego me nunc denique natum
>   Gratulor."

All this activity has added to the value of life, and
to the scope of the intellect.   I will not say that
American institutions have given a new enlargement to our idea of a finished man, but they have
added important features to the sketch.

Observe the marked ethical quality of the innovations urged or adopted.   The new claim of woman
to a political status is itself an honorable testimony
to the civilization which has given her a civil
status new in history.   Now that by the increased
humanity of law she controls her property, she inevitably takes the next step to her share in power.
The war gave us the abolition of slavery, the success of the Sanitary Commission and of the Freed-
men's Bureau.   Add to these the new scope of
social science ; the abolition of capital punishment

and of imprisonment for debt; the improvement of prisons; the efforts for the suppression of intemperance; the search for just rules affecting labor; the co-operative societies; the insurance of life and limb; the free-trade league; the improved almshouses; the enlarged scale of charities to relieve local famine, or burned towns, or the suffering Greeks; the incipient series of international congresses; — all, one may say, in a high degree revolutionary, teaching nations the taking of government into their own hands, and superseding kings.

The spirit is new. A silent revolution has impelled, step by step, all this activity. A great many full-blown conceits have burst. The coxcomb goes to the wall. To his astonishment he has found that this country and this age belong to the most liberal persuasion; that the day of ruling by scorn and sneers is past; that good sense is now in power, and *that* resting on a vast constituency of intelligent labor, and, better yet, on perceptions less and less dim of laws the most sublime. Men are now to be astonished by seeing acts of good-nature, common civility, and Christian charity proposed by statesmen, and executed by justices of the peace, — by policemen and the constable. The fop is unable to cut the patriot in the street; nay, he lies at his mercy in the ballot of the club.

Mark, too, the large resources of a statesman, of

a socialist, of a scholar, in this age. When classes are exasperated against each other, the peace of the world is always kept by striking a new note. Instantly the units part, and form in a new order, and those who were opposed are now side by side. In this country the prodigious mass of work that must be done has either made new divisions of labor or created new professions. Consider, at this time, what variety of issues, of enterprises public and private, what genius of science, what of administration, what of practical skill, what masters, each in his several province, the railroad, the telegraph, the mines, the inland and marine explorations, the novel and powerful philanthropies, as well as agriculture, the foreign trade and the home trade (whose circuits in this country are as spacious as the foreign), manufactures, the very inventions, all on a national scale too, have evoked! — all implying the appearance of gifted men, the rapid addition to our society of a class of true nobles, by which the self-respect of each town and State is enriched.

Take as a type the boundless freedom here in Massachusetts. People have in all countries been burned and stoned for saying things which are commonplaces at all our breakfast-tables. Every one who was in Italy thirty-five years ago will remember the caution with which his host or guest in any house looked around him, if a political topic were broached. Here the tongue is free, and the hand; and the freedom of action goes to the brink, if not over the brink, of license.

A controlling influence of the times has been the wide and successful study of Natural Science. Steffens said, " The religious opinions of men rest on their views of nature." Great strides have been made within the present century. Geology, astronomy, chemistry, optics, have yielded grand results. The correlation of forces and the polarization of light have carried us to sublime generalizations, — have affected an imaginative race like poetic inspirations. We have been taught to tread familiarly on giddy heights of thought, and to wont ourselves to daring conjectures. The narrow sectarian cannot read astronomy with impunity. The creeds of his church shrivel like dried leaves at the door of the observatory, and a new and healthful air regenerates the human mind, and imparts a sympathetic enlargement to its inventions and method. That cosmical west-wind which, meteorologists tell us, constitutes, by the revolution of the globe, the upper current, is alone broad enough to carry to every city and suburb, to the farmer's house, the miner's shanty, and the fisher's boat, the inspirations of this new hope of mankind. Now, if any one say we have had enough of these boastful recitals, then I say, Happy is the land wherein benefits like these have grown trite and commonplace.

We confess that in America everything looks new and recent. Our towns are still rude, the make-shifts of emigrants, and the whole architecture tent-like when compared with the monumental solidity of medieval and primeval remains in Europe and Asia. But geology has effaced these distinctions. Geology, a science of forty or fifty summers, has had the effect to throw an air of novelty and mushroom speed over entire history. The oldest empires, — what we called venerable antiquity, — now that we have true measures of duration, show like creations of yesterday. It is yet quite too early to draw sound conclusions. The old six thousand years of chronology become a kitchen clock, no more a measure of time than an hour-glass or an egg-glass since the duration of geologic periods has come into view. Geology itself is only chemistry with the element of time added ; and the rocks of Nahant or the dikes of the White Hills disclose that the world is a crystal, and the soil of the valleys and plains a continual decomposition and recomposition. Nothing is old but the mind.

But I find not only this equality between new and old countries, as seen by the eye of science, but also a certain equivalence of the ages of history; and as the child is in his playthings working incessantly at problems of natural philosophy, working as hard and as successfully as Newton, so it were ignorance not to see that each nation and period has done its full part to make up the result of existing civility. We are all agreed that we have not on the instant better men to show than Plutarch's heroes. The world is always equal to itself. We cannot yet afford to drop Homer, nor Æschylus, nor Plato, nor Aristotle, nor Archimedes. Later, each European nation, after the breaking up of the Roman Empire, had its romantic era, and the productions of that era in each rose to about the same height. Take for an example in literature the *Romance of Arthur*, in Britain, or in the opposite province of Brittany; the *Chanson de Roland*, in France; the Chronicle of the Cid, in Spain; the *Niebelungen Lied*, in Germany; the Norse Sagas, in Scandinavia; and, I may add, the Arabian Nights, on the African coast. But if these works still survive and multiply, what shall we say of names more distant, or hidden through their very superiority to their coëvals, — names of men who have left remains that certify a height of genius in their several directions not since surpassed, and which men in proportion to their wisdom still cherish, — as Zoroaster, Con-

fucius, and the grand scriptures, only recently
known to Western nations, of the Indian Vedas,
the Institutes of Menu, the Puranas, the poems
of the Mahabarat and the Ramayana?

In modern Europe, the Middle Ages were called
the Dark Ages. Who dares to call them so now?
They are seen to be the feet on which we walk,
the eyes with which we see. It is one of our
triumphs to have reinstated them. Their Dante
and Alfred and Wickliffe and Abelard and Bacon;
their Magna Charta, decimal numbers, mariner's
compass, gunpowder, glass, paper, and clocks;
chemistry, algebra, astronomy; their Gothic architecture, their painting, are the delight and tuition
of ours. Six hundred years ago Roger Bacon explained the precession of the equinoxes and the
necessity of reform in the calendar; looking over
how many horizons as far as into Liverpool and
New York, he announced that machines can be
constructed to drive ships more rapidly than a
whole galley of rowers could do, nor would they
need anything but a pilot to steer; carriages, to
move with incredible speed, without aid of animals; and machines to fly into the air like birds.
Even the races that we still call savage or semi-
savage, and which preserve their arts from im-
memorial traditions, vindicate their faculty by
the skill with which they make their yam-cloths,

pipes, bows, boats, and carved war-clubs. The war-proa of the Malays in the Japanese waters struck Commodore Perry by its close resemblance to the yacht "America."

As we find thus a certain equivalence in the ages, there is also an equipollence of individual genius to the nation which it represents. It is a curious fact that a certain enormity of culture makes a man invisible to his contemporaries. It is always hard to go beyond your public. If they are satisfied with cheap performance, you will not easily arrive at better. If they know what is good, and require it, you will aspire and burn until you achieve it. But, from time to time in history, men are born a whole age too soon. The founders of nations, the wise men and inventors who shine afterwards as their gods, were probably martyrs in their own time. All the transcendent writers and artists of the world, — 't is doubtful who they were, they are lifted so fast into mythology; Homer, Menu, Viasa, Dædalus, Hermes, Zoroaster, even Swedenborg and Shakspeare. The early names are too typical, — Homer, or *blind man;* Menu, or *man;* Viasa, *compiler;* Dædalus, *cunning;* Hermes, *interpreter;* and so on. Probably the men were so great, so self-fed, that the recognition of them by others was not necessary to them. And every one has heard the remark (too often, I fear, politely made), that the philosopher was above his audience. I think I have seen two or three great men who, for that reason, were of no account among scholars.

But Jove is in his reserves. The truth, the hope of any time, must always be sought in the minorities. Michel Angelo was the conscience of Italy. We grow free with his name, and find it ornamental now; but in his own days his friends were few; and you would need to hunt him in a conventicle with the Methodists of the era, namely, Savonarola, Vittoria Colonna, Contarini, Pole, Occhino; superior souls, the religious of that day, drawn to each other and under some cloud with the rest of the world; reformers, the radicals of the hour, banded against the corruptions of Rome, and as lonely and as hated as Dante before them.

I find the single mind equipollent to a multitude of minds, say to a nation of minds, as a drop of water balances the sea; and under this view the problem of culture assumes wonderful interest. Culture implies all which gives the mind possession of its own powers; as languages to the critic, telescope to the astronomer. Culture alters the political status of an individual. It raises a rival royalty in a monarchy. 'T is king against king. It is ever the romance of history in all dynasties, — the co-presence of the revolutionary force in intellect. It creates a personal independence which the monarch cannot look down, and to which he must often succumb. If a man know the laws of nature better than other men, his nation cannot spare him; nor if he know the power of numbers, the secret of geometry, of algebra; on which the computations of astronomy, of navigation, of machinery, rest. If he can converse better than any other, he rules the minds of men wherever he goes ; if he has imagination, he intoxicates men. If he has wit, he tempers despotism by epigrams : a song, a satire, a sentence, has played its part in great events. Eloquence a hundred times has turned the scale of war and peace at will. The history of Greece is at one time reduced to two persons, — Philip, or the successor of Philip, on one side, and Demosthenes, a private citizen, on the other. If he has a military genius, like Belisarius, or administrative faculty, like Chatham or Bismarck, he is the king's king. If a theologian of deep convictions and strong understanding carries his country with him, like Luther, the state becomes Lutheran, in spite of the Emperor ; as Thomas à Becket overpowered the English Henry. Wit has a great charter. Popes and kings and Councils of Ten are very sharp with their censorships and inquisitions, but it is on dull people. Some Dante or Angelo, Rabelais, Hafiz, Cervantes, Erasmus, Béranger, Bettine von Arnim, or whatever genuine wit of the old inimitable class, is always allowed. Kings feel that this is that which they themselves represent; this is no red-kerchiefed, red-shirted rebel, but loyalty, kingship. This is real kingship, and their own only titular. Even manners are a distinction which, we some-times see, are not to be overborne by rank or offi-cial power, or even by other eminent talents, since they too proceed from a certain deep innate percep-tion of fit and fair.

It is too plain that a cultivated laborer is worth many untaught laborers; that a scientific engineer, with instruments and steam, is worth many hun-dred men, many thousands; that Archimedes or Napoleon is worth for labor a thousand thousands, and that in every wise and genial soul we have England, Greece, Italy, walking, and can dispense with populations of *navvies*.

Literary history and all history is a record of the power of minorities, and of minorities of one. Every book is written with a constant secret refer-ence to the few intelligent persons whom the writer believes to exist in the million. The artist has al-ways the masters in his eye, though he affect to flout them. Michel Angelo is thinking of Da Vinci, and Raffaelle is thinking of Michel Angelo. Tennyson would give his fame for a verdict in his favor from Wordsworth. Agassiz and Owen and

Huxley affect to address the American and English people, but are really writing to each other. Everett dreamed of Webster. McKay, the shipbuilder, thinks of George Steers; and Steers, of Pook, the naval constructor. The names of the masters at the head of each department of science, art, or function are often little known to the world, but are always known to the adepts; as Robert Brown in botany, and Gauss in mathematics. Often the master is a hidden man, but not to the true student; invisible to all the rest, resplendent to him. All his own work and culture form the eye to see the master. In politics, mark the importance of minorities of one, as of Phocion, Cato, Lafayette, Arago. The importance of the one person who has the truth over nations who have it not, is because power obeys reality, and not appearance; according to quality, and not quantity. How much more are men than nations! the wise and good souls, the stoics in Greece and Rome, Socrates in Athens, the saints in Judea, Alfred the king, Shakspeare the poet, Newton the philosopher, the perceiver and obeyer of truth, — than the foolish and sensual millions around them! So that, wherever a true man appears, everything usually reckoned great dwarfs itself; he is the only great event, and it is easy to lift him into a mythological personage.

Then the next step in the series is the equivalence of the soul to nature. I said that one of the distinctions of our century has been the devotion of cultivated men to natural science. The benefits thence derived to the arts and to civilization are signal and immense. They are felt in navigation, in agriculture, in manufactures, in astronomy, in mining, and in war. But over all their utilities, I must hold their chief value to be metaphysical. The chief value is not the useful powers he obtained, but the test it has been of the scholar. He has accosted this immeasurable nature, and got clear answers. He understood what he read. He found agreement with himself. It taught him anew the reach of the human mind, and that it was citizen of the universe.

The first quality we know in matter is centrality, — we call it gravity, — which holds the universe together, which remains pure and indestructible in each mote as in masses and planets, and from each atom rays out illimitable influence. To this material essence answers Truth, in the intellectual world, — Truth, whose centre is everywhere and its circumference nowhere, whose existence we cannot disimagine; the soundness and health of things, against which no blow can be struck but it recoils on the striker; Truth, on whose side we always heartily are. And the first measure of a mind is its centrality, its capacity of truth, and its adhesion to it.

When the correlation of the sciences was announced by Oersted and his colleagues, it was no surprise; we were found already prepared for it. The fact stated accorded with the auguries or divinations of the human mind. Thus, if we should analyze Newton's discovery, we should say that if it had not been anticipated by him, it would not have been found. We are told that in posting his books, after the French had measured on the earth a degree of the meridian, when he saw that his theoretic results were approximating that empirical one, his hand shook, the figures danced, and he was so agitated that he was forced to call in an assistant to finish the computation. Why agitated? — but because, when he saw, in the fall of an apple to the ground, the fall of the earth to the sun, of the sun and of all suns to the centre, that perception was accompanied by the spasm of delight by which the intellect greets a fact more immense still, a fact really universal, — holding in intellect as in matter, in morals as in intellect, — that atom draws to atom throughout nature, and truth to truth throughout spirit? His law was only a particular of the more universal law of centrality. Every law in nature, as gravity, centripetence, repulsion, polarity, undulation, has a counterpart in the intellect. The laws above are sisters of the laws below. Shall we study the mathematics of the sphere, and not its causal essence also? Nature is a fable whose moral blazes through it. There is no use in Copernicus if the robust periodicity of the solar system does not show its equal perfection in the mental sphere, the periodicity, the compensatory errors, the grand reactions. I shall never believe that centrifugence and centripetence balance, unless mind heats and meliorates, as well as the surface and soil of the globe.

On this power, this all-dissolving unity, the emphasis of heaven and earth is laid. Nature is brute but as this soul quickens it; Nature, always the effect, mind the flowing cause. Nature, we find, is ever as is our sensibility; it is hostile to ignorance, — plastic, transparent, delightful, to knowledge. Mind carries the law; history is the slow and atomic unfolding. All things admit of this extended sense, and the universe at last is only prophetic, or, shall we say, symptomatic, of vaster interpretation and results. Nature is an enormous system, but in mass and in particle curiously available to the humblest need of the little creature that walks on the earth! The immeasurableness of Nature is not more astounding than his power to gather all her omnipotence into a manageable rod or wedge, bringing it to a hair-point for the eye and hand of the philosopher.

Here stretches out of sight, out of conception

even, this vast Nature, daunting, bewildering, but
all penetrable, all self-similar; an unbroken unity,
and the mind of man is a key to the whole. He
finds that the universe, as Newton said, was "made
at one cast;" the mass is like the atom, — the
same chemistry, gravity and conditions. The as-
teroids are the chips of an old star, and a meteoric
stone is a chip of an asteroid. As language is in
the alphabet, so is entire Nature, the play of all its
laws, in one atom. The good wit finds the law
from a single observation, — the law, and its limi-
tations, and its correspondences, — as the farmer
finds his cattle by a footprint. "State the sun,
and you state the planets, and conversely."

Whilst its power is offered to his hand, its laws
to his science, not less its beauty speaks to his
taste, imagination, and sentiment. Nature is sana-
tive, refining, elevating. How cunningly she hides
every wrinkle of her inconceivable antiquity under
roses and violets and morning dew! Every inch
of the mountains is scarred by unimaginable convulsions, yet the new day is purple with the bloom
of youth and love. Look out into the July night
and see the broad belt of silver flame which flashes
up the half of heaven, fresh and delicate as the
bonfires of the meadow-flies. Yet the powers of
numbers cannot compute its enormous age, lasting
as space and time, embosomed in time and space.

And time and space, — what are they? Our first problems, which we ponder all our lives through, and leave where we found them; whose outrunning immensity, the old Greeks believed, astonished the gods themselves; of whose dizzy vastitudes all the worlds of God are a mere dot on the margin; impossible to deny, impossible to believe. Yet the moral element in man counterpoises this dismaying immensity and bereaves it of terror. The highest flight to which the muse of Horace ascended was in that triplet of lines in which he described the souls which can calmly confront the sublimity of Nature: —

> " Hunc solem, et stellas, et decedentia certis
>   Tempora momentis, sunt qui formidine nulla
>   Imbuti spectant."

The sublime point of experience is the value of a sufficient man. Cube this value by the meeting of two such, of two or more such, who understand and support each other, and you have organized victory. At any time, it only needs the contemporaneous appearance of a few superior and attractive men to give a new and noble turn to the public mind.

The benefactors we have indicated were exceptional men, and great because exceptional. The question which the present age urges with increasing emphasis, day by day, is, whether the high qualities which distinguished them can be imparted. The poet Wordsworth asked, "What one is, why may not millions be?" Why not? Knowledge exists to be imparted. Curiosity is lying in wait for every secret. The inquisitiveness of the child to hear runs to meet the eagerness of the parent to explain. The air does not rush to fill a vacuum with such speed as the mind to catch the expected fact. Every artist was first an amateur. The ear outgrows the tongue, is sooner ripe and perfect; but the tongue is always learning to say what the ear has taught it, and the hand obeys the same lesson.

There is anything but humiliation in the homage men pay to a great man; it is sympathy, love of the same things, effort to reach them, — the expression of their hope of what they shall become when the obstructions of their mal-formation and mal-education shall be trained away. Great men shall not impoverish, but enrich us. Great men, — the age goes on their credit; but all the rest, when their wires are continued and not cut, can do as signal things, and in new parts of nature. "No angel in his heart acknowledges any one superior to himself but the Lord alone." There is not a person here present to whom omens that should astonish have not predicted his future, have not uncovered his past. The dreams of the night supplement by their divination the imperfect experiments of the day. Every soliciting instinct is only a hint of a coming fact, as the air and water that hang invisibly around us hasten to become solid in the oak and the animal. But the recurrence to high sources is rare. In our daily intercourse, we go with the crowd, lend ourselves to low fears and hopes, become the victims of our own arts and implements, and disuse our resort to the Divine oracle. It is only in the sleep of the soul that we help ourselves by so many ingenious crutches and machineries. What is the use of telegraphs? What of newspapers? To know in each social crisis how men feel in Kansas, in California, the wise man waits for no mails, reads no telegrams. He asks his own heart. If they are made as he is, if they breathe the like air, eat of the same wheat, have wives and children, he knows that their joy or resentment rises to the same point as his own. The inviolate soul is in perpetual telegraphic communication with the Source of events, has earlier information, a private despatch, which relieves him of the terror which presses on the rest of the community.

The foundation of culture, as of character, is at last the moral sentiment. This is the fountain of power, preserves its eternal newness, draws its own rent out of every novelty in science. Science corrects the old creeds; sweeps away, with every new perception, our infantile catechisms, and necessitates a faith commensurate with the grander orbits and universal laws which it discloses. Yet it does not surprise the moral sentiment. That was older, and awaited expectant these larger insights.

The affections are the wings by which the intellect launches on the void, and is borne across it. Great love is the inventor and expander of the frozen powers, the feathers frozen to our sides. It was the conviction of Plato, of Van Helmont, of Pascal, of Swedenborg, that piety is an essential condition of science, that great thoughts come from the heart. It happens sometimes that poets do not believe their own poetry; they are so much the less poets. But great men are sincere. Great men are they who see that spiritual is stronger than any material force, that thoughts rule the world. No hope so bright but is the beginning of its own fulfilment. Every generalization shows the way to a larger. Men say, Ah! if a man could impart his talent, instead of his performance, what mountains of guineas would be paid! Yes, but in the measure of his absolute veracity he does impart it. When he does not play a part, does not wish to shine,— when he talks to men with the unrestrained frankness which children use with each other, he communicates himself, and not his vanity. All

vigor is contagious, and when we see creation we
also begin to create.   Depth of character, height
of genius, can only find nourishment in this soil.
The miracles of genius always rest on profound
convictions which refuse to be analyzed.   Enthusiasm is the leaping lightning, not to be measured by
the horse-power of the understanding.   Hope never
spreads her golden wings but on unfathomable seas.
The same law holds for the intellect as for the will.
When the will is absolutely surrendered to the
moral sentiment, that is virtue; when the wit is
surrendered to intellectual truth, that is genius.
Talent for talent's sake is a bauble and a show.
Talent working with joy in the cause of universal
truth lifts the possessor to new power as a benefactor.   I know well to what assembly of educated, re-
flecting, successful and powerful persons I speak.
Yours is the part of those who have received much.
It is an old legend of just men, *Noblesse oblige;*
or, superior advantages bind you to larger generosity.   Now I conceive that, in this economical world,
where every drop and every crumb is husbanded,
the transcendent powers of mind were not meant
to be misused.   The Divine Nature carries on its
administration by good men.   Here you are set
down, scholars and idealists, as in a barbarous age;
amidst insanity, to calm and guide it; amidst fools
and blind, to see the right done; among violent

proprietors, to check self-interest, stone-blind and stone-deaf, by considerations of humanity to the workman and to his child ; amongst angry politicians swelling with self-esteem, pledged to parties, pledged to clients, you are to make valid the large considerations of equity and good sense ; under bad governments to force on them, by your persistence, good laws. Around that immovable persistency of yours, statesmen, legislatures, must revolve, denying you, but not less forced to obey.

We wish to put the ideal rules into practice, to offer liberty instead of chains, and see whether liberty will not disclose its proper checks ; believing that a free press will prove safer than the censorship ; to ordain free trade, and believe that it will not bankrupt us; universal suffrage, believing that it will not carry us to mobs, or back to kings again. I believe that the checks are as sure as the springs. It is thereby that men are great and have great allies. And who are the allies? Rude opposition, apathy, slander, — even these. Difficulties exist to be surmounted. The great heart will no more complain of the obstructions that make success hard, than of the iron walls of the gun which hinder the shot from scattering. It was walled round with iron tube with that purpose, to give it irresistible force in one direction. A strenuous soul hates cheap successes. It is the ardor of the assailant that makes the vigor of the defender. The great are not tender at being obscure, despised, insulted. Such only feel themselves in adverse fortune. Strong men greet war, tempest, hard times, which search till they find resistance and bottom. They wish, as Pindar said, " to tread the floors of hell, with necessities as hard as iron." Periodicity, reaction, are laws of mind as well as of matter. Bad kings and governors help us, if only they are bad enough. In England, it was the game laws which exasperated the farmers to carry the Reform Bill. It was what we call *plantation manners* which drove peaceable forgiving New England to emancipation without phrase. In the Rebellion, who were our best allies? Always the enemy. The community of scholars do not know their own power, and dishearten each other by tolerating political baseness in their members. Now nobody doubts the power of manners, or that wherever high society exists it is very well able to exclude pretenders. The intruder finds himself uncomfortable, and quickly departs to his own gang.

It has been our misfortune that the politics of America have been often immoral. It has had the worst effect on character. We are a complaisant, forgiving people, presuming, perhaps, on a feeling of strength. But it is not by easy virtue, where the public is concerned, that heroic results are obtained. We have suffered our young men of ambition to play the game of politics and take the immoral side without loss of caste, — to come and go without rebuke. But that kind of loose association does not leave a man his own master. He cannot go from the good to the evil at pleasure, and then back again to the good. There is a text in Swedenborg which tells in figure the plain truth. He saw in vision the angels and the devils; but these two companies stood not face to face and hand in hand, but foot to foot, — these perpendicular up, and those perpendicular down.

Brothers, I draw new hope from the atmosphere we breathe to-day, from the healthy sentiment of the American people, and from the avowed aims and tendencies of the educated class. The age has new convictions. We know that in certain historic periods there have been times of negation, — a decay of thought, and a consequent national decline; that in France, at one time, there was almost a repudiation of the moral sentiment in what is called, by distinction, society, — not a believer within the Church, and almost not a theist out of it. In England the like spiritual disease affected the upper class in the time of Charles II., and down into the reign of the Georges. But it honorably distinguishes the educated class here, that they believe in the succor which the heart yields to the intellect, and draw greatness from its inspirations. And when I say the educated class, I know what a benignant breadth that word has, — new in the world, — reaching millions instead of hundreds. And more, when I look around me, and consider the sound material of which the cultivated class here is made up, — what high personal worth, what love of men, what hope, is joined with rich information and practical power, and that the most distinguished by genius and culture are in this class of benefactors, — I cannot distrust this great knighthood of virtue, or doubt that the interests of science, of letters, of politics and humanity, are safe. I think their hands are strong enough to hold up the Republic. I read the promise of better times and of greater men.

PERSIAN POETRY.

To Baron von Hammer Purgstall, who died in Vienna in 1856, we owe our best knowledge of the Persians. He has translated into German, besides the "Divan" of Hafiz, specimens of two hundred poets who wrote during a period of five and a half centuries, from A.D. 1050 to 1600. The seven masters of the Persian Parnassus — Firdusi, Enweri, Nisami, Jelaleddin, Saadi, Hafiz, and Jami — have ceased to be empty names; and others, like Ferideddin Attar and Omar Khayyam, promise to rise in Western estimation. That for which mainly books exist is communicated in these rich extracts. Many qualities go to make a good telescope, — as the largeness of the field, facility of sweeping the meridian, achromatic purity of lenses, and so forth; but the one eminent value is the space-penetrating power; and there are many virtues in books, but the essential value is the adding of knowledge to our stock by the record of new facts, and, better, by the record of intuitions which distribute facts, and are the formulas which supersede all histories.

Oriental life and society, especially in the Southern nations, stand in violent contrast with the multitudinous detail, the secular stability, and the vast average of comfort of the Western nations.   Life in the East is fierce, short, hazardous, and in extremes.   Its elements are few and simple, not exhibiting the long range and undulation of European existence, but rapidly reaching the best and the worst.   The rich feed on fruits and game, — the poor, on a watermelon's peel.   All or nothing is the genius of Oriental life.   Favor of the Sultan, or his displeasure, is a question of Fate.   A war is undertaken for an epigram or a distich, as in Europe for a duchy.   The prolific sun and the sudden and rank plenty which his heat engenders, make subsistence easy.   On the other side, the desert, the simoon, the mirage, the lion and the plague endanger it, and life hangs on the contingency of a skin of water more or less.   The very geography of old Persia showed these contrasts.   " My father's empire," said Cyrus to Xenophon, " is so large that people perish with cold at one extremity whilst they are suffocated with heat at the other."   The temperament of the people agrees with this life in extremes.   Religion and poetry are all their civilization.   The religion teaches an inexorable Destiny. It distinguishes only two days in each man's history, — his birthday, called *the Day of the Lot,*

and the Day of Judgment. Courage and absolute submission to what is appointed him are his
virtues.

The favor of the climate, making subsistence
easy and encouraging an outdoor life, allows to the
Eastern nations a highly intellectual organization,
— leaving out of view, at present, the genius of the
Hindoos (more Oriental in every sense), whom no
people have surpassed in the grandeur of their
ethical statement. The Persians and the Arabs,
with great leisure and few books, are exquisitely
sensible to the pleasures of poetry. Layard has
given some details of the effect which the *improv-
visatori* produced on the children of the desert.
" When the bard improvised an amatory ditty, the
young chief's excitement was almost beyond control.
The other Bedouins were scarcely less moved by
these rude measures, which have the same kind of
effect on the wild tribes of the Persian mountains.
Such verses, chanted by their self-taught poets or
by the girls of their encampment, will drive warriors to the combat, fearless of death, or prove an
ample reward on their return from the dangers of
the *ghazon*, or the fight. The excitement they
produce exceeds that of the grape. He who would
understand the influence of the Homeric ballads in
the heroic ages should witness the effect which
similar compositions have upon the wild nomads of

the East." Elsewhere he adds, " Poetry and flowers are the wine and spirits of the Arab ; a couplet
is equal to a bottle, and a rose to a dram, without
the evil effect of either."

The Persian poetry rests on a mythology whose
few legends are connected with the Jewish history
and the anterior traditions of the Pentateuch. The
principal figure in the allusions of Eastern poetry
is Solomon. Solomon had three talismans: first,
the signet-ring by which he commanded the spirits,
on the stone of which was engraven the name of
God; second, the glass in which he saw the secrets
of his enemies and the causes of all things, figured;
the third, the east-wind, which was his horse. His
counsellor was Simorg, king of birds, the all-wise
fowl who had lived ever since the beginning of the
world, and now lives alone on the highest summit
of Mount Kaf. No fowler has taken him, and none
now living has seen him. By him Solomon was
taught the language of birds, so that he heard
secrets whenever he went into his gardens. When
Solomon travelled, his throne was placed on a carpet of green silk, of a length and breadth sufficient
for all his army to stand upon, — men placing
themselves on his right hand, and the spirits on his
left. When all were in order, the east-wind, at his
command, took up the carpet and transported it
with all that were upon it, whither he pleased, —

the army of birds at the same time flying overhead and forming a canopy to shade them from the sun. It is related that when the Queen of Sheba came to visit Solomon, he had built, against her arrival, a palace, of which the floor or pavement was of glass, laid over running water, in which fish were swimming. The Queen of Sheba was deceived thereby, and raised her robes, thinking she was to pass through the water. On the occasion of Solomon's marriage, all the beasts, laden with presents, appeared before his throne. Behind them all came the ant, with a blade of grass: Solomon did not despise the gift of the ant. Asaph, the vizier, at a certain time, lost the seal of Solomon, which one of the Dews or evil spirits found, and, governing in the name of Solomon, deceived the people.

Firdusi, the Persian Homer, has written in the *Shah Nameh* the annals of the fabulous and heroic kings of the country: of Karun (the Persian Crœsus), the immeasurably rich gold-maker, who, with all his treasures, lies buried not far from the Pyramids, in the sea which bears his name ; of Jamschid, the binder of demons, whose reign lasted seven hundred years; of Kai Kaus, in whose palace, built by demons on Alburz, gold and silver and precious stones were used so lavishly that in the brilliancy produced by their combined effect, night and day appeared the same ; of Afrasiyab, strong as an ele-

phant, whose shadow extended for miles, whose
heart was bounteous as the ocean and his hands
like the clouds when rain falls to gladden the earth.
The crocodile in the rolling stream had no safety
from Afrasiyab.   Yet when he came to fight against
the generals of Kaus, he was but an insect in the
grasp of Rustem, who seized him by the girdle and
dragged him from his horse.   Rustem felt such
anger at the arrogance of the King of Mazinderan
that every hair on his body started up like a spear.
The gripe of his hand cracked the sinews of an
enemy.

These legends, with Chiser, the fountain of life,
Tuba, the tree of life; the romances of the loves of
Leila and Medschnun, of Chosru and Schirin, and
those of the nightingale for the rose; pearl-diving,
and the virtues of gems; the cohol, a cosmetic by
which pearls and eyebrows are indelibly stained
black, the bladder in which musk is brought, the
down of the lip, the mole on the cheek, the eyelash;
lilies, roses, tulips, and jasmines, — make the staple
imagery of Persian odes.

The Persians have epics and tales, but, for the
most part, they affect short poems and epigrams.
Gnomic verses, rules of life conveyed in a lively
image, especially in an image addressed to the eye
and contained in a single stanza, were always current in the East; and if the poem is long, it is only

a string of unconnected verses. They use an incon-
secutiveness quite alarming to Western logic, and
the connection between the stanzas of their longer
odes is much like that between the refrain of our
old English ballads, —

> "The sun shines fair on Carlisle wall,"

or

> "The rain it raineth every day," —

and the main story.

Take, as specimens of these gnomic verses, the
following : —

> "The secret that should not be blown
>   Not one of thy nation must know ;
> You may padlock the gate of a town,
>   But never the mouth of a foe : "

or this of Omar Khayyam : —

> " On earth's wide thoroughfares below
>   Two only men contented go :
> Who knows what 's right and what 's forbid,
>   And he from whom is knowledge hid."

Here is a poem on a melon, by Adsched of
Meru : —

> "Color, taste, and smell, smaragdus, sugar, and musk,
>   Amber for the tongue, for the eye a picture rare,
> If you cut the fruit in slices, every slice a crescent fair,
>   If you leave it whole, the full harvest moon is there."

Hafiz is the prince of Persian poets, and in his
extraordinary gifts adds to some of the attributes

of Pindar, Anacreon, Horace and Burns, the insight
of a mystic, that sometimes affords a deeper glance
at Nature than belongs to either of these bards.
He accosts all topics with an easy audacity. "He
only," he says, "is fit for company, who knows how
to prize earthly happiness at the value of a night-
cap. Our father Adam sold Paradise for two ker-
nels of wheat; then blame me not, if I hold it dear
at one grapestone." He says to the Shah, "Thou
who rulest after words and thoughts which no ear
has heard and no mind has thought, abide firm until thy young destiny tears off his blue coat from the
old graybeard of the sky." He says, —

> "I batter the wheel of heaven
> When it rolls not rightly by;
> I am not one of the snivellers
> Who fall thereon and die."

The rapidity of his turns is always surprising
us : —

> "See how the roses burn !
> Bring wine to quench the fire !
> Alas ! the flames come up with us,
> We perish with desire."

After the manner of his nation, he abounds in
pregnant sentences which might be engraved on a
sword-blade and almost on a ring.

"In honor dies he to whom the great seems ever
wonderful."

" Here is the sum, that, when one door opens, another shuts."

" On every side is an ambush laid by the robber-troops of circumstance ; hence it is that the horseman of life urges on his courser at headlong speed."

" The earth is a host who murders his guests."

" Good is what goes on the road of Nature.   On the straight way the traveller never misses."

> " Alas ! till now I had not known
>   My guide and Fortune's guide are one."

> " The understanding's copper coin
>   Counts not with the gold of love."

> " 'Tis writ on Paradise's gate,
>   ' Woe to the dupe that yields to Fate ! ' "

> " The world is a bride superbly dressed ; —
>   Who weds her for dowry must pay his soul."

" Loose the knots of the heart ; never think on thy fate :
No Euclid has yet disentangled that snarl."

> " There resides in the grieving
>   A poison to kill ;
>   Beware to go near them
>   'T is pestilent still."

Harems and wine-shops only give him a new ground of observation, whence to draw sometimes a deeper moral than regulated sober life affords, and this is foreseen : —

"I will be drunk and down with wine ;
Treasures we find in a ruined house."

Riot, he thinks, can snatch from the deeply hidden
lot the veil that covers it : —

"To be wise the dull brain so earnestly throbs,
Bring bands of wine for the stupid head."

"The Builder of heaven
  Hath sundered the earth,
So that no footway
  Leads out of it forth.

"On turnpikes of wonder
  Wine leads the mind forth,
Straight, sidewise, and upward,
  West, southward, and north.

"Stands the vault adamantine
  Until the Doomsday ;
The wine-cup shall ferry
  Thee o'er it away."

That hardihood and self-equality of every sound
nature, which result from the feeling that the spirit
in him is entire and as good as the world, which en-
title the poet to speak with authority, and make
him an object of interest and his every phrase and
syllable significant, are in Hafiz, and abundantly
fortify and ennoble his tone.

His was the fluent mind in which every thought
and feeling came readily to the lips. "Loose the
knots of the heart," he says.   We absorb elements

enough, but have not leaves and lungs for healthy perspiration and growth. An air of sterility, of incompetence to their proper aims, belongs to many who have both experience and wisdom. But a large utterance, a river that makes its own shores, quick perception and corresponding expression, a constitution to which every morrow is a new day, which is equal to the needs of life, at once tender and bold, with great arteries, — this generosity of ebb and flow satisfies, and we should be willing to die when our time comes, having had our swing and gratification. The difference is not so much in the quality of men's thoughts as in the power of uttering them. What is pent and smouldered in the dumb actor, is not pent in the poet, but passes over into new form, at once relief and creation.

The other merit of Hafiz is his intellectual liberty, which is a certificate of profound thought. We accept the religions and politics into which we fall, and it is only a few delicate spirits who are sufficient to see that the whole web of convention is the imbecility of those whom it entangles, — that the mind suffers no religion and no empire but its own. It indicates this respect to absolute truth by the use it makes of the symbols that are most stable and reverend, and therefore is always provoking the accusation of irreligion.

Hypocrisy is the perpetual butt of his arrows:

" Let us draw the cowl through the brook of wine."

He tells his mistress that not the dervish, or the monk, but the lover, has in his heart the spirit which makes the ascetic and the saint; and certainly not their cowls and mummeries but her glances can impart to him the fire and virtue needful for such self-denial. Wrong shall not be wrong to Hafiz for the name's sake. A law or statute is to him what a fence is to a nimble school-boy, — a temptation for a jump. "We would do nothing but good, else would shame come to us on the day when the soul must hie hence; and should they then deny us Paradise, the Houris themselves would forsake that and come out to us."

His complete intellectual emancipation he communicates to the reader. There is no example of such facility of allusion, such use of all materials. Nothing is too high, nothing too low for his occasion. He fears nothing, he stops for nothing. Love is a leveller, and Allah becomes a groom, and heaven a closet, in his daring hymns to his mistress or to his cupbearer. This boundless charter is the right of genius.

We do not wish to strew sugar on bottled spiders, or try to make mystical divinity out of the Song of Solomon, much less out of the erotic and bacchanalian songs of Hafiz. Hafiz himself is determined to defy all such hypocritical interpretation, and tears off his turban and throws it at the head of the meddling dervish, and throws his glass after the turban. But the love or the wine of Hafiz is not to be confounded with vulgar debauch. It is the spirit in which the song is written that imports, and not the topics. Hafiz praises wine, roses, maidens, boys, birds, mornings, and music, to give vent to his immense hilarity and sympathy with every form of beauty and joy; and lays the emphasis on these to mark his scorn of sanctimony and base prudence. These are the natural topics and language of his wit and perception. But it is the play of wit and the joy of song that he loves; and if you mistake him for a low rioter, he turns short on you with verses which express the poverty of sensual joys, and to ejaculate with equal fire the most unpalatable affirmations of heroic sentiment and contempt for the world. Sometimes it is a glance from the height of thought, as thus: —

"Bring wine; for in the audience-hall of the soul's independence, what is sentinel or Sultan? what is the wise man or the intoxicated?"

And sometimes his feast, feasters, and world are only one pebble more in the eternal vortex and revolution of Fate: —

"I am: what I am
My dust will be again."

A saint might lend an ear to the riotous fun of Falstaff ; for it is not created to excite the animal appetites, but to vent the joy of a supernal intelligence. In all poetry, Pindar's rule holds, —συνετοῖς φωνεῖ, it speaks to the intelligent ; and Hafiz is a poet for poets, whether he write, as sometimes, with a parrot's, or, as at other times, with an eagle's quill.

Every song of Hafiz affords new proof of the unimportance of your subject to success, provided only the treatment be cordial. In general what is more tedious than dedications or panegyrics addressed to grandees ? Yet in the " Divan " you would not skip them, since his muse seldom supports him better :

> " What lovelier forms things wear,
> Now that the Shah comes back ! "

And again : —

> " Thy foes to hunt, thy enviers to strike down,
> Poises Arcturus aloft morning and evening his spear."

It is told of Hafiz, that, when he had written a compliment to a handsome youth, —

> " Take my heart in thy hand, O beautiful boy of Shiraz !
> I would give for the mole on thy cheek Samarcand and Buchara ! " —

the verses came to the ears of Timour in his palace. Timour taxed Hafiz with treating disrespectfully his two cities, to raise and adorn which he had conquered nations. Hafiz replied, " Alas, my lord, if I had not been so prodigal, I had not been so poor!"

The Persians had a mode of establishing copyright the most secure of any contrivance with which we are acquainted. The law of the *ghaselle*, or shorter ode, requires that the poet insert his name in the last stanza. Almost every one of several hundreds of poems of Hafiz contains his name thus interwoven more or less closely with the subject of the piece. It is itself a test of skill, as this self-naming is not quite easy. We remember but two or three examples in English poetry: that of Chaucer, in the " House of Fame ; " Jonson's epitaph on his son, —

"Ben Jonson his best piece of poetry ; "

and Cowley's, —

"The melancholy Cowley lay."

But it is easy to Hafiz. It gives him the opportunity of the most playful self-assertion, always gracefully, sometimes almost in the fun of Falstaff, sometimes with feminine delicacy. He tells us, " The angels in heaven were lately learning his last pieces." He says, " The fishes shed their pearls, out of desire and longing as soon as the ship of Hafiz swims the deep."

"Out of the East, and out of the West, no man understands me ;
O, the happier I, who confide to none but the wind !

This morning heard I how the lyre of the stars resounded,
'Sweeter tones have we heard from Hafiz!'"

Again, —

"I heard the harp of the planet Venus, and it said
in the early morning, 'I am the disciple of the sweet-
voiced Hafiz!'"

And again, —

"When Hafiz sings, the angels hearken, and Anaitis,
the leader of the starry host, calls even the Messiah in
heaven out to the dance."

"No one has unvailed thoughts like Hafiz, since the
locks of the World-bride were first curled."

"Only he despises the verse of Hafiz who is not himself by nature noble."

But we must try to give some of these poetic
flourishes the metrical form which they seem to require : —

> "Fit for the Pleiads' azure chord
> The songs I sung, the pearls I bored."

Another : —

> "I have no hoarded treasure,
> Yet have I rich content ;
> The first from Allah to the Shah,
> The last to Hafiz went."

Another : —

> "High heart, O Hafiz ! though not thine
> Fine gold and silver ore ;

> More worth to thee the gift of song,
> And the clear insight more."

Again : —

> "O Hafiz ! speak not of thy need ;
> Are not these verses thine ?
> Then all the poets are agreed,
> No man can less repine."

He asserts his dignity as bard and inspired man of his people. To the vizier returning from Mecca he says, —

"Boast not rashly, prince of pilgrims, of thy fortune. Thou hast indeed seen the temple ; but I, the Lord of the temple. Nor has any man inhaled from the musk-bladder of the merchant or from the musky morning-wind that sweet air which I am permitted to breathe every hour of the day."

And with still more vigor in the following lines :—

> "Oft have I said, I say it once more,
> I, a wanderer, do not stray from myself.
> I am a kind of parrot ; the mirror is holden to me ;
> What the Eternal says, I stammering say again.
> Give me what you will; I eat thistles as roses,
> And according to my food I grow and I give.
> Scorn me not, but know I have the pearl,
> And am only seeking one to receive it."

And his claim has been admitted from the first. The muleteers and camel-drivers, on their way through the desert, sing snatches of his songs, not so much for the thought as for their joyful temper and tone; and the cultivated Persians know his poems by heart. Yet Hafiz does not appear to have set any great value on his songs, since his scholars collected them for the first time after his death.

In the following poem the soul is figured as the Phœnix alighting on Tuba, the Tree of Life : —

"My phœnix long ago secured
    His nest in the sky-vault's cope;
In the body's cage immured,
    He was weary of life's hope.

"Round and round this heap of ashes
    Now flies the bird amain,
But in that odorous niche of heaven
    Nestles the bird again.

"Once flies he upward, he will perch
    On Tuba's golden bough;
His home is on that fruited arch
    Which cools the blest below.

"If over this world of ours
    His wings my phœnix spread,
How gracious falls on land and sea
    The soul-refreshing shade !

"Either world inhabits he,
    Sees oft below him planets roll;
His body is all of air compact,
    Of Allah's love his soul."

Here is an ode which is said to be a favorite with all educated Persians : —

" Come ! — the palace of heaven rests on aery pillars, —
Come, and bring me wine ; our days are wind.
I declare myself the slave of that masculine soul
Which ties and alliance on earth once forever renounces.
Told I thee yester-morn how the Iris of heaven
Brought to me in my cup a gospel of joy ?
O high-flying falcon ! the Tree of Life is thy perch ;
This nook of grief fits thee ill for a nest.
Hearken ! they call to thee down from the ramparts of
    heaven ;
I cannot divine what holds thee here in a net.
I, too, have a counsel for thee ; O, mark it and keep it,
Since I received the same from the Master above :
Seek not for faith or for truth in a world of light-minded
    girls ;
A thousand suitors reckons this dangerous bride.
Cumber thee not for the world, and this my precept forget
    not,
'T is but a toy that a vagabond sweetheart has left us.
Accept whatever befalls ; uncover thy brow from thy locks;
Never to me nor to thee was option imparted ;
Neither endurance nor truth belongs to the laugh of the
    rose.
The loving nightingale mourns ; — cause enow for mourn-
    ing ; —
Why envies the bird the streaming verses of Hafiz ?
Know that a god bestowed on him eloquent speech."

The cedar, the cypress, the palm, the olive and
fig-tree, the birds that inhabit them, and the garden flowers, are never wanting in these musky
verses, and are always named with effect. " The
willows," he says, " bow themselves to every wind

out of shame for their unfruitfulness." We may
open anywhere on a floral catalogue.

> " By breath of beds of roses drawn,
>   I found the grove in the morning pure,
> In the concert of the nightingales
>   My drunken brain to cure.

> " With unrelated glance
>   I looked the rose in the eye :
> The rose in the hour of gloaming
>   Flamed like a lamp hard-by.

> " She was of her beauty proud,
>   And prouder of her youth,
> The while unto her flaming heart
>   The bulbul gave his truth.

> " The sweet narcissus closed
>   Its eye, with passion pressed ;
> The tulips out of envy burned
>   Moles in their scarlet breast.

> " The lilies white prolonged
>   Their sworded tongue to the smell ;
> The clustering anemones
>   Their pretty secrets tell."

Presently we have, —

> " All day the rain
> Bathed the dark hyacinths in vain,
> The flood may pour from morn till night
> Nor wash the pretty Indians white."

And so onward, through many a page.

This picture of the first days of Spring, from Enweri, seems to belong to Hafiz : —

" O'er the garden water goes the wind alone
 To rasp and to polish the cheek of the wave ;
The fire is quenched on the dear hearthstone,
 But it burns again on the tulips brave."

Friendship is a favorite topic of the Eastern poets, and they have matched on this head the absoluteness of Montaigne.

Hafiz says, —

" Thou learnest no secret until thou knowest friendship, since to the unsound no heavenly knowledge enters."

Ibn Jemin writes thus : —

" Whilst I disdain the populace,
I find no peer in higher place.
Friend is a word of royal tone,
Friend is a poem all alone.
Wisdom is like the elephant,
Lofty and rare inhabitant :
He dwells in deserts or in courts ;
With hucksters he has no resorts."

Jami says, —

" A friend is he, who, hunted as a foe,
 So much the kindlier shows him than before ;
Throw stones at him, or ruder javelins throw,
 He builds with stone and steel a firmer floor."

Of the amatory poetry of Hafiz we must be very sparing in our citations, though it forms the staple of the " Divan." He has run through the whole gamut of passion, — from the sacred to the borders, and over the borders, of the profane. The same confusion of high and low, the celerity of flight and allusion which our colder muses forbid, is habitual to him. From the plain text, —

> " The chemist of love
>   Will this perishing mould,
> Were it made out of mire,
>   Transmute into gold,"—

he proceeds to the celebration of his passion; and nothing in his religious or in his scientific traditions is too sacred or too remote to afford a token of his mistress. The Moon thought she knew her own orbit well enough; but when she saw the curve on Zuleika's cheek, she was at a loss : —

> " And since round lines are drawn
>   My darling's lips about,
> The very Moon looks puzzled on,
>   And hesitates in doubt
> If the sweet curve that rounds thy mouth
> Be not her true way to the South."

His ingenuity never sleeps : —

> " Ah, could I hide me in my song,
>   To kiss thy lips from which it flows ! "

and plays in a thousand pretty courtesies : —

" Fair fall thy soft heart !
   A good work wilt thou do ?
   O, pray for the dead
   Whom thine eyelashes slew ! "

And what a nest has he found for his bonny bird to take up her abode in ! —

" They strew in the path of kings and czars
   Jewels and gems of price :
But for thy head I will pluck down stars,
   And pave thy way with eyes.

" I have sought for thee a costlier dome
   Than Mahmoud's palace high,
And thou, returning, find thy home
   In the apple of Love's eye."

Then we have all degrees of passionate abandonment : —

" I know this perilous love-lane
   No whither the traveller leads,
Yet my fancy the sweet scent of
   Thy tangled tresses feeds.

" In the midnight of thy locks,
   I renounce the day ;
In the ring of thy rose-lips,
   My heart forgets to pray."

And sometimes his love rises to a religious sentiment : —

" Plunge in yon angry waves,
   Renouncing doubt and care ;
The flowing of the seven broad seas
   Shall never wet thy hair.

"Is Allah's face on thee
  Bending with love benign,
And thou not less on Allah's eye
  O fairest! turnest thine."

We add to these fragments of Hafiz a few specimens from other poets.

NISAMI.

"While roses bloomed along the plain,
  The nightingale to the falcon said,
  'Why, of all birds, must thou be dumb?
  With closed mouth thou utterest,
  Though dying, no last word to man.
  Yet sitt'st thou on the hand of princes,
  And feedest on the grouse's breast,
  Whilst I, who hundred thousand jewels
  Squander in a single tone,
  Lo! I feed myself with worms,
  And my dwelling is the thorn.'—
  The falcon answered, 'Be all ear:
  I, experienced in affairs,
  See fifty things, say never one;
  But thee the people prizes not,
  Who, doing nothing, say'st a thousand.
  To me, appointed to the chase,
  The king's hand gives the grouse's breast;
  Whilst a chatterer like thee
  Must gnaw worms in the thorn. Farewell!'"

The following passages exhibit the strong tendency of the Persian poets to contemplative and
religious poetry and to allegory.

ENWERI.

BODY AND SOUL.

" A painter in China once painted a hall ; —
Such a web never hung on an emperor's wall ; —
One half from his brush with rich colors did run,
The other he touched with a beam of the sun ;
So that all which delighted the eye in one side,
The same, point for point, in the other replied.
In thee, friend, that Tyrian chamber is found ;
Thine the star-pointing-roof, and the base on the ground :
Is one half depicted with colors less bright ?
Beware that the counterpart blazes with light ! "

IBN JEMIN.

" I read on the porch of a palace bold
    In a purple tablet letters cast, —
' A house though a million winters old,
    A house of earth comes down at last ;
Then quarry thy stones from the crystal All,
And build the dome that shall not fall.' "

" What need," cries the mystic Feisi, " of palaces
and tapestry ?   What need even of a bed ?

" The eternal Watcher, who doth wake
    All night in the body's earthen chest,
Will of thine arms a pillow make,
    And a bolster of thy breast."

Ferideddin Attar wrote the " Bird Conversations," a mystical tale, in which the birds, coming
together to choose their king, resolve on a pilgrim-
age to Mount Kaf, to pay their homage to the

Simorg. From this poem, written five hundred years ago, we cite the following passage, as a proof of the identity of mysticism in all periods. The tone is quite modern. In the fable, the birds were soon weary of the length and difficulties of the way, and at last almost all gave out. Three only persevered, and arrived before the throne of the Simorg.

> "The bird-soul was ashamed ;
> Their body was quite annihilated ;
> They had cleaned themselves from the dust,
> And were by the light ensouled.
> What was, and was not, — the Past, —
> Was wiped out from their breast.
> The sun from near-by beamed
> Clearest light into their soul ;
> The resplendence of the Simorg beamed
> As one back from all three.
> They knew not, amazed, if they
> Were either this or that.
> They saw themselves all as Simorg,
> Themselves in the eternal Simorg.
> When to the Simorg up they looked,
> They beheld him among themselves ;
> And when they looked on each other,
> They saw themselves in the Simorg.
> A single look grouped the two parties,
> The Simorg emerged, the Simorg vanished,
> This in that and that in this,
> As the world has never heard.
> So remained they, sunk in wonder,
> Thoughtless in deepest thinking,

And quite unconscious of themselves.
Speechless prayed they to the Highest
To open this secret,
And to unlock *Thou* and *We*.
There came an answer without tongue. —
'The Highest is a sun-mirror;
Who comes to Him sees himself therein,
Sees body and soul, and soul and body;
When you came to the Simorg,
Three therein appeared to you,
And, had fifty of you come,
So had you seen yourselves as many.
Him has none of us yet seen.
Ants see not the Pleiades.
Can the gnat grasp with his teeth
The body of the elephant?
What you see is He not;
What you hear is He not.
The valleys which you traverse,
The actions which you perform,
They lie under our treatment
And among our properties.
You as three birds are amazed,
Impatient, heartless, confused:
Far over you am I raised,
Since I am in act Simorg.
Ye blot out my highest being,
That ye may find yourselves on my throne;
Forever ye blot out yourselves,
As shadows in the sun. Farewell!'"

INSPIRATION.

INSPIRATION.

It was Watt who told King George III. that he dealt in an article of which kings were said to be fond, — Power. 'T is certain that the one thing we wish to know is, where power is to be bought. But we want a finer kind than that of commerce; and every reasonable man would give any price of house and land and future provision, for condensation, concentration, and the recalling at will of high mental energy. Our money is only a second best. We would jump to buy power with it, that is, intellectual perception moving the will. That is first best. But we don't know where the shop is. If Watt knew, he forgot to tell us the number of the street. There are times when the intellect is so active that everything seems to run to meet it. Its supplies are found without much thought as to studies. Knowledge runs to the man, and the man runs to knowledge. In spring, when the snow melts, the maple-trees flow with sugar, and you cannot get tubs fast enough; but it is only for a few days. The hunter on the prairie, at the right season, has no need of choosing his ground ; east, west, by the river, by the timber, he is everywhere near his game. But the favorable conditions are rather the exception than the rule.

The aboriginal man, in geology and in the dim lights of Darwin's microscope, is not an engaging figure. We are very glad that he ate his fishes and snails and marrow-bones out of our sight and hearing, and that his doleful experiences were got through with so very long ago. They combed his mane, they pared his nails, cut off his tail, set him on end, sent him to school and made him pay taxes, before he could begin to write his sad story for the compassion or the repudiation of his descendants, who are all but unanimous to disown him. We must take him as we find him, — pretty well on in his education, and, in all *our* knowledge of him, an interesting creature, with a will, an invention, an imagination, a conscience and an inextinguishable hope.

The Hunterian law of *arrested development* is not confined to vegetable and animal structure, but reaches the human intellect also. In the savage man, thought is infantile ; and, in the civilized, unequal and ranging up and down a long scale. In the best races it is rare and imperfect. In happy moments it is reinforced, and carries out what were rude suggestions to larger scope and to clear and grand conclusions. The poet cannot see a natural phenomenon which does not express to him a correspondent fact in his mental experience ; he is made aware of a power to carry on and complete the metamorphosis of natural into spiritual facts. Everything which we hear for the first time was expected by the mind ; the newest discovery was expected. In the mind we call this enlarged power Inspiration. I believe that nothing great and lasting can be done except by inspiration, by leaning on the secret augury. The man's insight and power are interrupted and occasional ; he can see and do this or that cheap task, at will, but it steads him not beyond. He is fain to make the ulterior step by mechanical means. It cannot so be done. That ulterior step is to be also by inspiration ; if not through him, then by another man. Every real step is by what a poet called " lyrical glances," by lyrical facility, and never by main strength and ignorance. Years of mechanic toil will only seem to do it ; it will not so be done.

Inspiration is like yeast. 'T is no matter in which of half a dozen ways you procure the infection ; you can apply one or the other equally well to your purpose, and get your loaf of bread. And every earnest workman, in whatever kind, knows some favorable conditions for his task. When I wish to write on any topic, 't is of no consequence what kind of book or man gives me a hint or a motion, nor how far off that is from my topic.

Power is the first good. Rarey can tame a wild horse; but if he could give speed to a dull horse, were not that better? The toper finds, without asking, the road to the tavern, but the poet does not know the pitcher that holds his nectar. Every youth should know the way to prophecy as surely as the miller understands how to let on the water or the engineer the steam. A rush of thoughts is the only conceivable prosperity that can come to us. Fine clothes, equipages, villa, park, social consideration, cannot cover up real poverty and insignificance, from my own eyes or from others like mine.

Thoughts let us into realities. Neither miracle nor magic nor any religious tradition, not the immortality of the private soul is incredible, after we have experienced an insight, a thought. I think it comes to some men but once in their life, sometimes a religious impulse, sometimes an intellectual insight. But what we want is consecutiveness. 'T is with us a flash of light, then a long darkness, then a flash again. The separation of our days by sleep almost destroys identity. Could we but turn these fugitive sparkles into an astronomy of Copernican worlds! With most men, scarce a link of memory holds yesterday and to-day together. Their house and trade and families serve them as ropes to give a coarse continuity. But they have forgotten the thoughts of yesterday; they say to-day what occurs to them, and something else to-morrow. This insecurity of possession, this quick ebb of power, — as if life were a thunder-storm wherein you can see by a flash the horizon, and then cannot see your hand, — tantalizes us. We cannot make the inspiration consecutive. A glimpse, a point of view that by its brightness excludes the purview is granted, but no panorama. A fuller inspiration should cause the point to flow and become a line, should bend the line and complete the circle. To-day the electric machine will not work, no spark will pass; then presently the world is all a cat's back, all sparkle and shock. Sometimes there is no sea-fire, and again the sea is aglow to the horizon. Sometimes the Æolian harp is dumb all day in the window, and again it is garrulous and tells all the secrets of the world. In June the morning is noisy with birds; in August they are already getting old and silent.

Hence arises the question, Are these moods in any degree within control? If we knew how to command them! But where is the Franklin with kite or rod for this fluid? — a Franklin who can draw off electricity from Jove himself, and convey it into the arts of life, inspire men, take them off their feet, withdraw them from the life of trifles and gain and comfort, and make the world transparent, so that they can read the symbols of nature? What metaphysician has undertaken to enumerate the tonics of the torpid mind, the rules for the recovery of inspiration? That is least within control which is best in them. Of the *modus* of inspiration we have no knowledge. But in the experience of meditative men there is a certain agreement as to the conditions of reception. Plato, in his seventh Epistle, notes that the perception is only accomplished by long familiarity with the objects of intellect, and a life according to the things themselves. "Then a light, as if leaping from a fire, will on a sudden be enkindled in the soul, and will then itself nourish itself." He said again, "The man who is his own master knocks in vain at the doors of poetry." The artists must be sacrificed to their art. Like bees, they must put their lives into the sting they give. What is a man good for without enthusiasm? and what is enthusiasm but this daring of ruin for its object? There are thoughts beyond the reaches of our souls; we are not the less drawn to them. The moth flies into the flame of the lamp; and Swedenborg must solve the problems that haunt him, though he be crazed or killed.

There is genius as well in virtue as in intellect. 'T is the doctrine of faith over works. The raptures of goodness are as old as history and new with this morning's sun. The legends of Arabia, Persia, and India are of the same complexion as the Christian. Socrates, Menu, Confucius, Zertusht, — we recognize in all of them this ardor to solve the hints of thought.

I hold that ecstasy will be found normal, or only an example on a higher plane of the same gentle gravitation by which stones fall and rivers run. Experience identifies. Shakspeare seems to you miraculous; but the wonderful juxtapositions, parallelisms, transfers, which his genius effected, were all to him locked together as links of a chain, and the mode precisely as conceivable and familiar to higher intelligence as the index-making of the literary hack. The result of the hack is inconceivable to the type-setter who waits for it.

We must prize our own youth. Later, we want heat to execute our plans: the good-will, the knowledge, the whole armory of means are all present, but a certain heat that once used not to fail, refuses its office, and all is vain until this capricious fuel is supplied. It seems a semi-animal heat; as if tea, or wine, or sea-air, or mountains, or a genial companion, or a new thought suggested in book or conversation could fire the train, wake the fancy and the clear perception. Pit-coal, — where to find it? 'T is of no use that your engine is made like a watch, — that you are a good workman, and know how to drive it, if there is no coal. We are waiting until some tyrannous idea emerging out of heaven shall seize and bereave us of this liberty with which we are falling abroad. Well, we have the same hint or suggestion, day by day. "I am not," says the man, "at the top of my condition to-day, but the favorable hour will come when I can command all my powers, and when that will be easy to do which is at this moment impossible." See how the passions augment our force, — anger, love, ambition! — sometimes sympathy, and the expectation of men. Garrick said that on the stage his great paroxysms surprised himself as much as his audience. If this is true on this low plane, it is true on the higher. Swedenborg's genius was the perception of the doctrine that "The Lord flows into the spirits of angels and of men;" and all poets have signalized their consciousness of rare moments when they were superior to themselves, — when a light, a freedom, a power came to them which lifted them to performances far better than they could reach at other times; so that a religious poet once told me that he valued his poems, not because they were his, but because they were not. He thought the angels brought them to him.

Jacob Behmen said : " Art has not wrote here, nor was there any time to consider how to set it punctually down according to the right understanding of the letters, but all was ordered according to the direction of the spirit, which often went on haste, — so that the penman's hand, by reason he was not accustomed to it, did often shake. And, though I could have written in a more accurate, fair, and plain manner, the burning fire often forced forward with speed, and the hand and pen must hasten directly after it, for it comes and goes as a sudden shower. In one quarter of an hour I saw and knew more than if I had been many years together at an university."

The depth of the notes which we accidentally sound on the strings of nature is out of all proportion to our taught and ascertained faculty, and might teach us what strangers and novices we are, vagabond in this universe of pure power, to which we have only the smallest key. Herrick said : —

> " 'T is not every day that I
> Fitted am to prophesy ;
> No, but when the spirit fills
> The fantastic panicles,
> Full of fire, then I write

> As the Godhead doth indite.
> Thus enraged, my lines are hurled,
> Like the Sibyl's, through the world :
> Look how next the holy fire
> Either slakes, or doth retire ;
> So the fancy cools, — till when
> That brave spirit comes again."

Bonaparte said : " There is no man more pusillanimous than I, when I make a military plan. I magnify all the dangers, and all the possible mischances. I am in an agitation utterly painful. That does not prevent me from appearing quite serene to the persons who surround me. I am like a woman with child, and when my resolution is taken, all is forgot except whatever can make it succeed."

There are, to be sure, certain risks in this presentiment of the decisive perception, as in the use of ether or alcohol : —

> " Great wits to madness nearly are allied ;
> Both serve to make our poverty our pride."

Aristotle said : " No great genius was ever without some mixture of madness, nor can anything grand or superior to the voice of common mortals be spoken except by the agitated soul." We might say of these memorable moments of life that we were in them, not they in us. We found ourselves by happy fortune in an illuminated portion or meteorous zone, and passed out of it again, so aloof was it from any will of ours. "It is a principle of war," said Napoleon, "that when you can use the lightning it is better than cannon."

How many sources of inspiration can we count? As many as our affinities. But to a practical purpose we may reckon a few of these.

1. Health is the first muse, comprising the magical benefits of air, landscape, and bodily exercise, on the mind. The Arabs say that "Allah does not count from life the days spent in the chase," that is, those are thrown in. Plato thought "exercise would almost cure a guilty conscience." Sydney Smith said: "You will never break down in a speech on the day when you have walked twelve miles."

I honor health as the first muse, and sleep as the condition of health. Sleep benefits mainly by the sound health it produces; incidentally also by dreams, into whose farrago a divine lesson is sometimes slipped. Life is in short cycles or periods; we are quickly tired, but we have rapid rallies. A man is spent by his work, starved, prostrate; he will not lift his hand to save his life; he can never think more. He sinks into deep sleep and wakes with renewed youth, with hope, courage, fertile in resources, and keen for daring adventure.

> " Sleep is like death, and after sleep
> The world seems new begun ;

> White thoughts stand luminous and firm,
>   Like statues in the sun ;
> Refreshed from supersensuous founts,
> The soul to clearer vision mounts." [1]

A man must be able to escape from his cares and fears, as well as from hunger and want of sleep; so that another Arabian proverb has its coarse truth : " When the belly is full, it says to the head, Sing, fellow ! " The perfection of writing is when mind and body are both in key; when the mind finds perfect obedience in the body. And wine, no doubt, and all fine food, as of delicate fruits, furnish some elemental wisdom. And the fire, too, as it burns in the chimney; for I fancy that my logs, which have grown so long in sun and wind by Walden, are a kind of muses. So of all the particulars of health and exercise and fit nutriment and tonics. Some people will tell you there is a great deal of poetry and fine sentiment in a chest of tea.

2. The experience of writing letters is one of the keys to the *modus* of inspiration. When we have ceased for a long time to have any fulness of thoughts that once made a diary a joy as well as a necessity, and have come to believe that an image or a happy turn of expression is no longer at our command, in writing a letter to a friend we may find that we rise to thought and to a cordial power

[1] Allingham.

of expression that costs no effort, and it seems to us that this facility may be indefinitely applied and resumed. The wealth of the mind in this respect of seeing is like that of a looking-glass, which is never tired or worn by any multitude of objects which it reflects. You may carry it all round the world, it is ready and perfect as ever for new millions.

3. Another consideration, though it will not so much interest young men, will cheer the heart of older scholars, namely that there is diurnal and secular rest. As there is this daily renovation of sensibility, so it sometimes if rarely happens that after a season of decay or eclipse, darkening months or years, the faculties revive to their fullest force. One of the best facts I know in metaphys ical science is Niebuhr's joyful record that after his genius for interpreting history had failed him for several years, this divination returned to him. As this rejoiced me, so does Herbert's poem " The Flower." His health had broken down early, he had lost his muse, and in this poem he says : —

> " And now in age I bud again,
>   After so many deaths I live and write ;
> I once more smell the dew and rain,
> And relish versing : O my only light,
>   It cannot be
>   That I am he
> On whom thy tempests fell all night."

His poem called " The Forerunners " also has supreme interest. I understand "The Harbingers "
to refer to the signs of age and decay which he detects in himself, not only in his constitution, but in
his fancy and his facility and grace in writing verse ;
and he signalizes his delight in this skill, and his
pain that the Herricks, Lovelaces, and Marlows, or
whoever else, should use the like genius in language
to sensual purpose, and consoles himself that his
own faith and the divine life in him remain to him
unchanged, unharmed.

4. The power of the will is sometimes sublime ;
and what is will for, if it cannot help us in emer-
gencies ? Seneca says of an almost fatal sickness
that befell him, " The thought of my father, who
could not have sustained such a blow as my death,
restrained me; I commanded myself to live."
Goethe said to Eckermann, " I work more easily
when the barometer is high than when it is low.
Since I know this, I endeavor, when the barometer
is low, to counteract the injurious effect by greater
exertion, and my attempt is successful."

" To the persevering mortal the blessed immortals
are swift." Yes, for they know how to give you in
one moment the solution of the riddle you have
pondered for months. " Had I not lived with
Mirabeau," says Dumont, " I never should have
known all that can be done in one day, or, rather,

in an interval of twelve hours. A day to him was of more value than a week or a month to others. To-morrow to him was not the same impostor as to most others."

5. Plutarch affirms that " souls are naturally endowed with the faculty of prediction, and the chief cause that excites this faculty and virtue is a certain temperature of air and winds." My anchorite thought it " sad that atmospheric influences should bring to our dust the communion of the soul with the Infinite." But I am glad that the atmosphere should be an excitant, glad to find the dull rock itself to be deluged with Deity, — to be theist, Christian, poetic. The fine influences of the morning few can explain, but all will admit. Goethe acknowledges them in the poem in which he dislodges the nightingale from her place as Leader of the Muses : —

MUSAGETES.

" Often in deep midnights
I called on the sweet muses.
No dawn shines,
And no day will appear:
But at the right hour
The lamp brings me pious light,
That it, instead of Aurora or Phœbus,
May enliven my quiet industry.
But they left me lying in sleep
Dull, and not to be enlivened,

And after every late morning
Followed unprofitable days.

"When now the Spring stirred,
I said to the nightingales:
'Dear nightingales, trill
Early, O, early before my lattice,
Wake me out of the deep sleep
Which mightily chains the young man.'
But the love-filled singers
Poured by night before my window
Their sweet melodies, —
Kept awake my dear soul,
Roused tender new longings
In my lately touched bosom,
And so the night passed,
And Aurora found me sleeping;
Yea, hardly did the sun wake me.
At last it has become summer,
And at the first glimpse of morning
The busy early fly stings me
Out of my sweet slumber.
Unmerciful she returns again:
When often the half-awake victim
Impatiently drives her off,
She calls hither the unscrupulous sisters,
And from my eyelids
Sweet sleep must depart.
Vigorous, I spring from my couch,
Seek the beloved Muses,
Find them in the beech grove,
Pleased to receive me;
And I thank the annoying insect

For many a golden hour.
Stand, then, for me, ye tormenting creatures,
Highly praised by the poet
As the true Musagetes."

The French have a proverb to the effect that not the day only, but all things have their morning, — " *Il n'y a que le matin en toutes choses.*" And it is a primal rule to defend your morning, to keep all its dews on, and with fine foresight to relieve it from any jangle of affairs — even from the question, Which task? I remember a capital prudence of old President Quincy, who told me that he never went to bed at night until he had laid out the studies for the next morning. I believe that in our good days a well-ordered mind has a new thought awaiting it every morning. And hence, eminently thoughtful men, from the time of Pythagoras down, have insisted on an hour of solitude every day, to meet their own mind and learn what oracle it has to impart. If a new view of life or mind gives us joy, so does new arrangement. I don't know but we take as much delight in finding the right place for an old observation, as in a new thought.

6. Solitary converse with nature ; for thence are ejaculated sweet and dreadful words never uttered in libraries. Ah! the spring days, the summer dawns, the October woods ! I confide that my reader knows these delicious secrets, has perhaps

"Slighted Minerva's learned tongue,
But leaped with joy when on the wind the shell of Clio rung."

Are you poetical, impatient of trade, tired of labor and affairs? Do you want Monadnoc, Aglocochook, or Helvellyn, or Plinlimmon, dear to English song, in your closet? Caerleon, Provence, Ossian, and Cadwallon? Tie a couple of strings across a board and set it in your window, and you have an instrument which no artist's harp can rival. It needs no instructed ear; if you have sensibility it admits you to sacred interiors; it has the sadness of nature, yet, at the changes, tones of triumph and festal notes ringing out all measures of loftiness. "Did you never observe," says Gray, "'while rocking winds are piping loud,' that pause, as the gust is recollecting itself, and rising upon the ear in a shrill and plaintive note, like the swell of an Æolian harp? I do assure you there is nothing in the world so like the voice of a spirit." Perhaps you can recall a delight like it, which spoke to the eye, when you have stood by a lake in the woods in summer, and saw where little flaws of wind whip spots or patches of still water into fleets of ripples, — so sudden, so slight, so spiritual, that it was more like the rippling of the Aurora Borealis at night than any spectacle of day.

7. But the solitude of nature is not so essential as solitude of habit. I have found my advantage

in going in summer to a country inn, in winter to a city hotel, with a task which would not prosper at home. I thus secured a more absolute seclusion; for it is almost impossible for a housekeeper who is in the country a small farmer, to exclude interruptions and even necessary orders, though I bar out by system all I can, and resolutely omit, to my constant damage, all that can be omitted. At home, the day is cut into short strips. In the hotel, I have no hours to keep, no visits to make or receive, and I command an astronomic leisure. I forget rain, wind, cold, and heat. At home, I remember in my library the wants of the farm, and have all too much sympathy. I envy the abstraction of some scholars I have known, who could sit on a curbstone in State Street, put up their back, and solve their problem. I have more womanly eyes. All the conditions must be right for my success, slight as that is. What untunes is as bad as what cripples or stuns me. Novelty, surprise, change of scene, refresh the artist, — " break up the tiresome old roof of heaven into new forms," as Hafiz said. The sea-shore and the taste of two metals in contact, and our enlarged powers in the presence, or rather at the approach and at the departure of a friend, and the mixture of lie in truth, and the experience of poetic creativeness which is not found in staying at home nor yet in travelling, but in transitions from one to the other, which must therefore be adroitly managed to present as much transitional surface as possible, — these are the types or conditions of this power. " A ride near the sea, a sail near the shore," said the ancient. So Montaigne travelled with his books, but did not read in them. " *La Nature aime les croisements,*" says Fourier.

I know there is room for whims here; but in regard to some apparent trifles there is great agreement as to their annoyance. And the machine with which we are dealing is of such an inconceivable delicacy that whims also must be respected. Fire must lend its aid. We not only want time, but warm time. George Sand says, " I have no enthusiasm for nature which the slightest chill will not instantly destroy." And I remember that Thoreau, with his robust will, yet found certain trifles disturbing the delicacy of that health which composition exacted, — namely, the slightest irregularity, even to the drinking too much water on the preceding day. Even a steel pen is a nuisance to some writers. Some of us may remember, years ago, in the English journals, the petition, signed by Carlyle, Browning, Tennyson, Dickens and other writers in London, against the license of the organ-grinders, who infested the streets near their houses, to levy on them blackmail.

Certain localities, as mountain-tops, the sea-side, the shores of rivers and rapid brooks, natural parks of oak and pine, where the ground is smooth and unencumbered, are excitants of the muse. Every artist knows well some favorite retirement. And yet the experience of some good artists has taught them to prefer the smallest and plainest chamber, with one chair and table and with no outlook, to these picturesque liberties. William Blake said, "Natural objects always did and do weaken, deaden, and obliterate imagination in me." And Sir Joshua Reynolds had no pleasure in Richmond; he used to say "the human face was his landscape." These indulgences are to be used with great caution. Allston rarely left his studio by day. An old friend took him, one fine afternoon, a spacious circuit into the country, and he painted two or three pictures as the fruits of that drive. But he made it a rule not to go to the city on two consecutive days. One was rest; more was lost time. The times of force must be well husbanded, and the wise student will remember the prudence of Sir Tristam in *Morte d'Arthur*, who, having received from the fairy an enchantment of six hours of growing strength every day, took care to fight in the hours when his strength increased; since from noon to night his strength abated. What prudence again does every artist, every scholar need in the security of his

easel or his desk! These must be remote from the
work of the house, and from all knowledge of the
feet that come and go therein. Allston, it is said,
had two or three rooms in different parts of Boston, where he could not be found. For the delicate muses lose their head if their attention is once
diverted. Perhaps if you were successful abroad in
talking and dealing with men, you would not come
back to your book-shelf and your task. When the
spirit chooses you for its scribe to publish some
commandment, it makes you odious to men and
men odious to you, and you shall accept that loath-
someness with joy. The moth must fly to the
lamp, and you must solve those questions though
you die.

8. Conversation, which, when it is best, is a
series of intoxications. Not Aristotle, not Kant or
Hegel, but conversation, is the right metaphysical
professor. This is the true school of philosophy, —
this the college where you learn what thoughts are,
what powers lurk in those fugitive gleams, and
what becomes of them; how they make history.
A wise man goes to this game to play upon others
and to be played upon, and at least as curious to
know what can be drawn from himself as what can
be drawn from them. For, in discourse with a
friend, our thought, hitherto wrapped in our consciousness, detaches itself, and allows itself to be

seen as a thought, in a manner as new and entertaining to us as to our companions. For provocation of thought, we use ourselves and use each other. Some perceptions — I think the best — are granted to the single soul; they come from the depth and go to the depth and are the permanent and controlling ones. Others it takes two to find. We must be warmed by the fire of sympathy, to be brought into the right conditions and angles of vision. Conversation; for intellectual activity is contagious. We are emulous. If the tone of the companion is higher than ours, we delight in rising to it. 'T is a historic observation that a writer must find an audience up to his thought, or he will no longer care to impart it, but will sink to their level or be silent. Homer said, "When two come together, one apprehends before the other;" but it is because one thought well that the other thinks better: and two men of good mind will excite each other's activity, each attempting still to cap the other's thought. In enlarged conversation we have suggestions that require new ways of living, new books, new men, new arts and sciences. By sympathy, each opens to the eloquence, and begins to see with the eyes of his mind. We were all lonely, thoughtless; and now a principle appears to all: we see new relations, many truths; every mind seizes them as they pass; each catches by the mane one of these strong coursers like horses of the prairie, and rides up and down in the world of the intellect. We live day by day under the illusion that it is the fact or event that imports, whilst really it is not that which signifies, but the use we put it to, or what we think of it. We esteem nations important, until we discover that a few individuals much more concern us ; then, later, that it is not at last a few individuals, or any sacred heroes, but the lowliness, the outpouring, the large equality to truth of a single mind, — as if in the narrow walls of a human heart the whole realm of truth, the world of morals, the tribunal by which the universe is judged, found room to exist.

9. New poetry ; by which I mean chiefly, old poetry that is new to the reader. I have heard from persons who had practice in rhyming, that it was sufficient to set them on writing verses, to read any original poetry. What is best in literature is the affirming, prophesying, spermatic words of men-making poets. Only that is poetry which cleanses and mans me.

Words used in a new sense and figuratively, dart a delightful lustre ; and *every* word admits a new use, and hints ulterior meanings. We have not learned the law of the mind, — cannot control and domesticate at will the high states of contem-plation and continuous thought. " Neither by sea nor by land," said Pindar, "canst thou find the way to the Hyperboreans;" neither by idle wishing, nor by rule of three or rule of thumb. Yet I find a mitigation or solace by providing always a good book for my journeys, as Horace or Martial or Goethe, — some book which lifts me quite out of prosaic surroundings, and from which I draw some lasting knowledge. A Greek epigram out of the anthology, a verse of Herrick or Lovelace, are in harmony both with sense and spirit.

You shall not read newspapers, nor politics, nor novels, nor Montaigne, nor the newest French book. You may read Plutarch, Plato, Plotinus, Hindoo mythology and ethics. You may read Chaucer, Shakspeare, Ben Jonson, Milton, — and Milton's prose as his verse; read Collins and Gray; read Hafiz and the Trouveurs; nay, Welsh and British mythology of Arthur, and (in your ear) Ossian; fact-books, which all geniuses prize as raw material, and as antidote to verbiage and false poetry. Fact-books, if the facts be well and thoroughly told, are much more nearly allied to poetry than many books are that are written in rhyme. Only our newest knowledge works as a source of inspiration and thought, as only the outmost layer of *liber* on the tree. Books of natural science, especially those written by the ancients, — geography, botany, agriculture, explorations of the sea, of meteors, of astronomy, — all the better if written without literary aim or ambition. Every book is good to read which sets the reader in a working mood. The deep book, no matter how remote the subject, helps us best.

Neither are these all the sources, nor can I name all. The receptivity is rare. The occasions or predisposing circumstances I could never tabulate; but now one, now another landscape, form, color, or companion, or perhaps one kind of sounding word or syllable, "strikes the electric chain with which we are darkly bound," and it is impossible to detect and wilfully repeat the fine conditions to which we have owed our happiest frames of mind. The day is good in which we have had the most perceptions. The analysis is the more difficult, because poppy-leaves are strewn when a generalization is made; for I can never remember the circumstances to which I owe it, so as to repeat the experiment or put myself in the conditions: —

> " 'T is the most difficult of tasks to keep
> Heights which the soul is competent to gain."

I value literary biography for the hints it furnishes from so many scholars, in so many countries, of what hygiene, what ascetic, what gymnastic, what social practices their experience suggested and approved. They are, for the most part, men who needed only a little wealth. Large estates, political relations, great hospitalities, would have been impediments to them. They are men whom a book could entertain, a new thought intoxicate and hold them prisoners for years perhaps. Aubrey and Burton and Wood tell me incidents which I find not insignificant.

These are some hints towards what is in all education a chief necessity, — the right government, or, shall I not say? the right obedience to the powers of the human soul. Itself is the dictator; the mind itself the awful oracle. All our power, all our happiness consists in our reception of its hints, which ever become clearer and grander as they are obeyed.

GREATNESS.

GREATNESS.

THERE is a prize which we are all aiming at, and the more power and goodness we have, so much more the energy of that aim. Every human being has a right to it, and in the pursuit we do not stand in each other's way. For it has a long scale of degrees, a wide variety of views, and every aspirant, by his success in the pursuit, does not hinder but helps his competitors. I might call it completeness, but that is later, — perhaps adjourned for ages. I prefer to call it Greatness. It is the fulfilment of a natural tendency in each man. It is a fruitful study. It is the best tonic to the young soul. And no man is unrelated; therefore we admire eminent men, not for themselves, but as representatives. It is very certain that we ought not to be and shall not be contented with any goal we have reached. Our aim is no less than greatness; that which invites all, belongs to us all, — to which we are all sometimes untrue, cowardly, faithless, but of which we never quite despair, and which, in every sane moment, we resolve to make our own.

It is also the only platform on which all men can meet. What anecdotes of any man do we wish to hear or read? Only the best. Certainly not those in which he was degraded to the level of dulness or vice, but those in which he rose above all competition by obeying a light that shone to him alone. This is the worthiest history of the world.

Greatness, — what is it? Is there not some injury to us, some insult in the word? What we commonly call greatness is only such in our barbarous or infant experience. 'T is not the soldier, not Alexander or Bonaparte or Count Moltke surely, who represent the highest force of mankind; not the strong hand, but wisdom and civility, the creation of laws, institutions, letters, and art. These we call by distinction the *humanities;* these, and not the strong arm and brave heart, which are also indispensable to their defence. For the scholars represent the intellect, by which man is man; the intellect and the moral sentiment, — which in the last analysis can never be separated. Who can doubt the potency of an individual mind, who sees the shock given to torpid races — torpid for ages — by Mahomet; a vibration propagated over Asia and Africa? What of Menu? what of Buddha? of Shakspeare? of Newton? of Franklin?

There are certain points of identity in which these masters agree. Self-respect is the early form in which greatness appears. The man in the tavern maintains his opinion, though the whole crowd takes the other side ; we are at once drawn to him. The porter or truckman refuses a reward for finding your purse, or for pulling you drowning out of the river. Thereby, with the service, you have got a moral lift. You say of some new person, That man will go far, — for you see in his manners that the recognition of him by others is not necessary to him. And what a bitter-sweet sensation when we have gone to pour out our acknowledgment of a man's nobleness, and found him quite indifferent to our good opinion ! They may well fear Fate who have any infirmity of habit or aim ; but he who rests on what he is, has a destiny above destiny, and can make mouths at Fortune. If a man's centrality is incomprehensible to us, we may as well snub the sun. There is something in Archimedes or in Luther or Samuel Johnson that needs no protection. There is somewhat in the true scholar which he cannot be laughed out of, nor be terrified or bought off from. Stick to your own ; don't inculpate yourself in the local, social, or national crime, but follow the path your genius traces like the galaxy of heaven for you to walk in.

A sensible person will soon see the folly and wickedness of thinking to please. Sensible men are very rare. A sensible man does not brag, avoids introducing the names of his creditable companions, omits himself as habitually as another man obtrudes himself in the discourse, and is content with putting his fact or theme simply on its ground. You shall not tell me that your commercial house, your partners, or yourself are of importance; you shall not tell me that you have learned to know men; you shall make me feel that; your saying so unsays it. You shall not enumerate your brilliant acquaintances, nor tell me by their titles what books you have read. I am to infer that you keep good company by your better information and manners, and to infer your reading from the wealth and accuracy of your conversation.

Young men think that the manly character requires that they should go to California, or to India, or into the army. When they have learned that the parlor and the college and the counting-room demand as much courage as the sea or the camp, they will be willing to consult their own strength and education in their choice of place.

There are to each function and department of nature supplementary men : to geology, sinewy, out-of-doors men, with a taste for mountains and rocks, a quick eye for differences and for chemical changes. Give such, first a course in chemistry, and then a geological survey. Others find a charm and a profession in the natural history of man and the mammalia or related animals; others in ornithology, or fishes, or insects; others in plants; others in the elements of which the whole world is made. These lately have stimulus to their study through the extraordinary revelations of the spectroscope that the sun and the planets are made in part or in whole of the same elements as the earth is. Then there is the boy who is born with a taste for the sea, and must go thither if he has to run away from his father's house to the forecastle; another longs for travel in foreign lands; another will be a lawyer; another, an astronomer; another, a painter, sculptor, architect, or engineer. Thus there is not a piece of nature in any kind but a man is born, who, as his genius opens, aims slower or faster to dedicate himself to that. Then there is the poet, the philosopher, the politician, the orator, the clergyman, the physician. 'T is gratifying to see this adaptation of man to the world, and to every part and particle of it.

Many readers remember that Sir Humphry Davy said, when he was praised for his important discoveries, " My best discovery was Michael Faraday." In 1848 I had the privilege of hearing Professor Faraday deliver, in the Royal Institution in London, a lecture on what he called Diamagnetism, — by which he meant *cross-magnetism;* and he showed us various experiments on certain gases, to prove that whilst ordinarily magnetism of steel is from north to south, in other substances, gases, it acts from east to west. And further experiments led him to the theory that every chemical substance would be found to have its own, and a different, polarity. I do not know how far his experiments and others have been pushed in this matter, but one fact is clear to me, that diamagnetism is a law of the *mind*, to the full extent of Faraday's idea; namely, that every mind has a new compass, a new north, a new direction of its own, differencing its genius and aim from every other mind; — as every man, with whatever family resemblances, has a new countenance, new manner, new voice, new thoughts, and new character. Whilst he shares with all mankind the gift of reason and the moral sentiment, there is a teaching for him from within which is leading him in a new path, and, the more it is trusted, separates and signalizes him, while it makes him more important and necessary to society. We call this specialty the *bias* of each individual. And none of us will ever accomplish anything excellent or commanding except when he listens to this whisper which is heard by him alone. Swedenborg called it the *proprium*, — not a thought shared with others, but constitutional to the man. A point of education that I can never too much insist upon is this tenet that every individual man has a bias which he must obey, and that it is only as he feels and obeys this that he rightly develops and attains his legitimate power in the world. It is his magnetic needle, which points always in one direction to his proper path, with more or less variation from any other man's. He is never happy nor strong until he finds it, keeps it; learns to be at home with himself; learns to watch the delicate hints and insights that come to him, and to have the entire assurance of his own mind. And in this self-respect or hearkening to the privatest oracle, he consults his ease I may say, or need never be at a loss. In morals this is conscience; in intellect, genius; in practice, talent; — not to imitate or surpass a particular man in *his* way, but to bring out your own new way; to each his own method, style, wit, eloquence. It is easy for a commander to command. Clinging to Nature, or to that province of nature which he knows, he makes no mistakes, but works after her laws and at her own pace, so that his doing, which is perfectly natural, appears miraculous to dull people. Montluc, the great Marshal of France, says of the Genoese admiral, Andrew Doria, " It seemed as if the sea stood in awe of this man." And a kindred genius, Nelson, said, " I feel that I am fitter to do the action than to describe it." Therefore I will say that another trait of greatness is facility.

This necessity of resting on the real, of speaking *your* private thought and experience, few young men apprehend. Set ten men to write their journal for one day, and nine of them will leave out their thought, or proper result, — that is, their net experience, — and lose themselves in misreporting the supposed experience of other people. Indeed I think it an essential caution to young writers, that they shall not in their discourse leave out the one thing which the discourse was written to say. Let that belief which you hold alone, have free course. I have observed that in all public speaking, the rule of the orator begins, not in the array of his facts, but when his deep conviction, and the right and necessity he feels to convey that conviction to his audience, — when these shine and burn in his address; when the thought which he stands for gives its own authority to him, adds to him a grander personality, gives him valor, breadth, and new intellectual power, so that not he, but mankind, seems to speak through his lips. There is a certain transfiguration; all great orators have it, and men who wish to be orators simulate it.

If we should ask ourselves what is this self-respect, it would carry us to the highest problems. It is our practical perception of the Deity in man. It has its deep foundations in religion. If you have ever known a good mind among the Quakers, you will have found *that* is the element of their faith. As they express it, it might be thus: "I do not pretend to any commandment or large revelation, but if at any time I form some plan, propose a journey or a course of conduct, I perhaps find a silent obstacle in my mind that I cannot account for. Very well, — I let it lie, thinking it may pass away, but if it do not pass away I yield to it, obey it. You ask me to describe it. I cannot describe it. It is not an oracle, nor an angel, nor a dream, nor a law ; it is too simple to be described, it is but a grain of mustard-seed, but such as it is, it is something which the contradiction of all mankind could not shake, and which the consent of all mankind could not confirm."

You are rightly fond of certain books or men that you have found to excite your reverence and emulation. But none of these can compare with the greatness of that counsel which is open to you in happy solitude. I mean that there is for you the following of an inward leader, — a slow discrimination that there is for each a Best Counsel which enjoins the fit word and the fit act for every moment. And the path of each, pursued, leads to greatness. How grateful to find in man or woman a new emphasis of their own.

But if the first rule is to obey your native bias, to accept that work for which you were inwardly formed, — the second rule is concentration, which doubles its force. Thus if you are a scholar, be that. The same laws hold for you as for the laborer. The shoemaker makes a good shoe because he makes nothing else. Let the student mind his own charge ; sedulously wait every morning for the news concerning the structure of the world which the spirit will give him.

No way has been found for making heroism easy, even for the scholar. Labor, iron labor, is for him. The world was created as an audience for him ; the atoms of which it is made are opportunities. Read the performance of Bentley, of Gibbon, of Cuvier, Geoffroy St. Hilaire, Laplace. "He can toil terribly," said Cecil of Sir Walter Raleigh. These few words sting and bite and lash us when we are frivolous. Let us get out of the way of their blows by making them true of ourselves. There is so much to be done that we ought to begin quickly to bestir ourselves. This day-labor of ours, we confess, has hitherto a certain emblematic air, like the annual ploughing and sowing of the Emperor of China. Let us make it an honest sweat. Let the scholar measure his valor by his power to cope with intellectual giants. Leave others to count votes and calculate stocks. His courage is to weigh Plato, judge Laplace, know Newton, Faraday, judge of Darwin, criticise Kant and Swedenborg, and on all these arouse the central courage of insight. The scholar's courage should be as terrible as the Cid's, though it grow out of spiritual nature, not out of brawn. Nature, when she adds difficulty, adds brain.

With this respect to the bias of the individual mind add, what is consistent with it, the most catholic receptivity for the genius of others. The day will come when no badge, uniform, or medal will be worn; when the eye, which carries in it planetary influences from all the stars, will indicate rank fast enough by exerting power. For it is true that the stratification of crusts in geology is not more precise than the degrees of rank in minds. A man will say : 'I am born to this position ; I must take it, and neither you nor I can help or hinder me. Surely, then, I need not fret myself to guard my own dignity.' The great man loves the conversation or the book that convicts him, not that which soothes or flatters him. He makes himself of no reputation; he conceals his learning, conceals his charity. For the highest wisdom does not concern itself with particular men, but with man enamored with the law and the Eternal Source. Say with Antoninus, " If the picture is good, who cares who made it ? What matters it by whom the good is done, by yourself or another ? " If it is the truth, what matters who said it ? If it was right, what signifies who did it? All greatness is in degree, and there is more above than below. Where were your own intellect, if greater had not lived? And do you know what the right meaning of Fame is? It is that sympathy, rather that fine element by which the good become partners of the greatness of their superiors.

Extremes meet, and there is no better example than the haughtiness of humility. No aristocrat, no prince born to the purple, can begin to compare with the self-respect of the saint. Why is he so lowly, but that he knows that he can well afford it, resting on the largeness of God in him? I have read in an old book that Barcena the Jesuit confessed to another of his order that when the Devil appeared to him in his cell one night, out of his profound humility he rose up to meet him, and prayed him to sit down in his chair, for he was more worthy to sit there than himself.

Shall I tell you the secret of the true scholar? It is this: Every man I meet is my master in some point, and in that I learn of him. The populace will say, with Horne Tooke, " If you would be powerful, pretend to be powerful." I prefer to say, with the old Hebrew prophet, " Seekest thou great things? — seek them not; " or, what was said of the Spanish prince, "The more you took from him, the greater he appeared," *Plus on lui ôte, plus il est grand.*

Scintillations of greatness appear here and there in men of unequal character, and are by no means confined to the cultivated and so-called moral class. It is easy to draw traits from Napoleon, who was not generous nor just, but was intellectual and knew the law of things. Napoleon commands our respect by his enormous self-trust, the habit of seeing with his own eyes, never the surface, but to the heart of the matter, whether it was a road, a cannon, a character, an officer, or a king, — and by the speed and security of his action in the premises, always new. He has left a library of manuscripts, a multitude of sayings, every one of widest application. He was a man who always fell on his feet. When one of his favorite schemes missed, he had the faculty of taking up his genius, as he said, and of carrying it somewhere else. " Whatever they may tell you, believe that one fights with cannon as with fists ; when once the fire is begun, the least want of ammunition renders what you have done already useless." I find it easy to translate all his technics into all of mine, and his official advices are to me more literary and philosophical than the memoirs of the Academy. His advice to his brother, King Joseph of Spain, was : " I have only one counsel for you, — *Be Master.*" Depth of intellect relieves even the ink of crime with a fringe of light. We perhaps look on its crimes as experiments of a universal student; as he may read any book who reads all books, and as the English judge in old times, when learning was rare, forgave a culprit who could read and write. It is difficult to find greatness pure. Well, I please myself with its diffusion; to find a spark of true fire amid much corruption. It is some guaranty, I hope, for the health of the soul which has this generous blood. How many men, detested in contemporary hostile history, of whom, now that the mists have rolled away, we have learned to correct our old estimates, and to see them as, on the whole, instruments of great benefit. Diderot was no model, but unclean as the society in which he lived; yet was he the best-natured man in France, and would help any wretch at a pinch. His humanity knew no bounds. A poor scribbler who had written a lampoon against him and wished to dedicate it to a pious Duc d'-Orleans, came with it in his poverty to Diderot, and Diderot, pitying the creature, wrote the dedication for him, and so raised five-and-twenty louis to save his famishing lampooner alive.

Meantime we hate snivelling. I do not wish you to surpass others in any narrow or professional or monkish way. We like the natural greatness of health and wild power. I confess that I am as much taken by it in boys, and sometimes in people not normal, nor educated, nor presentable, nor church-members, — even in persons open to the suspicion of irregular and immoral living, in Bohemians, — as in more orderly examples. For we must remember that in the lives of soldiers, sailors and men of large adventure, many of the stays and guards of our household life are wanting, and yet the opportunities and incentives to sublime daring and performance are often close at hand. We must have some charity for the sense of the people, which admires natural power, and will elect it over virtuous men who have less. It has this excuse, that natural is really allied to moral power, and may always be expected to approach it by its own instincts. Intellect at least is not stupid, and will see the force of morals over men, if it does not itself obey. Henry VII. of England was a wise king. When Gerald, Earl of Kildare, who was in rebellion against him, was brought to London, and examined before the Privy Council, one said, " All Ireland cannot govern this Earl." " Then let this Earl govern all Ireland," replied the King.

It is noted of some scholars, like Swift and Gibbon and Donne, that they pretended to vices which they had not, so much did they hate hypocrisy. William Blake the artist frankly says, " I never knew a bad man in whom there was not something very good." Bret Harte has pleased himself with noting and recording the sudden virtue blazing in the wild reprobates of the ranches and mines of California.

Men are ennobled by morals and by intellect; but those two elements know each other and always beckon to each other, until at last they meet in the man, if he is to be truly great. The man who sells you a lamp shows you that the flame of oil, which contented you before, casts a strong shade in the path of the petroleum which he lights behind it; and this again casts a shadow in the path of the electric light. So does intellect when brought into the presence of character; character puts out that light. Goethe, in his correspondence with his Grand Duke of Weimar, does not shine. We can see that the Prince had the advantage of the Olympian genius. It is more plainly seen in the correspondence between Voltaire and Frederick of Prussia. Voltaire is brilliant, nimble, and various, but Frederick has the superior tone. But it is curious that Byron *writes down* to Scott; Scott writes up to him. The Greeks surpass all men till they face the Romans, when Roman character prevails over Greek genius. Whilst degrees of intellect interest only classes of men who pursue the same studies, as chemists or astronomers, mathematicians or linguists, and have no attraction for the crowd, there are always men who have a more catholic genius, are really great as men, and inspire universal enthusiasm. A great style of hero draws equally all classes, all the extremes of society, till we say the very dogs believe in him. We have had such examples in this country, in Daniel Webster, Henry Clay, and the seamen's preacher, Father Taylor; in England, Charles James Fox; in Scotland, Robert Burns; and in France, though it is less intelligible to us, Voltaire. Abraham Lincoln is perhaps the most remarkable example of this class that we have seen, — a man who was at home and welcome with the humblest, and with a spirit and a practical vein in the times of terror that commanded the admiration of the wisest. His heart was as great as the world, but there was no room in it to hold the memory of a wrong.

These may serve as local examples to indicate a magnetism which is probably known better and finer to each scholar in the little Olympus of his own favorites, and which makes him require geniality and humanity in his heroes. What are these but the promise and the preparation of a day when the air of the world shall be purified by nobler society, when the measure of greatness shall be usefulness in the highest sense, — greatness consisting in truth, reverence, and good-will?

Life is made of illusions, and a very common one is the opinion you hear expressed in every village: 'O yes, if I lived in New York or Philadelphia,

Cambridge or New Haven or Boston or Andover, there might be fit society ; but it happens that there are no fine young men, no superior women in my town.' You may hear this every day; but it is a shallow remark. Ah! have you yet to learn that the eye altering alters all; that " the world is an echo which returns to each of us what we say?" It is not examples of greatness, but sensibility to see them, that is wanting. The good botanist will find flowers between the street pavements, and any man filled with an idea or a purpose will find examples and illustrations and coadjutors wherever he goes. Wit is a magnet to find wit, and character to find character. Do you not know that people are as those with whom they converse? And if all or any are heavy to me, that fact accuses me. Why complain, as if a man's debt to his inferiors were not at least equal to his debt to his superiors? If men were equals, the waters would not move; but the difference of level which makes Niagara a cataract, makes eloquence, indignation, poetry, in him who finds there is much to communicate. With self-respect then there must be in the aspirant the strong fellow-feeling, the humanity, which makes men of all classes warm to him as their leader and representative.

We are thus forced to express our instinct of the truth by exposing the failures of experience. The

man whom we have not seen, in whom no regard of
self degraded the adorer of the laws, — who by governing himself governed others; sportive in manner, but inexorable in act; who sees longevity in
his cause; whose aim is always distinct to him;
who is suffered to be himself in society; who carries fate in his eye; — he it is whom we seek, en-
couraged in every good hour that here or hereafter
he shall be found.

IMMORTALITY.

IMMORTALITY.

In the year 626 of our era, when Edwin, the Anglo-Saxon king, was deliberating on receiving the Christian missionaries, one of his nobles said to him : " The present life of man, O king, compared with that space of time beyond, of which we have no certainty, reminds me of one of your winter feasts, where you sit with your generals and ministers. The hearth blazes in the middle and a grateful heat is spread around, while storms of rain and snow are raging without. Driven by the chilling tempest, a little sparrow enters at one door and flies delighted around us till it departs through the other. Whilst it stays in our mansion it feels not the winter storm ; but when this short moment of happiness has been enjoyed, it is forced again into the same dreary tempest from which it had escaped, and we behold it no more. Such is the life of man, and we are as ignorant of the state which preceded our present existence as of that which will follow it. Things being so, I feel that if' this new faith can give us more certainty, it deserves to be received. "

In the first records of a nation in any degree thoughtful and cultivated, some belief in the life beyond life would of course be suggested. The Egyptian people furnish us the earliest details of an established civilization, and I read in the second book of Herodotus this memorable sentence : " The Egyptians are the first of mankind who have affirmed the immortality of the soul." Nor do I read it with less interest that the historian connects it presently with the doctrine of metempsychosis ; for I know well that where this belief once existed it would necessarily take a base form for the savage and a pure form for the wise ; — so that I only look on the counterfeit as a proof that the genuine faith had been there. The credence of men, more than race or climate, makes their manners and customs ; and the history of religion may be read in the forms of sepulture. There never was a time when the doctrine of a future life was not held. Morals must be enjoined, but among rude men moral judgments were rudely figured under the forms of dogs and whips, or of an easier and more plentiful life after death. And as the savage could not detach in his mind the life of the soul from the body, he took great care for his body. Thus the whole life of man in the first ages was ponderously determined on death ; and, as we know, the polity of the Egyptians, the by-laws of towns, of streets and houses, respected burial. It made every man an undertaker, and the priesthood a senate of sextons. Every palace was a door to a pyramid : a king or rich man was a *pyramidaire.* The labor of races was spent on the excavation of catacombs. The chief end of man being to be buried well, the arts most in request were masonry and embalming, to give imperishability to the corpse.

The Greek, with his perfect senses and perceptions, had quite another philosophy, He loved life and delighted in beauty. He set his wit and taste, like elastic gas, under these mountains of stone, and lifted them. He drove away the embalmers ; he built no more of those doleful mountainous tombs. He adorned death, brought wreaths of parsley and laurel ; made it bright with games of strength and skill, and chariot-races. He looked at death only as the distributor of imperishable glory. Nothing. can excel the beauty of his sarcophagus. He carried his arts to Rome, and built his beautiful tombs at Pompeii. The poet Shelley says of these delicately carved white marble cells, "They seem not so much hiding places of that which must decay, as voluptuous chambers for immortal spirits." In the same spirit the modern Greeks, in their songs, ask that they may be buried where the sun can see them, and that a little window may be cut in the sepulchre, from which the swallow might be seen when it comes back in the spring.

Christianity brought a new wisdom. But learning depends on the learner. No more truth can be conveyed than the popular mind can bear, and the barbarians who received the cross took the doctrine of the resurrection as the Egyptians took it. It was an affair of the body, and narrowed again by the fury of sect ; so that grounds were sprinkled with holy water to receive only orthodox dust ; and to keep the body still more sacredly safe for resurrection, it was put into the walls of the church ; . and the churches of Europe are really sepulchres. I read at Melrose Abbey the inscription on the ruined gate : —

> " The Earth goes on the Earth glittering with gold ;
> The Earth goes to the Earth sooner than it wold ;
> The Earth builds on the Earth castles and towers ;
> The Earth says to the Earth, All this is ours. "

Meantime the true disciples saw, through the letter, the doctrine of eternity, which dissolved the poor corpse and nature also, and gave grandeur to the passing hour. The most remarkable step in the religious history of recent ages is that made by the genius of Swedenborg, who described the moral faculties and affections of man, with the hard realism of an astronomer describing the suns and planets of our system, and explained his opinion of the history and destiny of souls in a narrative form, as of one who had gone in a trance into the society of other worlds. Swedenborg described an intelligible heaven, by continuing the like employments in the like circumstances as those we know; men in societies, in houses, towns, trades, entertainments ; continuations of our earthly experience. We shall pass to the future existence as we enter into an agreeable dream. All nature will accompany us there. Milton anticipated the leading thought of Swedenborg, when he wrote, in "Paradise Lost,"—

> "What if Earth
> Be but the shadow of Heaven, and things therein
> Each to the other like more than on earth is thought ?"

Swedenborg had a vast genius and announced many things true and admirable, though always clothed in somewhat sad and Stygian colors. These truths, passing out of his system into general circulation, are now met with every day, qualifying the views and creeds of all churches and of men of no church. And I think we are all aware of a revolution in opinion. Sixty years ago, the books read, the sermons and prayers heard, the habits of thought of religious persons, were all directed on death. All were under the shadow of Calvinism and of the Roman Catholic purgatory, and death was dreadful. The emphasis of all the good books given to young people was on death. We were all taught that we were

born to die; and over that, all the terrors that
theology could gather from savage nations were
added to increase the gloom. A great change
has occurred. Death is seen as a natural event,
and is met with firmness. "A wise man in our
time caused to be written on his tomb, "Think
on living." That inscription describes a progress
in opinion. Cease from this antedating of your
experience. Sufficient to to-day are the duties of
to-day. Don't waste life in doubts and fears;
spend yourself on the work before you, well assured that the right performance of this hour's
duties will be the best preparation for the hours
or ages that follow it:

> "The name of death was never terrible
> To him that knew to live."

A man of thought is willing to die, willing to
live; I suppose because he has seen the thread
on which the beads are strung, and perceived that
it reaches up and down, existing quite independently of the present illusions. A man of affairs
is afraid to die, is pestered with terrors, because
he has not this vision, and is the victim of those
who have moulded the religious doctrines into
some neat and plausible system, as Calvinism,
Romanism, or Swedenborgism, for household use.
It is the fear of the young bird to trust its
wings. The experiences of the soul will fast out-

grow this alarm. The saying of Marcus Antoninus it were hard to mend: " It is well to die if there be gods, and sad to live if there be none." I think all sound minds rest on a certain preliminary conviction, namely, that if it be best that conscious personal life shall continue, it will continue; if not best, then it will not: and we, if we saw the whole, should of course see that it was better so. Schiller said, " What is so universal as death, must be benefit." A friend of Michel Angelo saying to him that his constant labor for art must make him think of death with regret, — " By no means," he said ; " for if life be a pleasure, yet since death also is sent by the hand of the same Master, neither should that displease us." Plutarch, in Greece, has a deep faith that the doctrine of the Divine Providence and that of the immortality of the soul rest on one and the same basis. Hear the opinion of Montesquieu: "If the immortality of the soul were an error, I should be sorry not to believe it. I avow that I am not so humble as the atheist ; I know not how they think, but for me, I do not wish to exchange the idea of immortality against that of the beatitude of one day. I delight in believing myself as immortal as God himself. Independently of revealed ideas, metaphysical ideas give me a vigorous hope of my

eternal well-being, which I would never renounce." [1]

I was lately told of young children who feel a
certain terror at the assurance of life without
end. " What! will it never stop ? " the child
said ; " what ! never die ? *never*, never ? It makes
me feel so tired." And I have in mind the expression of an older believer, who once said to
me, " The thought that this frail being is never
to end is so overwhelming that my only shelter
is God's presence." This disquietude only marks
the transition. The healthy state of mind is the
love of life. What is so good, let it endure.

I find that what is called great and powerful
life — the administration of large affairs, in commerce, in the courts, in the state, — is prone to
develop narrow and special talent; but, unless
combined with a certain contemplative turn, a
taste for abstract truth, for the moral laws, does
not build up faith or lead to content. There is
a profound melancholy at the base of men of
active and powerful talent, seldom suspected.
Many years ago, there were two men in the United
States Senate, both of whom are now dead.
I have seen them both ; one of them I personally knew. Both were men of distinction and
took an active part in the politics of their day

[1] *Pensées Diverses*, p. 223.

and generation. They were men of intellect, and one of them, at a later period, gave to a friend this anecdote. He said that when he entered the Senate he became in a short time intimate with one of his colleagues, and, though attentive enough to the routine of public duty, they daily returned to each other, and spent much time in conversation on the immortality of the soul and other intellectual questions, and cared for little else. When my friend at last left Congress, they parted, his colleague remaining there ; and, as their homes were widely distant from each other, it chanced that he never met him again until, twenty-five years afterwards, they saw each other through open doors at a distance in a crowded reception at the President's house in Washington. Slowly they advanced towards each other as they could, through the brilliant company, and at last met, — said nothing, but shook hands long and cordially. At last his friend said, " Any light, Albert ? " " None, " replied Albert. " Any light, Lewis ? " " None, " replied he. They looked in each other's eyes silently, gave one more shake each to the hand he held, and thus parted for the last time. Now I should say that the impulse which drew these minds to this inquiry through so many years was a better affirmative evidence than their failure to find a confirmation was negative. I ought to add that, though men of good minds, they were both pretty strong materialists in their daily aims and way of life. I admit that you shall find a good deal of skepticism in the streets and hotels and places of coarse amusement. But that is only to say that the practical faculties are faster developed than the spiritual. Where there is depravity there is a slaughter-house style of thinking. One argument of future life is the recoil of the mind in such company, — our pain at every skeptical statement. The skeptic affirms that the universe is a nest of boxes with nothing in the last box. All laughter at man is bitter, and puts us out of good activity. When Bonaparte insisted that the heart is one of the entrails, that it is the pit of the stomach that moves the world, — do we thank him for the gracious instruction? Our disgust is the protest of human nature against a lie.

The ground of hope is in the infinity of the world; which infinity reappears in every particle, the powers of all society in every individual, and of all mind in every mind. I know against all appearances that the universe can receive no detriment; that there is a remedy for every wrong and a satisfaction for every soul. Here is this wonderful thought. But whence came it? Who put it in the mind? It was not I, it was not you; it is elemental, — belongs to thought and virtue, and whenever we have either we see the beams of this light. When the Master of the universe has points to carry in his government he impresses his will in the structure of minds.

But proceeding to the enumeration of the few simple elements of the natural faith, the first fact that strikes us is our delight in permanence. All great natures are lovers of stability and permanence, as the type of the Eternal. After science begins, belief of permanence must follow in a healthy mind. Things so attractive, designs so wise, the secret workman so transcendently skilful that it tasks successive generations of observers only to find out, part with part, the delicate contrivance and adjustment of a weed, of a moss, to its wants, growth, and perpetuation; all these adjustments becoming perfectly intelligible to our study, — and the contriver of it all forever hidden! To breathe, to sleep, is wonderful. But never to know the Cause, the Giver, and infer his character and will! Of what import this vacant sky, these puffing elements, these insignificant lives full of selfsh loves and quarrels and ennui? Everything is prospective, and man is to live hereafter. That the world is for his education is the only sane solution of the enigma. And I think that the naturalist works not for himself, but for the believing mind, which turns his discoveries to revelations, receives them as private tokens of the grand good-will of the Creator.

The mind delights in immense time; delights in rocks, in metals, in mountain-chains, and in the evidence of vast geologic periods which these give; in the age of trees, say of the Sequoias, a few of which will span the whole history of mankind; in the noble toughness and imperishableness of the palm-tree, which thrives under abuse; delights in architecture, whose building lasts so long, — "A house," says Ruskin, "is not in its prime until it is five hundred years old," — and here are the Pyramids, which have as many thousands, and cromlechs and earth-mounds much older than these.

We delight in stability, and really are interested in nothing that ends. What lasts a century pleases us in comparison with what lasts an hour. But a century, when we have once made it familiar and compared it with a true antiquity, looks dwarfish and recent; and it does not help the matter adding numbers, if we see that it has an end, which it will reach just as surely as the shortest. A candle a mile long or a hundred miles long does not help the imagination; only a self-feeding fire, an inextinguishable lamp, like the sun and the star, that we have not yet found date and origin for. But the nebular theory threatens their duration also, bereaves them of this glory, and will make a shift to eke out a sort of eternity by succession, as plants and animals do.

And what are these delights in the vast and permanent and strong, but approximations and resemblances of what is entire and sufficing, creative and self-sustaining life ? For the Creator keeps his word with us. These long-lived or long-enduring objects are to us, as we see them, only symbols of somewhat in us far longer-lived. Our passions, our endeavors, have something ridiculous and mocking, if we come to so hasty an end. If not to *be*, how like the bells of a fool is the trump of fame ! Nature does not, like the Empress Anne of Russia, call together all the architectural genius of the Empire to build and finish and furnish a palace of snow, to melt again to water in the first thaw. Will you, with vast cost and pains, educate your children to be adepts in their several arts, and, as soon as they are ready to produce a masterpiece, call out a file of soldiers to shoot them down? We must infer our destiny from the preparation. We are driven by instinct to hive innumerable experiences which are of no visible value, and we may revolve through many lives before we shall assimilate or exhaust them. Now there is nothing in nature capricious, or whimsical, or accidental, or unsupported. Nature never moves by jumps, but always in steady and supported advances. The implanting of a desire indicates that the gratification of that desire is in the constitution of the creature that feels it; the wish for food, the wish for motion, the wish for sleep, for society, for knowledge, are not random whims, but grounded in the structure of the creature, and meant to be satisfied by food, by motion, by sleep, by society, by knowledge. If there is the desire to live, and in larger sphere, with more knowledge and power, it is because life and knowledge and power are good for us, and we are the natural depositaries of these gifts. The love of life is out of all proportion to the value set on a single day, and seems to indicate, like all our other experiences, a conviction of immense resources and possibilities proper to us, on which we have never drawn.

All the comfort I have found teaches me to confide that I shall not have less in times and places that I do not yet know. I have known admirable persons, without feeling that they exhaust the possibilities of virtue and talent. I have seen what glories of climate, of summer mornings and evenings, of midnight sky; I have enjoyed the benefits of all this complex machinery of arts and civilization, and its results of comfort. The good Power can easily provide me millions more as good. Shall I hold on with both hands to every paltry possession? All I have seen teaches me to trust the Creator for all I have not seen. Whatever it be which the great Providence prepares for us, it must be something large and generous, and in the great style of his works. The future must be up to the style of our faculties, — of memory, of hope, of imagination, of reason. I have a house, a closet which holds my books, a table, a garden, a field : are these, any or all, a reason for refusing the angel who beckons me away, — as if there were no room or skill elsewhere that could reproduce for me as my like or my enlarging wants may require ? We wish to live for what is great, not for what is mean. I do not wish to live for the sake of my warm house, my orchard, or my pictures. I do not wish to live to wear out my boots.

As a hint of endless being, we may rank that novelty which perpetually attends life. The soul does not age with the body. On the borders of the grave, the wise man looks forward with equal elasticity of mind, or hope ; and why not, after millions of years, on the verge of still newer existence ? — for it is the nature of intelligent beings to be forever new to life. Most men are insolvent, or promise by their countenance and conversation and by their early endeavor much more than they ever perform, — suggesting a design still to be carried out ; the man must have new motives, new companions, new condition, and another term. Frank-

lin said, " Life is rather a state of embryo, a preparation for life. A man is not completely born until
he has passed through death." Every really able
man, in whatever direction he work, — a man of
large affairs, an inventor, a statesman, an orator, a
poet, a painter, — if you talk sincerely with him,
considers his work, however much admired, as far
short of what it should be. What is this Better,
this flying Ideal, but the perpetual promise of his
Creator ?

The fable of the Wandering Jew is agreeable to
men, because they want more time and land in
which to execute their thoughts. But a higher
poetic use must be made of the legend. Take us
as we are, with our experience, and transfer us to a
new planet, and let us digest for its inhabitants
what we could of the wisdom of this. After we
have found our depth there, and assimilated what
we could of the new experience, transfer us to a new
scene. In each transfer we shall have acquired, by
seeing them at a distance, a new mastery of the old
thoughts, in which we were too much immersed.
In short, all our intellectual action, not promises
but bestows a feeling of absolute existence. We
are taken out of time and breathe a purer air. I
know not whence we draw the assurance of pro-
longed life, of a life which shoots that gulf we call
death and takes hold of what is real and abiding,

by so many claims as from our intellectual history. Salt is a good preserver; cold is: but a truth cures the taint of mortality better, and "preserves from harm until another period." A sort of absoluteness attends all perception of truth, — no smell of age, no hint of corruption. It is self-sufficing, sound, entire.

Lord Bacon said: "Some of the philosophers who were least divine denied generally the immortality of the soul, yet came to this point, that whatsoever motions the spirit of man could act and perform without the organs of the body, might remain after death; which were only those of the understanding, and not of the affections; so immortal and incorruptible a thing did knowledge seem to them to be." And Van Helmont, the philosopher of Holland, drew his sufficient proof purely from the action of the intellect. "It is my greatest desire," he said, "that it might be granted unto atheists to have tasted, at least but one only moment, what it is intellectually to understand; whereby they may feel the immortality of the mind, as it were by touching." A farmer, a laborer, a mechanic, is driven by his work all day, but it ends at night; it has an end. But, as far as the mechanic or farmer is also a scholar or thinker, his work has no end. That which he has learned is that there is much more to be learned. The wiser he is, he feels only the more his incompetence. "What we know is a point to what we do not know." A thousand years,—tenfold, a hundredfold his faculties, would not suffice. The demands of his task are such that it becomes omnipresent. He studies in his walking, at his meals, in his amusements, even in his sleep. Montesquieu said, "The love of study is in us almost the only eternal passion. All the others quit us in proportion as this miserable machine which holds them approaches its ruin." "Art is long," says the thinker, "and life is short." He is but as a fly or a worm to this mountain, this continent, which his thoughts inhabit. It is a perception that comes by the activity of the intellect; never to the lazy or rusty mind. Courage comes naturally to those who have the habit of facing labor and danger, and who therefore know the power of their arms and bodies; and courage or confidence in the mind comes to those who know by use its wonderful forces and inspirations and returns. Belief in its future is a reward kept only for those who use it. "To me," said Goethe, "the eternal existence of my soul is proved from my idea of activity. If I work incessantly till my death, nature is bound to · give me another form of existence, when the present can no longer sustain my spirit."

It is a proverb of the world that good-will makes intelligence, that goodness itself is an eye; and the one doctrine in which all religions agree is that new light is added to the mind in proportion as it uses that which it has. " He that doeth the will of God abideth forever." Ignorant people confound reverence for the intuitions with egotism. There is no confusion in the things themselves. The health of the mind consists in the perception of law. Its dignity consists in being under the law. Its goodness is the most generous extension of our private interests to the dignity and generosity of ideas. Nothing seems to me so excellent as a belief in the laws. It communicates nobleness, and, as it were, an asylum in temples to the loyal soul.

I confess that everything connected with our personality fails. Nature never spares the individual ; we are always balked of a complete success : no prosperity is promised to our self-esteem. We have our indemnity only in the moral and intellectual reality to which we aspire. That is immortal, and we only through that. The soul stipulates for no private good. That which is private I see not to be good. " If truth live, I live ; if justice live, I live," said one of the old saints, " and these by any man's suffering are enlarged and enthroned."

The moral sentiment measures itself by sacrifice. It risks or ruins property, health, life itself, without hesitation, for its thought, and all men justify tho man by their praise for this act. And Mahomet in the same mind declared, " Not dead but living ye are to account all those who are slain in the way of God."

On these grounds I think that wherever man ripens, this audacious belief presently appears, — in the savage, savagely; in the good, purely. As soon as thought is exercised, this belief is inevitable; as soon as virtue glows, this belief confirms itself. It is a kind of summary or completion of man. It cannot rest on a legend; it cannot be quoted from one to another; it must have the assurance of a man's faculties that they can fill a larger theatre and a longer term than nature here allows him. Goethe said : " It is to a thinking being quite impossible to think himself non-existent, ceasing to think and live; so far does every one carry in himself the proof of immortality, and quite spontaneously. But so soon as the man will be objective and go out of himself, so soon as he dogmatically will grasp a personal duration to bolster up in cockney fashion that inward assurance, he is lost in contradiction." The doctrine is not sentimental, but is grounded in the necessities and forces we possess. Nothing will hold but that which we must be and must do : —

> " Man's heart the Almighty to the Future set
> By secret but inviolable springs."

The revelation that is true is written on the palms of the hands, the thought of our mind, the desire of our heart, or nowhere. My idea of heaven is that there is no melodrama in it at all; that it is wholly real. Here is the emphasis of conscience and experience; this is no speculation, but the most practical of doctrines. Do you think that the eternal chain of cause and effect which pervades nature, which threads the globes as beads on a string, leaves this out of its circuit, — leaves out this desire of God and men as a waif and a caprice, altogether cheap and common, and falling without reason or merit?

We live by desire to live; we live by choice; by will, by thought, by virtue, by the vivacity of the laws which we obey, and obeying share their life, — or we die by sloth, by disobedience, by losing hold of life, which ebbs out of us. But whilst I find the signatures, the hints and suggestions, noble and wholesome, — whilst I find that all the ways of virtuous living lead upward and not downward, — yet it is not my duty to prove to myself the immortality of the soul. That knowledge is hidden very cunningly. Perhaps the archangels cannot find the secret of their existence, as the eye cannot see itself; — but, ending or endless, to live whilst I live.

There is a drawback to the value of all state-

ments of the doctrine, and I think that one ab-
stains from writing or printing on the immortality
of the soul, because, when he comes to the end of
his statement, the hungry eyes that run through it
will close disappointed; the listeners say, That is
not here which we desire; — and I shall be as
much wronged by their hasty conclusions, as they
feel themselves wronged by my omissions. I mean
that I am a better believer, and all serious souls
are better believers in the immortality, than we can
give grounds for. The real evidence is too subtle,
or is higher than we can write down in proposi-
tions, and therefore Wordsworth's "Ode" is the
best modern essay on the subject.

We cannot prove our faith by syllogisms. The
argument refuses to form in the mind. A conclu-
sion, an inference, a grand augury, is ever hover-
ing, but attempt to ground it, and the reasons are
all vanishing and inadequate. You cannot make a
written theory or demonstration of this as you can
an orrery of the Copernican astronomy. It must
be sacredly treated. Speak of the mount in the
mount. Not by literature or theology, but only by
rare integrity, by a man permeated and perfumed
with airs of heaven, — with manliest or womanliest
enduring love, — can the vision be clear to a use
the most sublime. And hence the fact that in the
minds of men the testimony of a few inspired souls

has had such weight and penetration. You shall not say, "O my bishop, O my pastor, is there any resurrection? What do you think? Did Dr. Channing believe that we should know each other? did Wesley? did Butler? did Fénelon?" What questions are these! Go read Milton, Shakspeare, or any truly ideal poet. Read Plato, or any seer of the interior realities. Read St. Augustine, Swedenborg, Immanuel Kant. Let any master simply recite to you the substantial laws of the intellect, and in the presence of the laws themselves you will never ask such primary-school questions.

Is immortality only an intellectual quality, or, shall I say, only an energy, there being no passive? He has it, and he alone, who gives life to all names, persons, things, where he comes. No religion, not the wildest mythology dies for him; no art is lost. He vivifies what he touches. Future state is an illusion for the ever-present state. It is not length of life, but depth of life. It is not duration, but a taking of the soul out of time, as all high action of the mind does: when we are living in the sentiments we ask no questions about time. The spiritual world takes place; — that which is always the same. But see how the sentiment is wise. Jesus explained nothing, but the influence of him took people out of time, and they felt eternal. A great integrity makes us immortal;

an admiration, a deep love, a strong will, arms us
above fear.   It makes a day memorable.   We say
we lived years in that hour.   It is strange that
Jesus is esteemed by mankind the bringer of the
doctrine of immortality.   He is never once weak or
sentimental; he is very abstemious of explanation,
he never preaches the personal immortality; whilst
Plato and Cicero had both allowed themselves to
overstep the stern limits of the spirit, and gratify
the people with that picture.

How ill agrees this majestical immortality of our
religion with the frivolous population!   Will you
build magnificently for mice?   Will you offer empires to such as cannot set a house or private affairs
in order?   Here are people who cannot dispose of
a day; an hour hangs heavy on their hands; and
will you offer them rolling ages without end?   But
this is the way we rise.   Within every man's
thought is a higher thought, — within the character
he exhibits to-day, a higher character.   The youth
puts off the illusions of the child, the man puts off
the ignorance and tumultuous passions of youth;
proceeding thence puts off the egotism of manhood,
and becomes at last a public and universal soul.
He is rising to greater heights, but also rising to
realities; the outer relations and circumstances
dying out, he entering deeper into God, God into
him, until the last garment of egotism falls, and he

is with God, — shares the will and the immensity of the First Cause.

It is curious to find the selfsame feeling, that it is not immortality, but eternity, — not duration, but a state of abandonment to the Highest, and so the sharing of His perfection, — appearing in the farthest east and west. The human mind takes no account of geography, language, or legends, but in all utters the same instinct.

Yama, the lord of Death, promised Nachiketas, the son of Gautama, to grant him three boons at his own choice. Nachiketas, knowing that his father Gautama was offended with him, said, "O Death! let Gautama be appeased in mind, and forget his anger against me: this I choose for the first boon." Yama said, "Through my favor, Gautama will remember thee with love as before." For the second boon, Nachiketas asks that the fire by which heaven is gained be made known to him; which also Yama allows, and says, "Choose the third boon, O Nachiketas!" Nachiketas said, there is this inquiry. Some say the soul exists after the death of man; others say it does not exist. This I should like to know, instructed by thee. Such is the third of the boons. Yama said, "For this question, it was inquired of old, even by the gods; for it is not easy to understand it. Subtle is its nature. Choose another boon, O Nachiketas! Do not compel me to this." Nachiketas said, "Even by the gods was it inquired. And as to what thou sayest, O Death, that it is not easy to understand it, there is no other speaker to be found like thee. There is no other boon like this." Yama said, "Choose sons and grandsons who may live a hundred years; choose herds of cattle; choose elephants and gold and horses; choose the wide expanded earth, and live thyself as many years as thou listeth. Or, if thou knowest a boon like this, choose it, together with wealth and far-extending life. Be a king, O Nachiketas! On the wide earth I will make thee the enjoyer of all desires. All those desires that are difficult to gain in the world of mortals, all those ask thou at thy pleasure;—those fair nymphs of heaven with their chariots, with their musical instruments; for the like of them are not to be gained by men. I will give them to thee, but do not ask the question of the state of the soul after death." Nachiketas said, "All those enjoyments are of yesterday. With thee remain thy horses and elephants, with thee the dance and song. If we should obtain wealth, we live only as long as thou pleasest. The boon which I choose I have said." Yama said, "One thing is good, another is pleasant. Blessed is he who takes the good, but he who chooses the pleasant loses the object of man. But thou, considering the objects of desire, hast abandoned them. These two, **ignorance** (whose object is what is pleasant) and knowledge (whose object is what is good), are known to be far asunder, and to lead to different goals. Believing this world exists, and not the other, the careless youth is subject to my sway. That knowledge for which thou hast asked is not to be obtained by argument. I know worldly happiness is transient, for that firm one is not to be obtained by what is not firm. The wise, by means of the union of the intellect with the soul, thinking him whom it is hard to behold, leaves both grief and joy. Thee, O Nachiketas! I believe a house whose door is open to Brahma. Brahma the supreme, whoever knows him obtains whatever he wishes. The soul is not born; it does not die; it was not produced from any one. Nor was any produced from it. Unborn, eternal, it is not slain, though the body is slain; subtler than what is subtle, greater than what is great, sitting it goes far, sleeping it goes everywhere. Thinking the soul as unbodily among bodies, firm among fleeting things, the wise man casts off all grief. The soul cannot be gained by knowledge, not by understanding, not by manifold science. It can be obtained by the soul by which it is desired. It reveals its own truths."

www.ingramcontent.com/pod-product-compliance
Lightning Source LLC
Chambersburg PA
CBHW031143120726
47905CB00006B/1803